THE DARK ANGEL

A Medieval Romance

By Kathryn Le Veque

The BATTLE LORDS
of DE VELT

KATHRYN LE VEQUE
NOVELS

ARE YOU SIGNED UP FOR KATHRYN'S BLOG?

You'll get the latest news and information on exclusive giveaways, exclusive excerpts, coming releases, sales, free books, cover reveals and more.

Kathryn's blog followers get it all first. No spam, no junk.

Get the latest info from the reigning Queen of English Medieval Romance!

Sign Up Here

kathrynleveque.com

The BATTLE LORDS of DE VELT

It's not often the House of de Velt sees both tragedy and comedy, but when Medieval hippies come to call on the darkest lord of all, Julian de Velt gets caught up in the Medieval mayhem…

But he pays a price.

Lista de la Mere is a young woman of beauty, sense, and education. Unfortunately, her mother and her aunt don't have the same sensibilities. Lista is an heiress, and a very wealthy one, and if her conniving, alcoholic mother and her sly, drug-addicted aunt have anything to say about it, she's going to marry the man that can provide them with unlimited coinage to feed their habits – and put them back on top of the social hierarchy.

Lista's mother was a friend of Kellington Coleby de Velt, Julian's mother, long ago. They pitch Lista to Kellington as a wife for Julian and although Julian has no intention of marrying anytime soon, he's rather intrigued with the lovely, bright young woman who is so capable of drawing him out of his shell.

But Lista's mother and aunt don't stop there. It's their intention to have a bidding war, the prize being Lista, and they pitch Lista to another knight, setting off a chain of events that could ruin everything. Julian, who is usually shy and quiet, must call forth the inner devil that his father managed to tame so ably.

Now, it's Julian's time to rise.

Join introverted, powerful Julian and sweet, intelligent Lista as they battle to save a love that too many people are trying to destroy.

It's peace, love, chaos and madness in Medieval England!

de Velt Motto: *Quoniam magnus coram mors*

Death before mercy

Author's Note

And finally, we have Julian's story…

I've actually really come to like Julian. He'd only appeared here and there in Cole and Cassian's stories, so I wasn't really sure what kind of a personality he had or how we would see his character growth. The worst thing an author can do is write about a character who is the same in the beginning as he (or she) is in the end. I feel that it's important to take a reader on the journey of a character, so I wasn't sure which direction to go with Julian. When that's the case, I let the character talk to me.

Julian had a lot to say.

Now – trigger warning! I will forewarn you of something, however, before we get started. I've always sworn I would never write the death of a major character but, in this case, it was important for Julian's growth as a man – as a knight – to experience his father's death. So if you are at all sensitive about the death of Jax de Velt, be very careful reading the prologue. I've written it as tastefully as I could, but let's face it – any death of a major character is heartbreaking and especially Jax's. We knew in my novel, *Godspeed*, that he'd fallen fighting King John's mercenaries. It was spoken about it in *The Splendid Hour* and in *The Dark Conqueror*. So, it's not like it's out of the blue. But now, we actually see it, so if it's going to upset you – be careful about reading it. Yes, it's important for Julian's growth, but you'll see his development anyway. But with Jax's death – it has so much more meaning. And to see him and Kellington together at the end… sigh…

Consider yourself warned.

Now, let's talk about the de Velt family a little –

Several years back, I published *Spectre of the Sword*. We met the hero's half-brother, Rod de Titouan, who was kind of a – how can I say this? – a butthead at times. Now, don't get me wrong. I really like Rod. I liked him so much that at the end of *Devil's Dominion*, he and Effington de Velt got together. It was further mentioned in a brief sentence:

But that didn't stop Effington. She followed Rod into the hall as well and, on a warm August night of the next year, after a serious adventure of their own, Rod and Effington celebrated their own marriage in Pelinom's keep the same day as Allaston gave birth to a big, healthy boy at Belford Castle.

To be clear, Rod and Effington were married a long time ago (in 1207 according to *Devil's Dominion*) – it was just never mentioned in other de Velt books nor have Effie and Rod had their own story told(yet!), so don't be confused when you see the marriage mentioned in this book. So far, anything with Rod and Effie has happened "off page".

Something more to discuss away from the de Velt family – books. Believe it or not, there were books in Medieval times. I've used them many times, but just a brief mention. In the High Middle Ages, they were called a codex, not a "book" as we do today. It was vellum pages between two boards and they were almost always, without fail, richly painted and works of art. It wasn't until the 15th century when books started to evolve into what we know today, but for the purposes of ease, I've called the codex a "book".

A quick reminder about Jax and Kellington's children:
Coleby "Cole" b. 1181
Julian b. 1183
Allaston b. 1186
Effington b. 1189

Addington b. 1191

Cassian b. 1193

On a personal note, this book was very difficult for me to finish. More than halfway through it, I lost my own father quite suddenly. Usually a healthy man, he was with us in the evening and then gone the next morning. To my recollection, I've only really written about the death of one major character – and a father – and it just happened to be in this book, so I struggled through this story greatly because of it. Had it not been on preorder, I would have thrown it out altogether. But in a sense, *The Dark Angel* will always be a special book to me, if not one of *the* most special because of the time in my life when I wrote it. My dad was a little leery of his daughter's writing (read into this: squeamish of sex scenes), but in the end, he was so proud of what I'd accomplished. He became my biggest supporter and I will miss that greatly.

At this point, I think that's about all of an author's note I can give. Not even a pronunciation guide because there's nothing odd in the book (and that's rare!).

Thank you so much for reading – and enjoy Julian and Lista's story.

Hugs,

DEDICATION

I don't usually do dedications because with as many books as I've written, I would run out of people to dedicate to. In this case, I'm making an exception and dedicating the book to my dad, William Ralph Bouse, Jr., who left us on January 5, 2022.

His friends called him Bill and his grandkids called him Bull.

It's difficult to summarize fifty-seven years of life with a man who, when you were a child, was your teacher. When you were a teenager, he was your worst enemy (at least, for a few years, he was mine in a classic love/hate fest), and when you were an adult, he became the wisest, most important man in your life other than your husband. That's probably the biggest thing I will remember about my father – his wisdom. I've tried to infuse every male hero I've written about with that same kind of wisdom. Some have my dad's sense of adventure, some have his sense of humor. Some are stubborn, just like he was. Matthew Wellesbourne from *The White Lord of Wellesbourne* had his love of fishing. William de Wolfe from *The Wolfe* even bears his name. Every hero I write about has a piece of my dad in them, so in that sense, he will continue to live on through my heroes.

That's a good legacy for any man.

At this point, that's as good a dedication as I can give, so I'll simply say this: Godspeed, Dad. It's been an amazing life with you. Thank you for impressing upon me all of the good qualities a father, and a man, should have.

See you on the other side.

PROLOGUE

January 1216
Pelinom Castle, Northumberland

THE BATTLE HAD been raging for nearly two days.

It was one of the most desolate, brutal things Julian de Velt had ever seen. He'd been in battles before, too many times to count, but he'd never had his home attacked as it was now. Pelinom was his family's home. He'd been born there, as had his siblings and even his mother. Certainly, they had trouble with Scots now and again, but those had always been quick or unspectacular raids because no man in his right mind would go after the seat of the most feared warlord in England.

The man known as The Dark Lord.

Except for, perhaps, the King of England himself.

That's where this bombardment came from. John Lackland, as he'd once been known, had been waging a horrific scorched earth campaign against his own warlords, those who were opposed to his rule and had been after more than fifteen years of dealing with a king who had little respect for the men who were sworn to him. Years and years of a king who refused to keep his word to his own vassals, who lied and cheated and swindled his way through his reign. When the warlords, like Jax de Velt, could take no more and refused to fight for John any longer, the king raised an army of mercenaries from the darkest corners of the earth.

Men who had only come to kill for the money it would bring them.

It was their only motivation. John paid them well with ill-gotten funds to kill his enemies and that's exactly what they did. They had no regard for England or her warlords, no respect for the land or the people. They'd moved from Winchester to Nottingham to York, fighting their way northward, before finally descending on Berwick Castle. Berwick was an outpost of the de Velt empire, at least temporarily, and Julian's older brother, Cole, was the garrison commander. But Cole fought valiantly against John's hired army of thugs so they moved off to the west, along the River Tweed, tearing into any castle they came across that wasn't loyal to John.

Northwood.

Wark.

Roxburgh.

And finally, Pelinom.

Northwood, Wark, and Roxburgh held against the onslaught, but not without significant damage. Northwood, in particular, had suffered a great deal, but in the end, John's army moved away, heading for that jewel called Pelinom. If they could take down Pelinom, the line of castles holding the Scots border would break and they very much wanted it to break. John was prepared to move into Scotland, all the way to Edinburgh and the Highlands, but he had to break the border first.

But the warlords held strong.

That only seemed to infuriate him.

Now, on the dawn of the third day, Julian stood at the keep entry, though the doors themselves were bolted and the iron grate, like a portcullis, had long been lowered and secured. Even if John's mercenaries made it into the bailey, there was no way to make it into the keep. The doors behind the grate could be burned, but the grate was too big and too heavy to be moved or destroyed. The nearest windows were slender lancet openings and unless a man was as thin as a reed, there was no way to slip through them.

The keep of Pelinom, containing Julian's mother and sisters, was tightly secured.

But that meant the army had been out in the open, exposed to the projectiles that John's army flung over the walls from time to time. At first, they were bundles of wood, tied together and soaked in oil and then flung over the walls in the hope of catching some structure on fire. All they managed to do was create nice, warm piles of kindling that the de Velt army warmed themselves on.

Then came the human cargo.

Literally, the mercenaries started flinging terrified squires or drunken soldiers over the walls in an attempt to get men on the inside. Pelinom's walls were so incredibly tall, with great crenelations that Jax himself had put all the way around the wall walk, that mounting the walls was a near impossibility. The mercenary army had tried for two days. They were still trying. The men who had come flying over the walls had all been killed either during the endeavor or shortly thereafter. Jax had ordered their bodies slung back over the walls and into Pelinom's substantial moat.

It had both demoralized and enraged the mercenaries.

And everyone knew it.

The smoke was heavy in the air as the sun began to rise, the smell of cooking fires mingled with the heavy, oily smell of burning bodies. It wasn't that anyone in Pelinom was burning bodies, for they'd suffered no casualties, but more that the mercenaries were burning their dead, unable to provide for storage or a place to bury them because the ground was frozen.

It was the beginning of the third day of an increasingly unpleasant standoff.

"Were you able to sleep?"

The question came from behind and Julian turned to see Sir Ashton de Royans approaching. Ashton, or Ash as he was known, was the son of Sir Juston de Royans of Bowes Castle, about one hundred miles to the south. Ashton and his older brother, Tristan, were both at Pelinom these days and had been well before any trouble with the king started. Tristan was actually the bastard child of King Henry II and Alys of France. Juston had taken the boy in and adopted him so the boys were raised together. Ash had always considered Tristan his brother.

While Tristan had luscious auburn hair and a bristly beard, with big, white teeth and a temper to match those sharp looks, Ashton had the enormous blond comeliness of the de Royans men. He was bright, powerful, calm in almost any circumstance, and had a bit of a wicked streak him in that Julian loved.

They'd been best friends for years.

"A little," Julian said, his eyes twinklingly wearily. "One does not sleep much when one's home is being attacked."

Ashton snorted softly. "Attacked," he said with disdain. "The nuns from Kelso could have done a better job of laying siege. Why don't they simply leave us alone? They'll never get in."

Julian flashed a grin, big dimples carving through both cheeks. "There is truth in that," he said, looking up at the battlements that were heavily lined with men. "My father was just saying how weak this entire attack has been but considering how many castles they have bombarded before us, there is little wonder that they have worn down."

Ashton shook his head. "They did not take any of the castles from here to Berwick," he said. "I have a feeling they may have expended all of their energy on Berwick. That fortress is key to holding the north. If John had captured it, he could use the river to bring more troops into the north."

Julian's grin faded. "I know," he said. "We know that Berwick held but not much beyond that."

"Your father has not received any reports?"

"We've been locked tight for the past three days. Nothing has been able to come through."

Ashton could feel Julian's concern. The de Velt family was inordinately close for the most part with the exception of Cassian, the youngest son, who spent his time in the south with the House of de Lohr. Cassian had gone there to foster and had simply never returned. It was well known that a certain de Lohr daughter was holding him there, leaving Cole and Julian to support their father's empire. Truthfully, Cole had his own agenda in life – garrison commander of Berwick, a wife, a family, and also serving William Marshal when the call came, but Julian was solely and exclusively devoted to his father.

He was, in fact, his father's shadow.

Ashton had known Julian for a few years, ever since he was sent north by his father, Juston, to support Pelinom during a time of constant raids from reivers. Ashton had liked the north so much that he'd remained, enjoying Jax and Julian and Cole when he came around. He'd come with his older brother, Tristan, who was even now on the opposite side of the fortress, in the kitchen yard because there was a low, squat, and heavily defended postern gate there, the only possible way John's men could infiltrate if they came across the moat and gained a foothold.

And no one would get in with Tristan at the gate.

In fact, Tristan had made himself indispensable to Jax since nearly his arrival, a bold and courageous man to the core. Julian was technically Jax's second in command, but Tristan was older and more aggressive and, truth be told, experienced. Julian was rather quiet, introverted, quieter still when Tristan began to gain steam. He was still young enough to be offended by forceful older knights, especially ones he saw as trying to take his father's attention away. Deep down, Julian de Velt had a confidence problem and Tristan only made it worse. But Ashton knew something Tristan didn't know.

Julian was smarter, better, and stronger than all of them.

He just needed the opportunity to show it.

"Well," Ashton finally said. "I would not worry. John's mercenaries are too exhausted to do much damage, so I do not imagine today will be much of an issue. I would suspect at some point in the next day or two, when they realize they cannot breach Pelinom, that they will simply move on to the next castle and leave us alone."

Julian's gaze came off of the battlements, focusing on Ashton again. "My father is not so sure," he said. "He does not think that John will give up so easily. He needs a castle from which to launch his attacks into Scotland and Pelinom seems to be his last chance."

Ashton shrugged. "There are others that he can probably take with more ease," he said. "Smaller outposts."

"My father seems to think he wants a larger castle, like Pelinom," Julian said. "It would be a trophy. What a boast it would be for John to tell all of England that he captured The Dark Lord's castle."

Ashton grinned, suggesting such a thing was not possible. "I do not think he would like The Dark Lord's reaction to having his castle taken," he said. "He and his mercenaries might very well find themselves speared on poles and propped up like Christians at a crucifixion. In fact, here comes that terrifying man in the flesh."

He was looking over Julian's shoulder, nodding his head in that direction. Julian turned to see his father approaching from the stables, an enormous knight with a head of shoulder-length dark hair that was dusted heavily with gray these days. He was in full protection, the same protection he'd worn all of these years – heavy mail coat, hauberk, steel braces on his forearms and shins, and the de Velt boar tunic. When he caught sight of Julian and Ashton, he headed in their direction.

"I've had the thatching from the stables' roof removed," he said, fussing with the fasten of a glove that had come loose. "In fact, I've had all of the thatching and hay put into the niches in the outer wall to protect them in case we have any more flaming projectiles or men tossed over the wall at us."

Julian couldn't quite see the stables from where he stood, but he craned his neck to get a peek at what his father was talking about. "I could have done that," he said. "You should not have to bother."

"It was no bother."

Julian cocked a dark blond eyebrow. "This is how the chain

of command works, Papa," he said seriously. "You command and I obey. Give me an order and I shall do it. You do not need to handle menial tasks like that. This is why you have a thousand men at your disposal."

Jax chuckled as he looked at his middle son. Julian had his handsome features, but his blond coloring was purely his mother's. "Is that why I have you?" he quipped. "Truly, Julian, I had no idea."

Julian's grin returned, now at his father. "At least let us earn our pay, Papa," he said. "Otherwise, we will all grow fat and lazy like John and his mercenaries."

Jax snorted, eyeing the battlements where the men were stationed. "I would not discount John and his mercenaries too easily," he said. "You are speaking of a Plantagenet, a man who fought against his father and brothers, at any given time, from a very young age. John may be many things but, in battle, he is no fool. Do not underestimate him."

Julian found himself looking at the battlements also. "He has had two days to breach our walls," he said. "Two days of attempts. The best he could do was try to sling men over the walls. I think that is a sign of his desperation."

"Or his genius," Jax said, looking at him. "The worst thing you can do in battle is underestimate any opponent, Julian. Do not let your confidence be your downfall."

Julian smiled weakly, averting his gaze. "No one could ever accuse me of that," he said. "I do not profess to have your experience, but I am not a novice."

"Nay, you are not, but you must listen to me when I tell you not to misjudge the king."

"My lord!" Men were shouting at Jax from the battlements. "A party approaches the drawbridge!"

That was a distinct surprise. Curiously, Jax and Julian and Ashton made their way to the enormous gatehouse of Pelinom, the one structure that was truly standing between them and annihilation. The gatehouse had two iron portcullises, which utterly demoralized any army attempting to breach it. Not only did they have to get through one, but they had to get through a second one to make headway into the bailey.

In fact, Jax acquired Pelinom in a siege thirty years earlier and there had only been one portcullis at the time, one he had been able to destroy. He was the one who added the second portcullis for just that reason. As he stood there with his son and knight, watching through both grates as the sun began to rise, they could see a small party of riders approaching.

Tension was immediately in the air.

The drawbridge had been burned away the first day of the siege because the mechanism raising it had jammed and they'd been unable to lift it. Therefore, Jax had ordered it doused with oil and burned, and it had mostly burned away. Chunks of it still smoldered, filling his vision, as he watched the party approach the moat but stop just shy of it. He found it interesting that they were in the range of his archers, making him doubly curious about their purpose.

"I come on behalf of the king!" someone shouted in a heavy accent. "We seek Ajax de Velt!"

Jax's eyes narrowed as he realized it wasn't a native Englishman speaking. Undoubtedly, it was a mercenary.

"I have no need to hear anything from you or the king," he said. "However, you will listen to me and listen well. I have over a thousand men in this castle who are begging to rush forth and put your entire army on poles and leave you to die. You know my reputation and you know this is not an idle threat, so I suggest you depart today or face my wrath."

The men on horseback weren't quite sure what to say to that until one of them, shoved back behind the group, suddenly dismounted and stepped forward. Dressed in expensive protection, he was also dressed quite finely. *Too* finely for a knight. He removed his helm, revealing dark, dirty hair and a droopy eye. It took Jax a moment to recognize the man.

He was looking at John, King of England.

"De Velt," John said, sounding hoarse and weary. "Surely our engagement will not come to such bloodshed. It does not need to."

Jax wasn't about to show any measure of respect to a man he deeply resented. There were years of hatred there, stoked by none other than John himself.

"Your father and I had an agreement," he said. "You and I also had an agreement early in your reign. What has happened to this bargain, John? Why attack Pelinom? You know this will not end well for you."

John, seeing Jax through the big iron fangs, grinned. "Jax, my old friend," he said affectionately. At least, it sounded like affection. "I always thought William Marshal and his Executioner Knights were the most necessary evil in my kingdom but I think you surpass even them. You are the most fearsome warlord in all of England, but you are not an unreasonable man. Surely we can come to an agreement. We have always been able to talk, you and I."

Jax wasn't falling for his mild-sounding words. "If you had anything to say, you would have done it prior to attacking my home," he said. "After two days of being unable to breach the walls of Pelinom, *now* you wish to converse? Truly, I have nothing to say to you."

John wasn't going to back down. "Join me and I shall gift you Berwick permanently," he said, moving directly to the point. "I will also gift you with Carlisle. You shall become the Earl of Carlisle and rule the north. Is this not appealing to you?"

Jax didn't even hesitate; he shook his head. "It means nothing," he said. "I have my home and my holdings. I do not want an earldom."

"But I need your help."

"You have the help of about fifteen hundred mercenaries. You do not need me."

"You are not being fair."

Jax sighed heavily. "We danced a similar dance a few years ago when you tried to take Berwick with the help of the Princes of the Isles," he said. "You tried to bring the Northmen into northern England to control your warlords and it did not work. We chased you out then and we shall chase you out now. You cannot have Pelinom and you cannot have me, so take your army and leave before I grow annoyed enough to open these gates and charge your army. I will not fight them – I will destroy them the way I have always destroyed armies. I have never put a king to the pole before but for you, I will make an exception."

John tried not to let his apprehension show because he knew the man was serious. Jax de Velt never said anything he didn't mean.

"I think The Marshal will have something to say about that," he said after a moment. "He may not love me, but he is sworn to me. For now."

"It does not matter."

"You would go against your ally?"

"I will defend what is mine and eliminate the threat. *You* are the threat."

The king could see that Jax would not be swayed. Not that he had expected he would be, but he had been hoping to intimidate or coerce de Velt enough for the man to want to compromise. He knew now that it had been a stupid hope because Jax de Velt had never compromised in his life.

They were at an impasse.

"Very well," John said, turning for his horse. "You only have yourself to blame for what happens next."

"The same could be said for you."

Annoyed, John was finished being polite. He leapt onto his horse and roughly turned the animal around, galloping back towards his encampment with his entourage.

Jax watched him fade from view.

"Reinforce the walls," he muttered to Julian and Ashton. "Inform Tristan of what has happened and reinforce the postern gate. That's the only..."

"*Attack!*"

The shout came from the kitchens, where the postern gate was. Men started to rush in that direction but Julian and Ashton stopped them, ordering them to hold their posts. Jax began to run towards the kitchen yard with Julian and Ashton on his heels.

"Damn," he hissed. "A ruse. That whole conversation was a ruse while they made their way to the postern gate. Get the men to their posts – everyone on the walls. *Go!*"

Julian and Ashton split off, with Ashton heading to the gatehouse and Julian rushing for the troop house to empty it of any men who might be inside. But those men had heard the shouting and were already spilling forth just about the time a hail of arrows sailed over the walls, straight into the bailey.

Very quickly, the quiet morning had turned deadly.

It was an all-out assault. Julian was nicked by a bolt, which clipped him in the shoulder, but he saw at least a dozen men go down with nasty bolts sticking out of them. He picked up the one that had hit him, inspecting it. They were big, freshly hewn bolts with enormous iron tips, newly fitted and forged. He could still smell the acrid heat from the forge on them. As he eyed the bolt, puzzled, another heavier barrage flew up and over the wall.

The shields, for the de Velt men, began to come out.

Tossing the bolt to the ground, Julian rushed to the armory to collect his shield. He also collected as many as he could carry, the only protection against the rain of arrows that were now bearing down on Pelinom. He had to find his father to make sure the man was protected and he rushed out of the armory, tossing shields to men as he went. A third wave was launched, heading straight for the battlements. He could see soldiers hiding behind the crenelations as a sea of bolts poured through any openings in the wall.

"They've got an army of archers!" Ashton bellowed down from the wall when he saw Julian approaching. "They just emerged from the trees. Hundreds of them!"

Julian mounted the ladder to the walls, meeting Ashton halfway and handing him one of two shields he still held. "They've been hiding for two days?" he demanded. "Those bolts are fresh, Ash. I inspected one and the tip is newly forged."

Ashton was grim as he took the offered shield. "It makes sense," he said. "They probably spent them all on the last few battles and had to replenish their arsenal. No wonder the past two days have been quiet. They were waiting for their archers to refill their damned quills!"

Another round of bolts flew over the walls, this time aiming for the bailey. Most everyone was already under cover except for the men who had been hit and there were several. They were trying to drag themselves to safety but most of them were bad off. Holding his shield over his head, Julian came off the ladder and ran for them.

The first man he grabbed had a big bolt in his chest. He was only half-conscious as Julian grabbed an arm and began to pull him towards the troop house. He had only taken a couple of steps when he began to hear his mother shouting for him.

"Julian!" Kellington de Velt was standing in the now open door to the keep. She was waving frantically at her son. "Bring them in here! Hurry!"

Enraged, Julian ran across the bailey, dragging the man behind him. "Why did you open the door?" he shouted. "Papa will be furious with you!"

Kellington ignored him. She was a strong woman, tough as few were, beautiful and intelligent. Only a woman of such strength and character could have survived marriage to The Dark Lord. Not only survived but thrived. Jax and Kellington had a love story for the ages. She stood aside as Julian brought the soldier to the door where servants took over and dragged him inside.

"Hurry, Julian," Kellington commanded, pointing to the wounded men in the bailey. "Bring them all in here."

Julian didn't have time to argue with her. He was angry that the door was open, but he supposed she had a point. They had wounded now, where they hadn't had any for two days, and his mother and sisters were prepared to tend them. He rushed back towards the wounded, grabbing another man, when he suddenly looked up and saw his father carrying one man over his broad shoulders while towing another man by the arm. As his father ran past him, Julian grabbed another victim by the wrist and began to run after his father.

"Papa!" he shouted. "Take my shield. You must protect yourself."

Jax dumped the man on his shoulder into the waiting arms of servants while still others pulled the man in his grip inside. He turned to Julian as the man rushed up dragging a body.

"No shield," Jax said, composed and focused as he always was. "It will only slow me down. These men must get inside."

"Jax, listen to him," Kellington said, bordering on scolding. "Use a shield to protect yourself. If they are firing bolts, then…"

She was cut off when another barrage flew over the wall, striking the sides of the keep. Jax pushed his wife inside the door, out of the line of fire, before rushing back to the wounded. More soldiers were dragging their colleagues inside now, some of them carrying shields to protect themselves, but it was chaos in the bailey of Pelinom. Men were shouting and running everywhere. Julian was behind his father, trying to shield his man from another hail of bolts.

"Papa, get inside," he pleaded. "Most of the men are inside and we can bring in the rest. You are needlessly exposing yourself!"

Before Jax could reply, more arrows hit a man near him, a man who was trying to carry a comrade to the keep. Jax rushed to help both of them when the worst happened – a bolt plowed into him, straight into his left shoulder blade in a prime location in his back. It was such a big bolt that the tip emerged on the left side of his abdomen, poking through the mail. Another barrage came over the wall and Julian threw himself on his father, shield lifted, but he wasn't in time. Another bolt caught Jax in the top of his right shoulder, burrowing nearly half its length straight down, straight into Jax's powerful body.

It had all happened so fast. Faster than Julian could comprehend. One moment, his father was well and in the next, he had two massive bolts sticking out of him. But he hadn't gone down; nay, Jax de Velt was too strong for that. He simply stood there and took it, as if the bolts meant nothing to him.

As if they didn't mean his very life.

But they meant something to Julian. After a split second of disbelief, he grabbed his father, trying to keep the shield over him but he couldn't because of the big bolt in Jax's right shoulder. It kept knocking the shield sideways.

Julian began screaming to the men around him.

"Help me!" he said. "Help me get him inside!"

Jax was in a bad way, but he had hold of a man on the ground with a bolt through his pelvis and he wouldn't release him. He was still walking, still dragging that man, but he was staggering.

He was weakening.

"Papa," Julian begged. "Let go of the soldier. Please let go."

Jax's face was ashen. All of the color was gone. But still, he wouldn't release the soldier. "I cannot," he said stoically. "I must get him to safety."

Julian was beside himself. "I must get *you* to safety," he said, struggling not to become hysterical. "Papa, drop the man. Someone else will help him. Please let me take you inside."

Jax ignored him, but he was grunting. An odd grunting sound was coming from him as each step became more and more difficult. More and more taxing. Blood was streaming from the entry and exit wounds and because both lungs had been pierced, he could hardly breathe. He coughed, spraying blood from his mouth. Men were starting to crowd around Jax including Ashton, who had come off the wall when he saw what happened. Between Ashton and Julian, they managed to break Jax's grip on the man he'd been trying so desperately to drag to safety.

Jax was still walking, but with great difficulty.

Julian had hold of him, guiding his father towards the keep entry. He could hear crying and sobbing, but he didn't take his eyes off his father. He knew the sound must have been coming from his sisters and even servants who were in the entry, watching the horrific and heartbreaking scene. Step by step, inch by inch, Jax continued to walk towards the keep with every bit of strength he had. He was focused on something straight ahead, something he'd been focused on for more than thirty years.

His wife.

Kellington had come out of the keep and Julian turned to see his mother, her arms outstretched to her husband. She was perfectly calm, perfectly collected, as she put her hands on her husband and directed him inside with her.

"Come along, Jax," she said steadily. "Come inside and let me help you."

She acted like there weren't two enormous bolts sticking out of the man. She was composed and soothing. But Jax had blood and saliva dripping from his mouth, down his chin, his face the color of snow.

"There are men who need help," he said breathlessly. "I must…"

"Julian will make sure they are collected," Kellington said, gently cutting him off. "I must take care of you now. You have been wounded and you must come with me."

Mercifully, he didn't argue. He went with her. They passed through the keep entry and Jax finally lost his strength. He plummeted to his knees and Kellington went down with him to help him, but he was such a large man that she couldn't support his weight as he pitched forward, falling on her. Kellington ended up on her bottom as Jax lay across her awkwardly because of the bolts that were sticking out of him. His head ended up against her breasts as her arms went around him.

"I am sorry," he said, spraying blood onto her chest. "This is not how I planned my day, Kelli."

Kellington cradled him as the surgeon, a man who had been with Jax's army for many years, rushed over to inspect the damage. Kellington managed to wrap her arms tightly around her husband, holding him against her as his blood stained her flesh, knowing that this was the end before the surgeon even told her that Jax would not survive his wounds.

Somehow, she just knew.

"I do not think any of us plan our days perfectly," she said, gazing down into his pale face. "But you were doing a very brave thing to help your wounded soldiers. I expect nothing less from you."

Jax tried to clear his throat but there was a good deal of blood clogging it. "They are my men," he said simply. "They are willing to die for me. I should be willing to die for them."

The surgeon was moving around her, quickly inspecting entry and exit wounds, but when she noticed the man had stopped, she glanced up at him. All she could see was a grim expression and she knew it was because there was no hope.

He didn't have to say a word.

She returned her gaze to Jax's dual-colored eyes, eyes she knew so well.

"You are the most noble man I know," she said, struggling against the grief and agony that threatened. It would do no good; it wouldn't heal Jax. And she very much wanted this moment between them to be peaceful and loving if it was to be their last. "When I first met you, you did not have a noble bone in your body, but you have redeemed yourself."

"Do you think so?"

"I do."

"I am afraid that God will not think so."

"He will," she assured him, warmth in her expression. Then she glanced up, seeing her daughters Effington and Addington kneeling beside Jax with tears all over their faces. Julian was at his father's hip and he reached out to take one of his bloodied hands. Kellington smiled at her children, at her husband. "Look at these fine, strong people you have raised, Jax. Glorious sons and beautiful daughters. Only a man blessed by God would have such magnificent offspring."

Jax tried to clear his throat again but all that came out was blood. "It was you," he muttered, speaking more slowly now. "Everything I am, everything they are... it is all you. I have loved you... from the beginning of time and I shall... love you... until the end. I want you to know that, Kelli. You've made my life... worth living."

Kellington pulled him closer, kissing his forehead. "And I shall love you even longer still," she whispered. "You are a great man, Jax de Velt. You are the greatest man I have ever known and it has been my honor and privilege to be your wife."

"Nay, love," he muttered thickly. "It is I who have been privileged. But for this ending, I... I am... sorry. I... had hoped to die an old man, with you... by my side. Forgive me."

She smoothed his hair away from his face, tenderly. "For

what?" she said. "We have had a wonderful life, you and I. It will not end here. I will see you again. But until I do, know that I shall miss you every hour of every day. I will miss your warmth and humor and stubbornness. I will miss everything about you. Even if we do not die together, old and gray, know I am the most fortunate woman in the world because of you."

His eyes, which had been drooping, suddenly opened again and he looked at her. "I do not want to leave you."

"I know."

"Do not leave me."

"I will not. I will stay right here."

"Are you... you still holding me?"

"I am, Jax."

"Hold me tighter."

Kellington squeezed him. "Is that better, my pet?"

Jax's eyes closed and a lone tear streamed from his right eye, down his temple. "Kelli?" he murmured.

"Aye?"

"Where are you?"

"Right here. I am with you. We are all with you."

"Where is Julian?"

Focus shifted to Julian, who had been watching the scene with complete horror and agony. He was so choked up that he could hardly speak. "I am here, Papa," he whispered. "I am right here."

Jax squeezed his hand weakly. "Do not be afraid, Julian," he muttered. "Whatever life brings you... do not be afraid."

Julian broke down, tears streaming from his eyes. "I won't, Papa, I promise."

"Your... your time will come. But you must... find that greatness yourself."

"I will try to, Papa."

"Tell your brothers... tell them I love them," he rasped. "Cass... he is my heart. Our last words were... in anger. Do... do not let him feel guilty because of it. And Cole... he is my soul. Tell them how proud I am of them."

"I will, Papa."

"Addie? Effie?"

The two younger daughters were sobbing quietly. "We're here, Papa," Effington, the older one, said as she touched his cheek. "We're here. We love you."

Jax's breathing was becoming erratic. "Be happy," he said breathlessly. "I... I love you both very much. Go with Julian now. I want... want to be alone with your mother."

Julian lifted his father's hand, kissing it, before leading his sisters away. The women were sobbing, heading off into the small solar of the keep, as Julian paused at the entry and watched them go. He was just so overwhelmed with everything that he felt as if he were living a nightmare. Everything was closing in on him, swallowing him up with grief until he could hardly breathe. After a moment, he turned to see Ashton standing in the keep entry.

The man had tears in his eyes.

"Back to the wall, Ash," he commanded quietly. "Tell Tristan what has happened, but do not tell them men. Some may have seen what happened, but most did not. It may kill their morale to know what has happened to my father, so do not... tell them yet."

Ashton quickly wiped his eyes. "I will not," he said. "Tristan and I will hold the line. You must be with your father at this time."

Julian simply nodded. Ashton put a comforting hand on his

shoulder before departing the keep, heading out to the wall and shouting to the men. Julian watched him go a moment before returning his attention to his father and mother. Kellington was still holding Jax tightly, her cheek against his forehead, rocking him gently.

The sight broke Julian's heart.

As he stood there and blinked back tears, the old surgeon came over to him.

"I cannot help your father, lad," he said in his usual raspy tone. "The wounds are too great. There was no chance."

"I know."

"He's a strong man. A lesser man would have been killed right away."

Julian struggled to swallow the lump in his throat. "My father is no ordinary man."

The surgeon, who had been with the de Velt army for several years, simply nodded. "I'll be with the men in the solar but send for me when your mother is ready."

"Ready for what?"

"To take your father away."

Julian couldn't believe he was hearing those words. So much of him was in denial at the moment that he simply couldn't grasp that his father was dying. It had all happened so fast. Five minutes ago, his father was alive and well, but now…

Now, he was passing into legend.

As he watched his parents in a scene he would never be able to forget, as if it were branded into his memory, he didn't see his father moving at all, so perhaps he was already dead. The battle that Julian had thought so ridiculously weak had become the worst battle he'd ever faced in his life. Most certainly the costliest.

Do not underestimate John, his father had said.

God help him, he'd been right.

But he couldn't allow the grief to fill him. If he did, he would be unable to function. There was still a battle going on and with his father down, it was now up to him. The timid knight who lacked self-confidence now found himself in command of mighty Pelinom Castle and John wasn't going to lay his goddamned hands on Pelinom while Julian had breath left his body.

Instead of grief filling his veins, hatred did.

Hatred for the king who killed his father.

With a lingering look to his parents, Julian headed out into the bailey where another barrage of arrows had come down but no one had been hit this time. Everyone was staying under cover now.

And that went on for the rest of the day.

When evening finally fell, John's army had retreated enough to convince Julian and Ashton and Tristan that they were finally pulling out. They'd been unable to break Pelinom, at least not in a way they could see. The walls stood, but inside, the damage had indeed been done. Terrible damage that was the worst possible outcome in the death of Jax de Velt. When Julian finally entered the keep after sunset to see what had become of his mother and father, he found his mother sitting on the ground where he'd left her, still holding what was now his father's cooling corpse and from what Julian was told, no one could make her release him.

Julian didn't even try.

In fact, he stood guard over his mother and father all night, a silent witness to their last embrace on this earth. A silent witness to the conclusion of a love story for the ages. Even when they finally managed to take Jax away to remove the bolts to prepare the man for burial, Kellington never left his side. The entire time, she never left him.

And neither did Julian.

For The Dark Lord, he showed him that respect.

For his father, he showed him that love.

Farewell, Papa…

CHAPTER ONE

September
Year of our Lord 1222
Berwick

O N THE BUSTLING city center of Berwick, an armed escort bearing the colors of black and red, with a fearsome boar on the center of the standard, made its way down High Street towards Woolmarket Street. There was a carriage in the midst of the escort, heavily fortified and also painted black and red, while several knights rode the perimeter. It was a large collection of knights for such a small escort.

But some of those knights were from Berwick.

Cole de Velt was one of them. Commander of Berwick Castle, he had received advanced word that his mother and youngest sister were heading into Berwick to go to the merchants along Woolmarket Street. He and his brother-in-law, an enormous and powerful knight by the name of Anteaus de Bourne, were waiting for the de Velt escort as it crossed the bridge near the castle. He hadn't seen his mother or brother, Julian, in a while and greeted his brother amiably as he met the escort.

These days, it was anyone's guess if Julian would be amiable in return, but he was.

Fortunately.

Cole, an enormous man with the same dual-colored eyes that all of the de Velt men had, grinned at his younger brother by eighteen months. They had an excellent and close relationship, something he treasured, but he also knew that over the past few years, Julian had changed somewhat. Gone was the quiet, efficient, and somewhat under confident knight.

Replacing him was a man with a heart of stone.

Not that Cole blamed him. Julian still hadn't gotten over the death of their father, something he blamed himself for, every hour of every day. In the days following that terrible event, Julian emerged with a massive guilt complex. He was convinced that he had been the cause of Jax's death and nothing anyone could say could convince him otherwise. Something in that sense of responsibility had knocked the warmth out of him, a warmth that Julian had always had. He had been the gentle brother, the kinder brother, but no more.

Something had changed in him on that terribly and dark day.

Even as Cole greeted him with a smile, Julian hardly met his eyes.

But that was normal.

As they rode into town with normally quiet Anteaus keeping up a steady stream of chatter to Ashton de Royans, who had accompanied Julian, Cole found himself looking at his younger brother. All of the de Velt sons followed the same physical structure that their father had – they were enormous men, though each had varying talents and physical attributes. For

Julian, though he was shorter than his eldest and youngest brother, it was his strength that sent him apart. The man had the strength of Samson. His brothers would tease him that even his muscles had muscles. He was a physical specimen of perfection, a knight of the highest order who had worked very hard for that physical perfection. He was fair, much like Cole was, with their mother's dark blonde hair, which Julian shaved on the sides of his head while leaving the top a little longer.

But his eyes...

That was where Julian stood out. He had the two-colored eyes that all of the males in his family had and almost the exact same splash pattern that his father had, only instead of having a muddy brown left eye and a half-brown right eye, the brown color of Julian's right eye was pale, very nearly the color of a topaz. That bright green burst was still very prevalent in his left eye, so big that it nearly covered the entire eye. Looking at the man, a first glimpse would make it seem as if he had one topaz-colored eye and one green eye.

It was an interesting look on an uncommonly handsome young knight who was, unfortunately, quite self-conscious about it. For that very reason, Julian had always had difficulty looking men in the eyes. Not because he was shifty or ill-mannered, but simply because he knew how he looked.

Unthoughtful men and women had commented on it enough times.

"How goes it at Pelinom these days?" Cole said, simply to break the silence between them over Anteaus' chatter to Ashton. "How are the harvests coming along?"

Julian's focus was on the roadway ahead. "Well enough," he said. "I'm setting aside about a third of it for you and your garrison. You should be well-supplied through the coming winter."

"Thank you," Cole said. "Cori will be pleased to hear that. She also says I do not do enough for you in return, so if you'd like me to send loads of fresh fish your way, all you need do is say so."

Cole was referring to his wife, Corisande, a woman his world revolved around. Julian cracked a smile.

"I hate fish," he said. "You know I hate fish."

"I know you do, but Mother does not."

Julian made a face. "She has the cook bake fish and it stinks up the entire castle," he said. "She will not let me ban fish, but I will not make it easier for her to cook it by accepting your loads of fish. Think of something better to send me."

Cole chuckled. "I have a large herd of sheep to the north," he said. "I could cull the herd and send some your way."

"I accept."

Cole grinned and Julian mirrored the gesture, actually looking his brother in the eyes. He seemed to loosen up a bit, simply by his expression, and Cole nodded his approval.

"That is what I like to see in you," he said. "Like the Julian of old."

"What do you mean?"

Cole snorted softly. "I thought you might have forgotten how to smile, you do it so rarely anymore."

Julian's smile faded. "I have not forgotten."

"And you love me still?"

"Of course I do."

Cole's smile faded as well. "Good," he said. "Because I have something I must speak to you about, but not in front of Mother."

Julian looked at him curiously. "What is it?"

Cole glanced over his shoulder to make sure there was no one within earshot of them, or at the very least, not paying attention to them. He lowered his voice.

"I received a missive last week from de Lohr," he said.

"Christopher?"

Cole nodded. "The Earl of Hereford and Worcester himself," he said. "It was about… Cassian."

That was the magic word with the de Velt family. *Cassian.* It was a subject so painful that it was rarely brought up and certainly not in front of Kellington. Cassian de Velt, the youngest de Velt son, had been serving at Lioncross Abbey Castle on the Welsh Marches for many years. He'd been sent there to foster at a young age but ended up remaining because it was well known that he was in love with one of the de Lohr daughters, Brielle.

Of course, Jax had never faulted Cassian for staying where his heart was, but shortly after Jax's death, Cassian disappeared on his journey north to pay his respects to his father. Both Cole and Christopher de Lohr had sent out scouts and soldiers to search for Cassian when he never showed up at Pelinom, but no trace of him had ever been found. Not only had Kellington lost her husband, but her youngest son, as well.

The de Velt family was still reeling from the blows.

That was why Cole didn't speak the name of his youngest brother lightly. Julian was looking at him with great curiosity and perhaps even great dread. He knew Cole wouldn't tell him until they had more privacy but he couldn't wait that long. Anything to do with Cassian had his great interest.

"What is it?" Julian finally hissed, pulling himself out of the escort and pushing his brother to the side of the road as the escort continued towards Woolmarket Street. "Tell me this instant, Cole. What about Cassian?"

Cole let the escort pass by, making sure the wagon was far enough away, before he answered. "I'm not quite sure how to tell you this and I'm certainly unsure how to tell Mother," he said. "But de Lohr wrote me on a serious matter."

Julian's dual-colored eyes were blazing. "God, what?" he said. "Have they discovered something about Cass? Have they located his body?"

Cole shook his head. "Nay, not that," he said. "It has nothing to do with his disappearance, but more a personal matter. Something very personal to Cass."

"What are you talking about?"

"Brielle," Cole said simply. "We all know that Cass was in love with Brielle de Lohr. They have loved one another since they were quite young."

"I know. *And?*"

"And it seems that Brielle gave birth to our brother's bastard," Cole said quietly. "A boy she has named Maxim."

Julian's jaw dropped. "*What?*" he hissed in shock. "My God… are you certain?"

"That is what de Lohr says."

"Cass has a *son?*"

"It seems that he does."

Julian closed his mouth, reeling with shock. "Holy Mother of God," he finally breathed. Then, his brow furrowed. "But this birth could not have been recent. How old is the boy?"

"Six years of age."

Now, Julian's brow furrowed. "*Six* years of age?" he repeated, aghast. "And Hereford is just telling us now?"

Cole could see his outrage. Truthfully, he'd had plenty of his own until he read de Lohr's reasons and his wife had helped him to see the logic in it. He held up a calming hand.

"He explained that they have been keeping it secret from everyone," he said. "They have told everyone that Max is merely an orphaned relative, so no one knows he is Brielle's son. For Brielle's sake, they have simply been trying to keep the child's identity secret but, evidently, the boy looks exactly like Cass. He even has his eyes. He felt that he could no longer, in good conscience, keep the child's existence from us any longer. He felt it was our right to know. It was time."

Julian understood, sort of. His initial shock cooled as he thought on the younger brother who had vanished those years ago. Truth be told, that sensitive knight in him hurt very much for his missing brother and always would. It had always been his father and Cole against him and Cassian. They'd always stuck together. But Cassian's disappearance right after their father's death had been an incredible shock that, to this day, still had him feeling it deeply. Any mention of Cassian and Julian could feel his heart begin to pound. The hurt was still fresh.

And now... now, Cassian had evidently left a son behind.

He could hardly believe it.

"So Cass has a son," he finally muttered, struggling to calm emotions he usually kept quite buried. "Who else knows other than Cori?"

Cole shook his head. "No one," he said. "But Cori says that we must tell Mother. It is her right to know."

Julian turned to watch the escort as it faded down the road, thinking of his mother and the pain she had endured to lose both a husband and son in such a short amount of time. The woman was a rock but even rocks could crack and Julian was very protective over her to the point of hovering. Ever since he'd spent his last night with his mother and father, vigilantly standing watch over them, his protective instincts towards his mother were nearly out of control.

"She will want to see the lad," he said after a moment. "But I do not know if that is such a good idea."

Cole was watching the escort, too, and in particular, that big carriage that held his mother and sister. "I agree," he said. "De Lohr says the boy looks just like Cass. I am concerned that it will be too painful for her, but Cori seems to think it will bring her comfort. A young lad in the image of the one she lost."

Julian looked at him. "Will it be of comfort?" he said. "Because I do not even know how I am going to feel if I see the lad. If he looks just like Cass, how can that not hurt? How can we not look at him and feel our loss to our very bones?"

Cole didn't have an answer. Like Julian, he wasn't sure if they could see the child and not feel those blows of grief. But for their mother, it would be worse – she was strong, stronger than any woman he'd ever known save his own wife, but the loss of her husband and youngest son all in the space of a year had put dents in her proverbial armor. Seeing Cassian's son might blow the armor off entirely.

Or not.

There was only one way to find out.

"I do not know how we will feel," he said after a moment. "The only way to know for certain is to see the boy for ourselves. Then we can decide if we should inform Mother."

"When do you want to do this?" Julian asked.

"As soon as possible. I probably will not be able to sleep until I see him."

Knowing there was a de Velt son out there had them both thinking the same thing. They were both eager to see the boy and dreading it. But Cole worried about his brother in particular; Julian, who had hardened so terribly since the death of their father, who pretended to be as cold and calculating as Jax de Velt had ever been. Perhaps he was in a sense, but inside that iron exterior beat that same tender heart he'd always had.

Something Julian tried very hard to ignore.

"Come along," Cole finally said. "Let us join Mother and Addie in town. There's a stall towards the river that makes the most remarkable fish pies that I have a craving for."

"I hate fish pies."

Cole snorted. "I know."

Julian looked at him, seeing he was being teased. That was the normal dynamic between Cole and Julian, but it had never been malicious. In fact, Julian took comfort in it. He loved his brother a great deal. Putting aside the revelation of his brother's bastard son for the moment, he spurred his steed after the escort with Cole following close behind.

And he was determined to avoid the fish pies.

CHAPTER TWO

S HE HATED COMING to the apothecary stalls.

There was a corner of Berwick where the strange and unusual gathered, with shops run by men who would forage on the Scottish Marches for the ingredients to their mystical potions and health incantations. Or, they would rush to meet the ragged cogs that would enter the mouth of the river and weigh anchor out in the cold, sandy waters. Ragged cogs that had been to London or Calais or Lisbon or Algiers. Cogs that endured the turbulent waters of the Mediterranean to bring both peculiar and mystifying items that demanding consumers would pay good money for.

Like her mother and aunt.

Lady Lista Rose de la Mere could hear them even now. They were just inside the door of a stall on Silver Street, one of the stalls on the very end of the avenue because it was the only place where the apothecaries were tolerated. In Berwick, they were bizarre men with bizarre habits that were considered just short of witchcraft, so they were not particularly welcome even if they were sought after.

Plenty of people wanted what they had.

Lista could hear her mother, Lady Meadow de la Mere and her loud-mouthed sister, Lady Flora d'Orbec, as they demanded a sample before purchasing. What they demanded was, in fact, a carefully cultivated product that the apothecary was unwilling to simply give away. But in the end, he handed over a small sample. He knew Lady Meadow and Lady Flora and he'd never won an argument yet. Besides... he'd made a good deal of money from them in the past so he was willing to go on a little faith. The house of de la Mere had money to spend and they did – often. Lista watched as her mother and aunt shoved the product into their mouths, chewing slowly.

"It tastes like dirt," Meadow said.

"It *is* dirt," Flora replied, her expression laced with dissatisfaction. "It is more than likely poisonous. The man is poisoning us."

This is where the situation could turn into a brawl because Flora was quite opinionated and she didn't care who she insulted. Her husband had been a wealthy French knight, dead these past nine years, but he had defended his brassy wife quite staunchly. He had also been a knight for King John and even if the man was dead, no one had the courage to stand up to Flora or one might get a dagger rammed into one's eyeball.

A little something her husband had taught her.

"I am sure no one is poisoning you, Flora," Lista said, stepping forward to calm the situation before it veered out of control. "Make your purchase and let us move along. There is much to see this day."

Flora looked at her niece. "I will not purchase anything until I know the results," she said. "We come here weekly. He knows what our expectations are for *mousseron*."

Lista struggled not to roll her eyes. Flora was referring to a type of growth, an edible fungus that grew in the fields and the crags that she and her mother indulged in quite regularly. The type they liked produced a sense of calm and tranquility, but it also produced "visions", as both her mother and aunt declared, and they swore they had visions of the past, present, and future. Worse still, they had visions from far-off places where the land and the people were foreign. They sometimes claimed to speak the language. They even claimed to be in communication with an emperor known as The Wu. All sorts of odd claims from a pair of sisters everyone in Berwick knew to be simply...

Odd.

Lista was well aware. With her mother and aunt, sometimes it was like trying to herd cats. They went every which way and tended to become agitated easily. It was always an exercise in patience any time they traveled into town.

The trick was getting them out of town in one piece.

"Let us continue with our shopping and return when you are satisfied with your results," Lista said, indicating the street next to the river where there were rows upon rows of fish drying on racks. "We still have some provisions to purchase, so let us get about our business and return when we are finished."

While Flora seemed to be moderately agreeable to moving on, Meadow had other ideas. Just as she took her aunt by the arm and directed her towards the exit, Meadow was bent over a table, licking something from the tabletop. Releasing Flora, Lista rushed over to her mother and grabbed her by the wrist.

"Mama," she hissed. "What on earth are you doing?"

Meadow pointed to the table, now with a wet streak on it. "The *mousseron* was here," she said. "It should not go to waste."

Lista didn't argue with her. She simply pulled the woman out of the stall with her, out to the street where Flora had moved to stand with their escort. She had a rather dazed expression and Lista knew it was because she was waiting for the reaction from the hallucinogenic fungi she had partaken of. She hated that her mother and aunt insisted on visiting the apothecary first, but that was usual with the pair. Now, it would only be a matter of time before she had two intoxicated women on her hands so it was best to take care of the rest of their business quickly.

Lista motioned to the soldier in charge of the six-man escort and men moved to help Meadow and Flora mount their small palfreys, but the women didn't want to ride. They wanted to walk. Lista also ended up walking, leading the group as it plodded along behind her.

She could hear her mother and aunt bickering.

But that was normal. All of this, in her experience, was normal, at least over the past few years. She was a young woman born into a good family with an older brother, a father, and a mother, only her father had died of a heart ailment a little over two years ago and her brother had managed to get himself killed two years ago in a gambling establishment in London known as Gomorrah.

Discovering what, exactly, had happened had been difficult because Gomorrah was one of those establishments that ran just outside of the legalities of both the church and proper society. It was secretive – they hadn't even been able to discover where it was located – and all they knew was that Simon de la Mere had been murdered because he'd cheated in a game. His body had been dragged out and dumped on the door of the nearest church.

Lista's mother had been somewhat strange before that, but not nearly as out of control as she was these days. The death of her husband was difficult to bear but the death of her son was impossible. Lista tried to be tolerant, but her mother found comfort in anything that could change her mental status – alcohol would do, but mostly she found diversion with any number of strange potions, herbs, and toadstools that the apothecaries in Berwick and elsewhere could supply. She burned strange-smelling weeds, ate fungus, and ingested potions. Anything to take away the pain.

But it had only turned her into a caricature of her former self.

"Mama?" Lista said, turning her head slightly to address Meadow. "Should we stop at the fish stall? You know, the man who brines the fish in wine and garlic? We could take a barrel of that back home with us."

"Home to Fuckington, you mean?"

Flora had spouted off, now giggling at her vulgar comment. Lista cast a withering look at her uncouth aunt.

"It's Felkington, as if you did not know that," she said with limited patience. "Felkington Castle."

"Fuckington Castle. Fuck, fuck, fuck."

Flora was off on a giggling jag and even the soldiers were starting to grin. But Lista didn't find anything amusing in the boorish reference to her beloved home.

"Call it what you will," she said. "But whatever you call it, *you* live there on our good graces, so I would not speak so rudely of it."

Flora stopped giggling and glared at her. "Do you let your daughter speak so terribly to me, Meadow?" she demanded. "Tell her that she must respect me."

Lista answered for her mother. "I'll respect you when you behave in a manner that warrants it," she said, ignoring Flora when the woman snarled at her. Instead, she was looking at her mother. "Well, Mama? Should we stop at the fish man?"

Meadow was a bit dull, a bit dazed. Whatever the apothecary had given her was beginning to take effect. She looked at her daughter as if startled by the fact that the woman was addressing her.

"Fish man?" she repeated as if she'd never heard it before. Then, she quickly nodded her head. "Aye, the fish man. I want the fish that he brines in the wine."

"I know, Mama."

"Let's get a hogshead of the stuff."

"I agree. Let's."

Flora, forgetting about Lista's lack of respect, eyed her sister. "We can eat the fish and drink the wine," she said, snorting. "Is garlic fish-wine any good?"

The fungus they'd chewed up at the apothecary's shop was finally having an impact on Flora, as well. Meadow threw up her hands.

"Who cares?" she said. "I'll drink the smelly fish-brine or fish-wine and be quite happy with it. *Wait!* We must return to the apothecary!"

Abruptly, she turned on her heel and began to race back down the small avenue with Flora shuffling after her. Meadow was short and rather round, while Flora was tall and slender, with trembling hands because of too much drink and the other things she ingested all day long. She moved faster than Meadow, but she didn't move in a straight line. She traversed a crooked path all the way back to the apothecary as Lista simply stood there and watched.

She didn't even try to go with them.

An armored body moved up beside her.

"Shall I go with them, my lady?"

Lista turned to see the captain of Felkington's guard, Sir Amaury de Varreville. He was a little younger than Lista's father would have been had he still been alive, a handsome and seasoned man who had lived in Northumberland his entire life and he'd served Felkington for over half of those years. He'd seen the de la Mere family go from a relatively normal, if not a little eccentric family, to the talk of the county because of the behavior of Lista's mother and aunt.

But it was so much more complicated than that.

"Nay," Lista said after a moment. "They know where they are going and they know where to return if they want an escort home. Let us go to the fish man and purchase the barrel of brined fish. Mayhap that will be our only food store purchase for the day because I have a feeling my mother will spend the rest of the money on her… comfort."

Amaury glanced at Lista, sympathy and resignation in his expression. Using the word "comfort" when it came to Lady Meadow's addictions was putting it kindly. But Amaury didn't say a word. He didn't need to. As he turned for the escort, he caught sight of a rather large group coming down Silver Street, heading in their direction.

"The garrison must be out on this day," he muttered.

Lista heard him. Distracted from her mother and aunt for the moment, she turned to see what had his attention. "What garrison?" she said.

Amaury pointed down the avenue. "See the standards?"

"Aye."

"That's de Velt," he said. "The red and black standards with the boar's head. De Velt holds Berwick Castle, so the garrison is moving into town. More than likely the garrison commander with that kind of escort. See the wagon?"

Lista strained to catch a glimpse of what he was talking about. She could see the party down the avenue, soldiers with their black and red tunics. She could also see mounted knights, warriors of the highest order, and there were at least three that she could count, possibly more. Felkington's small army and single knight didn't have nearly the clout or presence that de Velt's army had as they entered the bustling city center. It was crowded and people naturally moved out of their way, something they'd not done for de la Mere's paltry escort.

De Velt was on a whole different level.

"I do not think we've seen the garrison come into town for quite some time," she said. "Simon used to know the garrison commander, I think. What's his name?"

"Cole de Velt," Amaury said. "The eldest son of Ajax de Velt, the most feared warlord in England in his youth. I remember being terrified of that name when I was young."

"He died a few years ago, didn't he?"

"In battle against John," Amaury said. "Some say that John sealed his death warrant by killing de Velt. After that, the king did not survive the year. We are told he died of dysentery, but there are rumors that it was poison in revenge for de Velt."

"De Velt was well-liked, then?"

"Well-connected, as they say. Connected enough for his allies to kill a king."

"And you believe it?"

"With William Marshal and Christopher de Lohr involved? I do."

That was a rather impressive and intimidating thought. Lista lifted her hand, shielding the sun from her eyes as the de Velt escort drew closer. "My father did not speak much of him," she said. "I know the name, of course, but not much else. Papa was not in de Velt's social circle."

She grinned, thinking of her father, who hadn't been a warrior at all. Felkington was a smaller castle in a somewhat bucolic corner of Northumberland. Any raiding Scots seemed to avoid them, as they weren't strategic, and any battles or political intrigue never seemed to bother them. They lived in a safe little haven which, in Northumberland, was rare. Lista had never experienced a battle in her life and they only kept soldiers on because of the conventional need for protection. God only knew why Amaury remained because before he'd come to Felkington, he'd been a man of experience with the Earl of Northumberland's army. Lista's father had paid him well, and he had remained after her father's death.

"Your father may have not been in de Velt's social circle, but that doesn't mean he didn't know the happenings or the political players of Northumberland," Amaury said, cutting into her thoughts. "Your father was much more astute than you give him credit for."

Lista looked at him, smiling. "I give him all the credit in the world," she said. "But I wish, very much, that he were still here. He would have been able to help Mama cope with her grief from Simon's death, but now…"

She trailed off and averted her gaze. There was no use in verbalizing what they both knew and in wishing for something that would never happen. Lista had often wondered how her mother would have been had her father not perished before Simon had. Certainly, no one could have predicted the spiral Meadow was experiencing, leaving a daughter to manage a prosperous castle that she'd fortunately handled well.

"Your mother will find her balance someday," Amaury said

quietly. "But you must get her away from your aunt. That woman only seeks to drive her to ruin."

Lista knew that. Even now, she could see her aunt and mother emerging from the apothecary with small canvas bags. She knew what that meant – more herbs and weeds and fungi to chew on, to cause them both to float away on a haze of confusion. She was in for another week or two of wild behavior and not looking forward to it. Feeling despair, and disgust, she was about to turn away from the sight when the de Velt party, which had been far down the road only moments before, was now at the intersection of two avenues.

And her mother and aunt were walking right into them.

Lista could hear her mother screeching at the soldiers who had pushed her aside to allow the de Velt escort to pass. Since she knew her mother wasn't beyond unleashing a slap or two when aroused, she began to quickly walk in that direction with Amaury on her heels. About the time she reached the group, they had come to a halt because Meadow and Flora were in a full-blown brawl with two of the soldiers. As Lista watched in horror, one of the soldiers shoved her mother, hard, and the woman went skidding onto her backside. As Flora took a swing at the man, she was pushed roughly as well.

"Keep your hands off them!" Lista snarled as she put herself between the soldiers and her mother and aunt. "How dare you touch a noblewoman? Who are you? What is your name?"

The soldier wasn't inclined to answer, but a nearby knight did. "I assure you, my lady, that he did not start the fight," he said calmly. "These two women charged him, quite unprovoked."

Lista was furious as she turned to the knight. He was emerging from midway down the escort, astride the biggest horse she'd ever seen. In fact, the knight himself was the largest man she'd ever seen. At least, from what she *could* see. He was covered in well-used and expensive armor, a great helm upon his head and big weapons strapped to his body. Weapons he was undoubtedly skilled in using.

But Lista didn't back away.

"My mother would not have charged anyone unless she was rightfully baited," she said. "If this is your way of defending your undisciplined men, then you should be ashamed of yourself. A well-trained man would not have shoved a woman."

"You throw around accusations too easily without knowing the facts, my lady."

"And you hide your failure as a commander of men by blaming innocent women."

Suddenly, a brief encounter was becoming far more serious than it should have. The knight didn't say anything but another knight, one with rather elaborate armor, slid off his horse and put himself between the great-helmed knight and the woman before a brawl of epic proportions developed.

The insults were flying.

"My lady, no offense was intended," he said calmly. "I am Cole de Velt, the commander of Berwick Castle, and I can assure you that our men are well-trained and disciplined. What happened was an unfortunate mistake and our man will be punished for it. Please do not think us all ill-bred over one small incident."

Lista was placated somewhat, but she was still glaring daggers at the other knight. However, the commander's apology was fair and reasonable.

She backed down a little.

"I do not think you ill-bred, my lord," she said. "But I do

not think there is any excuse for a man becoming rough with a woman, no matter what has been said."

"You are correct, my lady."

"And I'll not be told that an unarmed woman was a threat to a man with weapons."

"Again, you are correct, my lady."

"Then someone should tell your knight not to blame women for the failure of men under his command."

The enormous knight didn't say anything for a moment, perhaps sizing her up behind that face plate. Lista couldn't see his eyes, but she could only imagine what he was thinking. She thought perhaps she might have said too much but, on the other hand, the sight of her mother being pushed around had inflamed her.

The big knight cleared his throat quietly.

"I have introduced myself," he said. "It would be polite for you to tell me your name, also."

He was right, which meant she couldn't be so self-righteous any longer. She'd had a failure in manners, too.

"I am Lady Lista de la Mere of Felkington Castle," she said. "This is my mother, Lady Felkington, and my aunt, Lady d'Orbec. If... if they got in your man's way, then I apologize, but it was unintentional."

That was as much of an apology as they were going to get from her. Her gaze moved to the soldier who had shoved her mother and then to the knight who had defended him. His helm was turned in her direction so she was positive he was looking at her. One wrong word from him and she could quite possibly take a stick to him. The commander of Berwick must have sensed that, so he tried to distract her.

"Felkington?" he repeated. "That is to the south, is it not?"

Not wanting to be rude to the man who had tried to ease the situation, Lista returned her focus to him.

"Aye, my lord," she said. "To the southwest."

"And your father? His name?"

"Edmund de la Mere, Lord Felkington. The castle was named for the title," Lista said. "I also had a brother, Simon, who perished two years ago. I believe you knew him."

That brought pause from the knight. "I did," he said, surprised. "Dead, you say? What happened?"

"He was murdered in London."

The knight's head bobbed up and down in understanding. "You have my sympathies," he said. "I did not know your brother well, but I met him on a few occasions."

"He thought well of you, my lord."

"Then I am pleased," the knight said. "And your father is dead also?"

"He is, my lord."

The knight nodded as if satisfied by the answers but before he could continue, the door to the carriage lurched open and a woman in a tight wimple stepped forth. She was an older woman, though quite lovely, and after her came a younger woman with long, dark hair, stylishly arranged.

"We may as well get out," the older woman said, pushing between the soldiers until she came to the knights and Lista in a strange sort of standoff. Her gaze fixed on Lista curiously. "Ah. I see why we have stopped. A social visit, is it?"

Lista had no idea who the woman was, though she seemed pleasant enough. Reaching up, the big knight removed his helm, revealing a handsome man with shoulder-length, dark blond hair and striking eyes that were two different colors.

"Nay, this is not a social visit," he said. "This is Lady Lista de la Mere. We've had a bit of a… misunderstanding, but I have made our apologies."

The woman in the wimple approached Lista, focusing on her intently. She was a beautiful woman for her age, fair-skinned, with brown eyes.

"De la Mere," she repeated. "Edmund de la Mere?"

Lista nodded. "He was my father, my lady."

That brought a smile to the woman's lips. "Your mother is Meadow?"

Lista was surprised. "Aye, my lady," she said. "Meadow is indeed my mother. Do you know her?"

The woman nodded. "I did, long ago," she said, looking around. "Is your mother here?"

Lista thought she was. She thought her mother and Flora were right behind her, but a quick perusal of the area failed to turn them up. She was about to shout her mother's name until she heard some bickering going on in the apothecary shop behind them.

That told her everything she needed to know.

"God's Bones," she hissed. "Please excuse me, my lady."

With that, she dashed inside the entry just as the apothecary was shoving Meadow and Flora out the door.

"And keep them out!" the man shouted at her. "They are trying to lick the corks of my phials. And they are stealing my hemp!"

Lista was mortified. She had hold of her mother and aunt, preparing to pull them out of the apothecary's shop when Meadow's face suddenly lit up.

"Kelli!" she gasped. "Kellington Coleby!"

She yanked from Lista's grasp and ran to the wimpled woman, throwing her arms around her and nearly knocking her over. Both knights, standing close by, had to reach out to steady the women so they wouldn't go over into the mud. Even when she was righted, Meadow continued to hug the well-dressed woman.

"Kelli, I've not seen you in years!" Meadow said happily, finally loosening her embrace to get a good look at her. "So many years have gone by, but I still recognized you. I would know your lovely brown eyes anywhere!"

Lady Kellington Coleby de Velt smiled at her old friend. "I am so happy to see you, too," she said. "It has been too long."

"Much too long."

"Whatever are you doing in Berwick?"

Meadow turned to gesture to her daughter and sister. "We have come into town to purchase a few things," she said. "We were just going to the man who sells the brined fish down by the river. What are *you* doing in Berwick?"

"The same thing you are."

"Shall we go together, then?"

Kellington wasn't too certain about that. She had a lot of people with her and didn't want to drag them along while she went off with a childhood friend, pleased as she was to see her.

"I am sure you have many other things to attend to, just as we do," she said. "But introduce me to your daughter. I've not met her. I do not think I remember your sister, either."

Meadow turned to the pair behind her, proudly. "My daughter, Lista," she said. "Isn't she beautiful?"

Kellington grinned at the young woman who was now starting to flush. "Quite," she said. "She looks like your mother a little."

Meadow nodded in agreement. "She is much prettier than my mother ever was," she said. "And she's very smart, as well.

She can read and do sums in her head. She can do anything you ask of her, for she is perfect."

Lista was hoping the ground would swallow her up right about then. But unfortunately, she was left exposed as her mother praised her. "My mother has far too much faith in me, my lady," she said, trying to shut her mother up because the woman was being too chatty due to the fungi she had ingested. "May I introduce my aunt, Lady Flora d'Orbec."

Flora was slightly more inebriated than Meadow, but she concealed it well when she wanted to.

She'd had practice.

"My lady," she greeted. "I recognize your name. I do not think we met as children, though I suspect it was because I went to foster before my sister did and there was never the opportunity. Where did you know her?"

Kellington smiled politely at the slender woman with the long face and hair piled neatly on top of her head. It made her head, in general, look extremely long.

"St. Helen's," she said. "I was born at Pelinom Castle and my father would take me for lessons with the priests at St. Helen's, where Meadow also received lessons."

"What sort of lessons?"

"Mostly biblical education, but we learned to read and also to write."

Flora smiled thinly. "Pity," she said. "My parents were never so gracious to me. They sent me away as soon as I became of age, though I cannot fathom why. They seemed to like to keep Meadow close to them."

If Kellington thought it was a strange comment, she didn't let on. "Where did you foster?" she asked politely.

"Alnwick," Flora said. "I met my husband there. He was a

retainer for the earl and, for a time, for John when he was king, though it is unpopular to say so. I rather enjoyed court."

Kellington kept her polite smile but it was clear she thought Flora was perhaps a little strange and a little much to take in all at once. She returned her attention to Meadow.

"I do not wish to keep you, but I hope you will accept an invitation to visit Pelinom," she said. "I would love to hear about your life since I last saw you."

Meadow was flying increasingly high with the fungi she had ingested, so it was a little difficult for her to maintain a coherent thought. She wasn't as adept as Flora was in concealing it so she clung to Kellington's hands, smiling dreamily at the woman.

"It has been tragic and eventful," she said. "But certainly, I have not done as well as you have. I heard you married a great warlord, long ago."

Kellington nodded. "I did," she said. "I married Ajax de Velt and these are two of our sons, Cole and Julian. Have you met them?"

Meadow shook her head, looking to Lista. "My daughter has," she said. "My dearest, sweetest girl was prepared to go fisty against them because their soldiers offended us."

She had used the slang for a fistfight. *Fisty.* That's what the lower class called such a brawl and Kellington looked at Cole with concern. "What is this?" she demanded. "We have offended my friend?"

Cole cleared his throat softly, throwing a glance in Julian's direction. "A misunderstanding, as I said," he replied. "I have made our apologies, I assure you."

"He has," Lista said before her mother could start something. "It was only a misunderstanding and Sir Cole has been very polite."

"And Julian?" Kellington wanted to know, looking to the second helmed knight. "Has he been polite, also? Surely you have met my Julian."

All eyes turned to the impossibly broad knight whom Lista had briefly sparred with. After a brief pause, perhaps one of resignation, the knight removed his helm, revealing close-cropped, dark blond hair on the sides of his skull and a square jaw. When he turned to look at Lista and the others head-on, the longer top of his hair hung down over his right eye, covering part of his face, but it didn't detract from his stunning good looks.

At least, Lista thought so.

The man was quite comely.

"We have not formally met your son, my lady," she said, feeling her cheeks growing pink to be in the presence of the handsome man she'd been so willing to fight. "Sir Julian, it is an honor."

Julian simply looked at her. The one eye that she could see was intense, riveted to her, but she was coming to feel uncomfortable that he'd not replied until Cole shot him a look that seemed to prompt him. He dipped his head politely.

"My lady," he said.

He had a deep voice that sounded as if it were being dragged over gravel. There was a hoarseness to it, but it was also bottomless in its tone. Deep, commanding, and controlled as she'd noticed from the first. She nodded her head in response, feeling rather shaken from that piercing eye and raspy voice. Her attention returned to Kellington.

"If Pelinom is too far for you to travel tonight, mayhap you will stop at Felkington and dine with my mother and me," she said. "We would be deeply honored by your visit."

Kellington had a warm smile for you. "You are very kind, my lady," she said. "But we will be staying at Berwick tonight with my eldest son and his wife. May... may I extend the invitation for you to dine with us at Berwick Castle tonight? I am certain that Cole and his wife will not mind and there is a great deal of room to accommodate you. Please say you will."

Lista was absolutely mortified by the invitation. By tonight, her mother and aunt would be flying with the night birds on all of the potions and weeds they'd purchased. That was certainly not what Lista wished to show Lady de Velt and her family. In fact, it would be an incredible embarrassment. But before she could politely decline, Meadow went to Kellington and took the woman's hand.

"You are very gracious, Kelli," she said, smiling. "May I call you Kelli? I used to, once. A little girl with long, blonde hair and skinny arms. What a terror you were!"

Kellington burst into giggles. "Of course you may call me Kelli," she said. "And I hope I will always be a terror."

Meadow threw her arms up as if to cheer. "Well said," she declared. "I hope I always am, as well. We shall accept your invitation to dine this evening. You are very kind."

Kellington laughed softly. "I am looking forward to it," she said. "Hurry, now – finish your shopping and come to the castle when you are finished. I will see you there."

Thrilled, Meadow kissed her loudly on the cheek and flitted off, rushing over to the de la Mere escort where Amaury was standing. He'd heard everything and he, too, was troubled by the fact that Lady de Velt, one of the most respected women in Northumberland, had just invited a pair of squirrels to dine with her in Meadow and Flora. The pair sauntered away, leaving Lista still standing with the de Velt escort.

Truly, she was torn. She wanted to decline the invitation in private because she could just tell that tonight would be a terrible night for her mother and aunt to be in a social situation where they would be expected to behave. She turned to look at Kellington, now standing with the young woman who had been in the carriage with her. They were speaking quietly as Lista summoned her courage and made her way over to them.

"Lady de Velt?" she said to catch the woman's attention. "My lady?"

Kellington and the young woman turned to her, expressions of kindness and interest on their faces.

"May I be of service, my lady?" Kellington asked. Then, she suddenly indicated the young woman next to her as if she had been most forgetful. "I did not introduce you to my daughter, Addington. Addie, this is the daughter of my old friend, Lady Lista."

Lista looked at the young woman who had the same two-color eyes that her eldest brother had, only hers were a different pattern. She had pale green around the pupils with a big, outer ring of muddy brown. But the green wasn't any green – it had gold and yellow in it, quite dynamic. Lista found herself looking into the face of a most beautiful and unusual looking young woman.

"I am honored to meet you, Lady Addington," she said. "I must say… you have such beautiful eyes. Has anyone ever told you that?"

Addington grinned. "My parents have told me often enough," she said. "But it is so much nicer coming from someone I have just met. Thank you very kindly, my lady. I am flattered."

Lista smiled timidly, already sensing something kind from

Addington de Velt. "It is true," she said. "Your brother has similar eyes. Is it a family trait?"

Addington nodded. "We all have it in different ways," she said. "My father had two-colored eyes, so we inherited it from him."

"I see," Lista said. "You are very fortunate. It makes your beauty most memorable."

"That is very kind of you, thank you."

With a final smile at Addington, Lista turned to Kellington. "My lady, I hope it will not be too much trouble, but I fear my mother was not thinking clearly when she accepted your invitation to sup," she said quickly and quietly. "You see, we came to Berwick today for… medicines. My mother has not been feeling well and I fear these medicines will make her say or do something to embarrass herself. Mayhap we should visit another time when she is feeling better."

Kellington looked over Lista's shoulder where Meadow and Flora were dancing with each other next to the escort. It appeared quite strange, as it had from the beginning. The moment she'd encountered Meadow and her odd sister, something just seemed… off. As she watched, they suddenly scurried off down the street as a big knight began to walk after them.

"I'm sorry to hear that she is ill," she said after a moment. "What is her ailment, if I may ask?"

Lista wanted to crawl into that hole she had once hoped would open up and swallow her. She didn't want to spill too much of the family secret, but with her mother and aunt clearly under the influence of something, she didn't see that she had too much choice.

But, God… it was embarrassing.

"My father died a few years ago and my brother was murdered shortly thereafter," she said. "The grief of my brother's demise has been too much for my mother to bear and she does... things to make her forget. Sometimes it is ale or wine, sometimes it is ingredients she purchases from the apothecary. She muddles her senses in such ways. Anything to forget her pain, so I am afraid today might not be a good day for her. I would hate to have her shame herself in front of you, or worse, make you angry."

Kellington's expression changed slightly. Her smile faded, but the warmth in her dark eyes was still there. Reaching out, she grasped Lista's hand gently.

"I lost my husband a few years ago and my youngest son shortly thereafter," she said softly. "Therefore, I understand your mother's grief. I know it all too well. Please come tonight. I would very much like to see her and mayhap... mayhap I can help her."

Lista wasn't at all sure she should. Her gaze moved to Addington, who smiled encouragingly, before returning her focus to Kellington.

"If you are certain," she murmured.

Kellington nodded firmly. "I am," she said. "Bring her. Come and visit with us. And mayhap you and Addie can become friends in the process."

Lista looked at Addington, who readily agreed. "I would like that," she said. "Won't you please come, Lady Lista? If you don't, I shall be forced to converse with Julian and he is terrible at conversation."

She only said it because Julian was closer to her than anyone else. She giggled, which made Lista giggle as she looked over at the enormous knight who had just put his helm back on.

"I am to save you from boredom, am I?" she asked.

If Julian heard them, he didn't acknowledge it. He simply went about his business. But Addington nodded as she continued to giggle, suggesting to Lista that the situation wasn't all that dire. It was clear that she was only jesting with her brother and Lista liked her spirit. She thought she might like to spend the evening conversing with a woman who didn't eat dirt and burn herbs.

Throwing caution to the wind, Lista sighed heavily.

"Very well," she said. "You have convinced me. But if my mother and aunt act strangely... thank you for making allowances."

Kellington's eyes were glimmering warmly. "We are quite understanding in such things," she said. But then she glanced over to where the de la Mere escort had been, noticing that they had all gone in pursuit of Meadow and Flora. "But it seems as if you are all alone, my lady. Julian will escort you to find your mother."

Before Lista could lodge a protest, Kellington was already turning to Julian and instructing him to escort her friend's daughter to find her mother. Lista watched as the helmed head turned in the direction of his mother, his impossibly broad shoulders slumped in resignation, and he gathered his horse's reins. No question, no protest.

Simply duty.

"But... truly, my lady," Lista said, stammering slightly. "I am sure they are just around the corner. I can find them easily."

Kellington wouldn't hear of it. "Nonsense," she said. "A young woman must have an escort. Julian will be happy to lend assistance."

Lista had to bite her tongue because any further protest

might make her sound ungrateful. She didn't want to get into an argument with Lady de Velt when she was doing something kind and proper. Moreover, the way Julian had immediately complied with his mother told her that any refusal would be futile.

Like it or not, she had an escort.

Therefore, Lista managed a smile, but it was more like a grimace. As Kellington and Addington moved away, they also removed the only barrier between her and the big knight she'd almost fought with. The one she'd insulted. For a moment, they simply looked at each other until Lista finally turned away, heading back towards the spot where she'd last seen the de la Mere escort.

Julian followed.

Lista had been hoping that the escort was only out of her line of sight, but when she reached the spot where she had last seen them, they were nowhere to be found. There was a crowd in Berwick on this day, as was usual during market days, so there were people everywhere, blocking her view in all directions.

"I am certain that I can find my escort from here, Sir Julian," Lista said. "You do not need to be troubled with me, truly. I can take care of myself."

He acted as if he hadn't heard her. "I saw them head east," he said. "Mayhap if we go that way, we shall locate them."

Lista eyed him. "I can find them on my own," she said, more firmly. "I have already troubled you too much today. You may return to your group. I insist."

He just started walking towards the east, leading his massive warhorse behind him. Lista watched him go and, frustrated that he had ignored her, she went in the opposite direction. In fact, she moved very quickly because she wanted to lose him. She was almost to the street that ran along the river when she suddenly heard the thunder of hooves come up behind her and a big horse abruptly blocked her path. Startled, she looked up to see Julian astride his big war beast.

He extended his hand to her.

"Come, my lady," he said. "Let me take you to your mother."

He was meaning to pull her onto his horse, but Lista didn't take his hand. Unfortunately, she had a stubborn streak in her and she didn't like the way he was ignoring her wishes.

"You do not seem to understand," she said. "I do not want your assistance. I did not ask for it. You may return to your party because I do not want your help. Is that clear?"

He didn't move his hand. "My mother has asked me to assist you and as far as I am concerned, that is as good as a command from God himself," he said. "We can do this the easy way or the difficult way, but either path you choose, I shall escort you back to your mother, so choose wisely."

So he was as stubborn as she was. She was digging in, he was digging in, but he was only succeeding in making her angry.

"Sir Julian," she said, her tone heavy with hazard. "If you truly saw what happened today between my mother and your soldier, then you know what I must deal with when it comes to my mother and my aunt. They are as skittish as colts, as unruly as foxes, and as difficult as wild boars. I do battle with them nearly every day and the truth is that I am sure they did provoke your soldier. I apologize for insulting you about it, but you understand that I must defend my mother. However, given what I have just told you, every moment they are out of my sight is a moment they could possibly be doing something outrageous and shameful, so I do not need to stand here and argue with the likes of you. I understand that you are an elite knight and I respect that greatly, but when I tell you that I do not need your help, I would appreciate the courtesy of having my wishes respected. You are the last person I need to do battle with."

She was nearly in tears by the time she finished although she had no idea why. It had something to do with embarrassing herself in front of a de Velt knight. A handsome knight who had probably never known a day of embarrassment or shame in his life. Quickly, she turned away and headed in the opposite direction, trying to get away from him and hoping he would simply leave her alone. She hadn't gotten very far when she heard a voice behind her.

"I do not wish to do battle with you, my lady, I swear it," Julian said. He was off his horse again, walking about ten paces behind her. "I promise you that I am not being stubborn. But I would be a callous man indeed if I did not make sure you were safe. There are all sorts of men in this town who would be happy to see you come to harm and if I can prevent that, I will. Besides... if I return to my mother and have not completed my task, she will be very unhappy with me and I do not wish to incur her wrath."

His response was far less stiff than he had been with her since their introduction. She had to admit that she was rather surprised by it. That deep, raspy voice that could be so hard could also be somewhat... pleasant.

She came to a halt and faced him.

"I appreciate your noble intention," she said. "And I do understand about your mother, truly. But I do believe it is customary to obey a lady's wish. *My* wish."

"Not if that wish will see her come to harm."

"Are you so certain it will?"

"Are you so certain it will not?"

He had her with that logic. Lista cocked an eyebrow. "I see that I will not be able to discourage you," she said with regret. "Tell me the truth. Are you really concerned for my safety more than you are afraid to return to your mother and tell her that I told you to leave me alone?"

"If I must choose, the latter, my lady."

Her lips twitched with a smile. "At least you are as honest as you are stubborn," she said. "Then I suppose if you are so grimly determined to be of service, I should let you."

"That would be wise, my lady."

Her smile broke through, as much as she tried to stop it. "Very well," she said. "And I meant what I said. I am sorry I was sharp with you, but it was my mother, after all."

"Understandable, my lady."

"Mayhap when we see each other tonight at the feast you will not view me so unfavorably."

"I would not view you unfavorably in any case, my lady."

He didn't seem much of a conversationalist so Lista didn't continue. She simply nodded her head as if to acknowledge that things were settled between them and there were no hard feelings before turning around and heading off towards the east. Julian trailed after her, following her for the next twenty minutes until she finally found her mother and aunt in a merchant stall.

Once Julian saw the de la Mere escort, he backed off and returned to the de Velt group, but not before casting a lingering glance at Lista as she tried to convince her mother and aunt that they didn't need whatever the vellum merchant was trying to sell them.

Julian never saw the lingering glance she cast him in return.

CHAPTER THREE

Berwick Castle

"SHE IS A beautiful woman," Ashton said. "Too bad she has the manners of a shrew."

By candlelight and in the reflection of a polished bronze mirror, Julian was shaving the stubble off his neck, which his hauberk was starting to irritate.

"Who?" he asked.

Ashton had just splashed water all over his face. "Today," he said, grabbing blindly for a towel. "The woman who told you that you were a poor commander."

Julian watched his reflection in the mirror as he carefully shaved. "The de la Mere lass?"

"The same."

They were in one of the many chambers of Berwick Castle, a vast complex of outbuildings, towers, chapels, and halls. Julian and Ashton were sharing a larger chamber in an apartment block near the southwest tower. There was some construction going on at the great donjon, which was synonymous with the great gatehouse, but there was also a keep on the northwest side of the castle where Cole and his family resided. In all, Berwick was a massive and impressive place, and Julian was always properly awed by his brother's command but at this moment, he wasn't thinking about Berwick.

He was thinking about a certain young woman who had insulted him.

"I suppose she is pretty enough," he said after a moment, carefully moving up his throat with a sharp razor. "I didn't think her manners were horrible."

Ashton frowned. "She all but condemned your ability as a commander," he said, agitated as he wiped his face. But he suddenly stopped. "And that's another thing – speaking of commanders, I swear to you that if de Bourne so much as looks at your sister in a manner I do not like, I will flay the man."

The change of subject was swift, from one young woman to another, and Julian grinned. "Anteaus de Bourne has as much right to look at Addie as you do," he said. "Christ, Ash, you've known my sister for ten years and you have had your chance. She's has grown tired of waiting for you."

Ashton turned his nose up at him. "I'm to inherit Bowes Castle and my father's titles," he sniffed. "What does de Bourne have to offer her? Nothing. Nothing but his big muscles. The man is as stupid as a post."

Julian burst out laughing. "He is more handsome than you are."

"He is *not*."

"Addie thinks so."

Ashton's eyes widened. "Did she say so?"

Julian was still chuckling as he rinsed off his razor in the basin. Ashton was quite beauteous with his blond de Royans looks, but it was always fun to poke at the man's pride.

"She did not," he said. "But Effie has said so."

Ashton sneered. "Effie has no bearing on the situation," he said. "She has a husband, the poor man. She should not be commenting on the comeliness of other men."

Julian snorted again, drying off his razor. "I like Rod," he said, referring to Effington's husband of several years. "And her husband is not a 'poor man'. He's skilled and wealthy. Rod de Titouan is a close ally of the Earl of Hereford and Worcester, you know."

"I know." Ashton tossed the towel aside. "I like Rod well enough, too, but Effington puts poison in Addie's ears. Her attitude is always quite different after she visits with her sister."

Julian glanced at him. "You mean that Effie tells Addie not to wait around for you?"

Ashton wasn't going to admit to anything. As Julian had mentioned, he'd known Addington for several years, only becoming interested in her over the last two. Addington was a beautiful girl, but since the death of her father, she'd stuck to her mother like flies to honey. She really didn't entertain suitors and the only reason she entertained Ashton was because he served at Pelinom. She saw him every day. But she was very much attached to her mother, something the family didn't really talk about much.

There was an underlying reason for that.

With the loss of Cassian, Addington was the baby of the family and there was something in her that couldn't seem to leave the nest, not just yet. She felt that her mother needed her more than a husband would. Ashton hadn't pushed, and that worked well in his favor since he wasn't entirely eager to marry yet, but when Cole's brother-in-law, Anteaus, started showing interest in Addington last year, Ashton was forced into the position of a dog protecting his bone.

It made for some humorous – and tense – moments at times.

"I do not care what Effington thinks," Ashton finally said, turning up his nose. "What's between Addie and me is our business, not hers."

"It's going to be Anteaus' business if you don't do something about it," Julian said.

Ashton shrugged, ever defiant. "It would serve Addie right if I married someone else," he said. "That woman from earlier today – the de la Mere girl – is quite pretty the more I think on it. And she'll be here tonight. Mayhap I should get to know her better and throw a little envy into Addie. If she sees me paying attention to another woman, mayhap it will drive her into my arms."

Julian shook his head at the logic. "Or drive her fist into her eye," he said. "Leave Lady Lista out of your manipulation. I have a feeling she has enough to deal with."

Ashton looked at him curiously. "What do you mean?"

"Did you see her mother and aunt?"

Ashton's eyebrows lifted in realization. "Oh, *that*," he said. "Those two were a pair. Mad, both of them."

"It seems so."

"If today was any indication, I have a feeling we are in for an interesting evening."

Julian tucked his razor away, his thoughts lingering on Lista de la Mere. Ashton was right – she was quite pretty. Magnificent, even. He thought on her long, dark hair with some wave to it, her sweetly oval face and pert nose, but most of all, he thought on her eyes. They were the purest shade he'd ever seen, the greenish-blue of the ocean when the water was clear and cold. There was something about her that would make any man take a second look at her, including him. But he thought it all rather futile.

A woman like that would never look at a man like him.

A not-unfamiliar sense of disappointment swept him.

Washed and shaved, because Cole's wife didn't like dirty, smelly knights at her table, Julian went to the window that overlooked the bailey of Berwick Castle. It was a vast, open space and he could see the men moving about now that night had fallen, hundreds of torches lighting up the bailey and the night sky. On the wall walk, he could see men moving about but the mist was starting to roll in from the sea, creating halos around the torches that were staving off the darkness.

"The mist is rolling in," he said. "It is going to be a cold and damp night."

Ashton already had his tunic over his head, putting his belt on. "Mayhap Addie will require extra warmth," he said, strapping a few weapons on his body. Broadswords were also forbidden in Berwick's hall. "I would not be disinclined to warm her should she ask."

Julian was still looking out of the window. "You should probably not tell me that," he said. "I have told you this before – any untoward behavior with my sister will not only incur my wrath, but Cole's as well. I do not think you can take us both on."

Ashton lifted his head from where he'd been fumbling with his buckle. "Nor would I want to," he said. "I did not mean that as a lascivious comment, only as a polite one."

Julian cast him a long look. "Lies do not become you."

Ashton snorted. "I am sorry I said anything at all," he said, throwing up his hands in surrender. "Sometimes I forget to whom I am speaking."

"You are speaking to Addington's older brother," Julian said, noting a party entering from the gatehouse, which had been closed up for the night. "I will be watching you tonight, Ash."

"You will only see proper behavior, I promise."

"And stay away from Anteaus."

Ashton didn't like that command, so he curled his lip unhappily at Julian and quit the chamber, heading out into the damp evening. Julian heard the door shut but didn't pay it any attention because the small party entering the bailey had his focus. The area was so well lit that it didn't take him long to see that it was the de la Mere party – six soldiers, a knight, and three women. They were met by a servant, a man who was in charge of all visitors, and he could see clearly when they were directed to leave their horses and head to the hall.

Perhaps it was a good time for him to head to the hall, too.

IT WAS THE nightmare she had feared.

Lista had just spent the past three hours in a tavern down by the river's edge, a grubby hovel of a place called The Silver Fish where there was a fight every hour, where women lifted their skirts and allowed men to do whatever they wished for a price, and where her mother and aunt could drink cheap wine that went straight to their heads.

An utter and complete nightmare.

After purchasing the brined fish and a few other things they needed from local merchants, the effects of the apothecary's ingredients had worn off and Meadow and Flora were on the lookout for their next thrill. They had been in The Silver Fish before and knew the barkeep, a man who always kept them well supplied, so they rushed to the tavern before Lista and Amaury could stop them. Amaury went so far as to try and remove them but that nearly started a fight when the rough-looking patrons thought the knight was trying to harass the women. Only Lista's intervention had prevented a bloodbath as Meadow and Flora went about drinking with the men.

They bought the entire tavern drinks.

After that, Amaury was forced to wait outside unless he wanted to start another fight and Lista was condemned to keeping an eye on her mother and aunt from inside the establishment. Too many men tried to speak with her, or buy her a drink, but she refused to speak and she refused to drink, kicking men in the groin who wouldn't leave her alone or gouging an eye or two if they came too close. For three long and horrific hours, she watched her mother and aunt drink themselves into oblivion until Lista finally reminded them that they were expected at the castle for supper. Only the thought of more food and drink got them out of the tavern and here they were, ready to continue drinking with Lady de Velt's expensive wine.

It was going to be another horrific evening in a long line of them.

The de la Mere party entered from one end of the great hall, with enormous metal doors that looked like chainmail, and traveled into the chamber with an enormous vaulted ceiling and stone floor. There was a colossal hearth about mid-hall, belching out smoke and sparks and a great amount of heat into the room. In addition to the table on the dais, there were several other large feasting tables, half of which were already full of men drinking and eating bread before the main meal got underway. While Amaury and the escort took Meadow and Flora into the hall and got them settled, Lista went in search of a servant who could deliver a message to Lady de Velt.

She wanted the woman to know what had transpired since they'd last met.

As Lista waited in the alcove for the servant who would come to take her message, she stood there and shivered. She was wet and cold from the ride from The Silver Fish, hoping for a few moments in front of that giant fire so she could warm up and dry out. Trembling, she rubbed at her damp arms, trying to bring some heat into her limbs, when Addington entered the alcove.

Surprised, Lista found herself looking into those mesmerizing eyes.

"My lady?" Addington said, equally surprised to see her. "A servant told me that you wished to send a message to my mother."

Lista was mortified. "I am very sorry if they sent for you instead," she said. "I did not ask them to. I simply wished to send your mother a message."

Addington smiled. "It was no trouble at all," she said. "I was coming to the hall, anyway. But why on earth are you so wet?"

Lista smiled weakly, her lips quivering with chill. "My mother forgot her cloak, so I gave mine to her," she said. "Unfortunately, it is rather wet out right now."

Addington was stricken. "We must get you into dry clothing immediately before you catch your death of chill," she said, reaching out to take Lista's ice-cold hand. "Come with me. I will find something dry for you to wear."

"Wait," Lista said, digging in her heels before Addington could whisk her away. "I must tell your mother that my mother and aunt are already... tipsy. I could not keep them out of a tavern this afternoon, so they are..."

"Full of sauce?" Addington finished for her.

Lista nodded, embarrassed. "I wish it was not so, but it is," she said. "I am so sorry. If you could simply give us a chamber, I will take them there and make them sleep it off. You will not see us again, I promise."

Addington's smile grew. "Then I would not have a chance to make a new friend," she said. "Where are they now?"

"In the hall, with our knight," Lista said. "He is keeping an eye on them."

"Good," Addington said. "Then they are well cared for at the moment. Come with me and let me care for you, too."

It was a very kind way of putting it, something Lista wasn't used to. She was so accustomed to being the one doing the caring that for someone to show her such regard nearly brought her to tears. She didn't know what to say, so she said nothing. She simply went with the woman when she tugged on her hand.

Berwick was a maze of corridors, doorways, chambers, and passages. Lista had no idea where Addington was taking her, but she simply followed along, trusting the woman who seemed very much to want to be her friend. Because of her mother and aunt, Lista really didn't have any friends. She was so focused on tending those two that any friendships had long since died away due to sheer neglect. Therefore, the prospect of a friend wasn't an unattractive one at all.

There were times when she desperately needed someone to talk to.

Somehow, they ended up at the big, block-like keep of Berwick. They had come out of a passageway and ended up on the front steps of the keep. Lista looked skyward, seeing how tall the building was. In fact, all of Berwick was ridiculously tall. She'd never seen such a big place in her entire life. Just as they were mounting the steps to enter, a worried servant stopped them.

"Lady Addington," the woman said. "We have a problem in the kitchen and I cannot find Lady Corisande or your mother. Will you help?"

Addington paused. "I do not know where Cori is," she said. "My mother was in her chamber the last I saw her."

"She's not there now, my lady. Will you come?"

Addington grunted unhappily. "I have a guest," she said, pointing out the obvious. "My mother is around here somewhere. You simply have to look for her."

The servant was wringing her big, chapped hands nervously. "It may be too late, my lady," she said. "We have a problem with the pig. The fire was too hot and we think it's ruined. We will have nothing to feed the men. Will you please come?"

Addington sighed heavily at what seemed to be a dire situation. She didn't see that she had much choice and was preparing to return Lista to the hall when someone crossing the bailey caught her eyes. She perked up, waving an arm to draw attention.

"Julian!" she shouted. "Julian, attend me!"

Startled, Lista turned to see Julian nearing the hall. There were so many torches in the bailey that it was easy to see the men moving through it. When Julian heard his sister, he paused, shifted, and headed in her direction.

Lista could feel her cheeks growing hot at the mere sight of him.

"Julian!" Addington sounded relieved. "Thank goodness. I

need your assistance with Lady Lista. She is soaking wet and I was going to find her a change of clothing, but I am needed in the kitchen and mother is nowhere to be found. Will you please take Lady Lista in-hand and see that she has something dry to wear?"

Lista could hardly look at Julian with that embarrassing request, but before she'd averted her gaze, she had noticed a few things about him – he was without his helm or any of his armor this night. He was wearing a buttery-soft leather tunic and breeches, with a belt of weapons around his trim waist. Earlier that day, she'd noticed how utterly muscular and massive the man was but she thought some of it might have been the protection he was wearing.

She was wrong.

All of that bulging muscle was his.

Much to her consternation, he was more handsome than she remembered. He looked as if he'd washed and shaved because he certainly didn't look like the man she'd seen earlier in the day. The front of his dark blond hair was still draping down the right side of his face, covering his right eye, and he made no move to push it aside as he looked at her.

"I would like to help, but I do not know anything about women's clothing," he said. "Mayhap I can help in the kitchen?"

Addington frowned. "A man in the kitchen?" she said as if it were the most ridiculous thing she'd ever heard. "Take the lady up to my chamber and let her pick out something dry. We are about the same size. Bring her back to the hall when she is properly dressed."

Julian didn't react or respond and Addington didn't wait for him to either resist or agree. She headed off with the servant, leaving Julian and Lista standing in awkward silence.

"Once again, you are being forced to assist me," Lista finally said, breaking the stillness between them. "I am terribly sorry. I can simply return to the hall and dry myself by the fire."

Julian's left eyebrow lifted. "And risk my sister seeing that you are in the same wet garment?" he said. "Not bloody likely. She'd tell my mother and we would both be in trouble. You'd better come along with me."

Before Lista could reply, he took her by the elbow and directed her into the keep. His enormous hand on her arm was like a firebrand – powerful, searing. She could feel it through the damp fabric. In fact, she could feel everything about him through that fabric – his size, his heat – everything.

It was enough to make her heart race.

"That is the second time you have expressed fear of your mother's wrath," she said as they entered the dimly lit innards. "Clearly, you have a healthy respect for your mother."

Julian grunted softly in agreement. "You will, too, once you come to know her."

"I hope I have the opportunity," Lista said. "Truthfully, this entire day has been rather strange. My mother is not usually so social as to accept an invitation to dine."

He directed her to a narrow spiral staircase that disappeared into the upper floors. He pointed to the steps and she headed up as he followed.

"Why not?" he asked. "She seemed pleasant enough."

Lista emerged on another dimly lit floor. "You are kind to say so," she said. "But you saw how she was today. I do not mean to keep bringing it up, but she is difficult to bear with some people so she and my aunt keep to themselves."

"And you?"

"I keep with them."

There was something decidedly lonely in that statement. Julian opened the first door they came to, revealing the lovely chamber beyond. There was a fire burning in the hearth and hides on the floor, making it all quite cozy and warm. Lista was so busy admiring the chamber that she didn't notice that Julian was looking at her with a good deal of interest.

As if he were trying to figure her out.

"Addie's wardrobe is over there," he said, pointing to the enormous cabinet against the wall. "Select something and I shall wait for you in the corridor."

"Nay," Lista said quickly, turning to him. "Please do not leave."

His brow rippled with confusion and perhaps even concern. "I cannot remain, my lady."

"Leave the door open and you can," she said. "I do not wish to be alone in this room with your sister's fine things. She does not truly know me and I do not know her, and I am uncomfortable enough going through her wardrobe. She is far too trusting, so I do not wish for there to ever be any question as to my actions. I would never want to violate that trust, so you will remain as a witness to my actions."

Julian understood and, in truth, he was impressed that she would be so forthright. Rather than throw him out and rifle through her sister's things, possibly even stealing something, she was determined to be transparent and honest, as a guest should.

Respect for the woman took root.

"As you wish," he said.

He planted himself in the doorway, not making any move to go further into the chamber, as Lista lit a big bank of tapers near the bed. As a soft, warm glow filled the room, she went to the old wardrobe and carefully opened the doors. Immediately, piles of clothing fell out, right onto her feet, and a cat jumped out, running onto the bed. Surprised, Lista looked at the clothing, the cat, and then burst into soft laughter.

Julian bit his lip to keep from grinning.

"My sister is a sweet woman, but she has never been the tidy sort," he said.

Lista put a hand over her mouth to stifle the giggles, but not before Julian caught a glimpse of straight, white teeth and a big dimple in her right cheek. "It is comforting to know that she is not as perfect as I thought she was," she said. "This wardrobe looks like mine, except I do not trap cats in it."

Julian let his grin break through, flashing his own dimples. "I would be careful sticking my hands in there," he said. "You just never know what more she has trapped in there, living or dead."

Lista feigned fear, a charming gesture as far as Julian was concerned, and proceeded cautiously. "Goodness," she said. "What more shall I find? A nest for fae?"

"More than likely a nest for trolls."

Lista giggled. "That is not a very nice thing to say about your sister," she said. "I am sure there are no trolls in here, nasty things."

"I would not be too sure."

She glanced at him, her sea-colored eyes twinkling, and he grinned and looked away. He was leaning against the door jamb, those enormous arms crossed, head lowered as he looked at his feet. Even though his hair was hanging over half his face, Lista could still see the smirk on his face. She could feel the brotherly love towards a sister.

She rather liked it.

"You have experience with trolls, then?" she asked, teasing him as she began to pick up the clothing at her feet. "Surely a knight of your caliber should have no trouble with them."

Julian saw what she was doing and broke his stance by the door, coming in to help. "No trouble with trolls," he said, picking up an armload of garments and tossing them onto the bed. "You?"

It was a rather witty comeback and she fought off a grin. "Not recently, no," she said, collecting a pile of scarves that had fallen out. "And you only have one sister?"

He shook his head, collecting some slippers that had tumbled out. "Three," he said. "Allaston, Effington, and Addington. Addie is the youngest."

"And one brother?"

Julian wasn't sure how to answer that. "I had three," he said, feeling his good mood fade. "We lost my youngest brother around the same time as we lost my father."

Lista put the scarves on the bed. "I am sorry," she said. "I did not mean to pry."

"You did not."

She wasn't so sure, but he was being polite about it, anyway. She turned back for the remainder of the pile on the floor. "I have no brothers or sisters anymore," she said. "I lost my brother, also. I understand how you feel."

Julian tilted his head to the side. "Then you have my condolences, as well," he said sincerely.

"It must be a good feeling to have a big family. It must make you feel as if you belong to something happy and loving."

"Or annoying and frustrating," he said, reaching down to pick up a cloak. "Especially if your sister embarrasses you in front of a guest."

He meant the pile of clothing but Lista grinned. "She did nothing of the sort," she insisted, picking up a final garment off the floor and seeing that it was a dark blue wool with silver embroidery on it. It seemed simple enough and a good fabric against the cold night. "Do you think your sister would mind if I borrowed this one?"

Julian looked at it. She was holding it against her and in the gentle glow of the tallow candles, he could see the dark blue color reflecting in her eyes. There was something so beautiful about her at the moment, something ethereal, that it took his breath away. He'd never had that kind of a reaction to a woman in his life. He could have stared at her all night but when she fixed on him, meeting his eyes, he quickly averted his gaze.

"I do not think she would," he said. "Is there anything else I can help you with, my lady? Should I send for a servant to help you dress?"

Lista's gaze lingered on him for a moment before she placed the dress carefully on the bed, disturbing the cat. She couldn't help but notice that while he would warm a little, he clearly had no intention of being anything other than politely friendly. Whenever their gazes would meet, he would quickly look away.

Sadly, she knew why. Or, at least she thought she did.

"That is not necessary," she said. "I do not need help dressing, though I appreciate your offer. I fear that, twice now, I have taken far too much of your valuable time. So if you wish to return to the hall, I will heartily encourage you to do so."

Julian shook his head. "I cannot," he said simply. "I will wait for you to change into dry clothing and escort you to the hall."

With that, he quit the chamber and shut the door behind him, leaving Lista feeling the least bit bewildered and also a little disappointed. He was such a handsome man, beautifully built, but there was absolutely nothing he saw in her that he liked. Truth be told, Lista hadn't been around many young knights, at least men of eligible marital age, so her time with Julian was quite rare.

But quite wonderful.

It took her away from her drunken mother and boorish aunt. It took her away from a life of managing an entire castle, her world consumed by tending to things that her mother should have taken care of. A world where everything depended on her and she, in turn, had no one that she could depend on. There *was* no one. Felkington was a wealthy castle but certainly no man in his right mind would want to marry her with the burden of her mother and aunt upon her shoulders. Now that Julian had seen the reality of her world, there was no way the man would ever be remotely interested.

But it wasn't just that she was hopeful for Julian, personally. He was far above her social station and she knew it. It was the fact that it could have been *any* man. Any man she had made an acquaintance of who had seen the reality of her life with her mother and aunt. It just happened to be Julian who had seen it and wanted nothing to do with it.

She didn't blame him in the least.

Looking up from the blue garment, Lista looked around the room. Even though she had a lavish chamber of her own back at Felkington, there was something different about Addington's. It was a luxurious room that clearly belonged to a woman who had a family to love her. A woman who surely must have had many marital prospects, a woman who could be herself and not have to worry about her fragile mother and misbehaving aunt.

A woman who had everything Lista had been denied.

That understanding had never been more painful than it was at this very moment.

She couldn't accept the dry dress. She couldn't accept anything of Addington's because it simply wasn't right. She was still damp, and still cold, but she wasn't going to change her clothing. In fact, she was going to gather her mother and aunt and find an inn somewhere in the village to spend the night before they headed home.

She wasn't going to impose on the perfect world of de Velt any longer.

Lista yanked the chamber door open and charged through, heading for the stairs. Julian had been standing right outside the door, startled when he saw her practically run to the steps. He called after her but she didn't answer him, taking the steps far too quickly. He was behind her and he seriously thought she was going to slip and fall all the way to the bottom, but she somehow managed to keep her footing.

Hitting the bottom of the steps, she began to run.

Puzzled, Julian ran after her.

The mist outside had turned into a wet blanket. Everything it touched was instantly sopping wet and that included Lista as she ran into the fog. Julian called after her twice, finally catching up to her about halfway to the stables. Reaching out, he grabbed her arm, forcing her to a halt. But even as they came to a stop, Lista was struggling to pull away from him.

"My lady?" he said, trying to hold on to her without hurting her. "Whatever is the matter? Why are you running?"

"Please," Lista said, trying to yank her arm free. "Please let me go. I must have our escort prepared."

Julian was looking at her with mounting concern. "But why?" he said. "What has happened?"

Lista stopped tugging because he clearly wasn't going to let her go. His grip was like iron. His hair, wet, had come away from the right side of his face and was now plastered against his right temple and cheek. Even in the torchlight of the bailey, which was still fairly bright, Lista could see the full scope of the man's face and she wasn't disappointed. He was glorious. But she also noticed that he had two different-colored eyes – one eye was bright green and the other was a light brown, almost a hazel. The hair draped over his eye had covered up the fact that the right eye was light brown.

But she didn't give it a second thought. If anything, it simply made him more handsome in her opinion. Handsome and kind and polite.

And he didn't want anything to do with her.

"Sir Julian," she said as steadily as she could. "I have troubled you for the last time. I want you to listen to me very carefully. Will you do this?"

His brow furrowed. "Of course I will, my lady. But why do you…?"

She cut him off before he could finish. "Please listen," she said again. "I want you to let my arm go."

He did, without hesitation. Lista straightened her sleeve before continuing. "Now," she said. "When we first met, I was sharp with you. I have apologized for that and I will do it yet again. I am sorry for the way I spoke to you. You and your mother were very kind to me and my mother and I will always be very grateful for that. Your mother was warm and welcoming to a woman she'd known as a child, but it never occurred to your mother that the woman she knew long ago is not the same woman of today. My mother is a reckless fool. It was a mistake to come here and impose upon your family. I am going to make sure our escort is prepared and then I am taking my mother and aunt away. We should not be here."

He was still frowning, unsure what had her so upset. "But I do not understand," he said. "You did not seem upset when I left you to change your clothing. Did I say something to offend you?"

She looked at him as if startled by the question. After a moment, a smile spread across her face, but it wasn't one of humor. The laugh that came from her mouth was one of great irony.

"Sir Julian, you do not have to pretend with me any longer," she said. "I understand that twice you have been forced into escorting me so you do not have to pretend it is something you are doing of your own free will. I am simply the daughter of a madwoman and what you have seen today is my life, every single day. Every morning is hell, every afternoon is exhaustion, and every night is spent wondering what is going to happen on the morrow. I've seen many a person turn away from my mother and me, so I know the expression well. I could see it in your face, too. I do not blame you. Though it has been my great honor to make your acquaintance, I ask that you go now and leave me alone. I have preparations to make."

With that, she turned on her heel and continued rushing towards the stables, leaving Julian standing there in confusion. He'd never heard a speech like that in his life, so he stood there a moment as he pondered every word. He had been thinking that he had been the one to send her running out into the mist, but now he was starting to realize that it wasn't him at all.

... or was it?

It took him a moment to realize that his wet hair had moved away from his right eye, exposing it. To those who had never seen his dual-toned eyes before, he knew how it looked. He'd had priests try to exorcise him, or throw holy water on him, or even herd people away from him. His father got the same reaction because his eye color was so pronounced. *The Devil's Eyes*, people used to say. Cole's eyes had the trait, but they were hardly noticeable, while Cassian had also possessed the trait to a larger degree. But Julian... his was quite obvious. Perhaps that trait had chased Lista de la Mere away but, somehow, she seemed tougher than that. She didn't seem the type to shy away from something different or superstitious. But then again, he didn't know her at all.

Perhaps he was wrong.

In any case, the woman was upset and he simply couldn't let it go.

He went in search of Addington.

"MY BROTHER THINKS that he has offended you."

Standing in the musty stables, Lista heard the soft female voice, turning to see Addington enter. She had been watching the grooms prepare the horses, unwilling to return to the hall just yet, so Addington's appearance had her uncertain and embarrassed.

"Nay, not at all," she said to Addington's blunt statement. "I simply asked him to leave me and let me go about my business."

"What business?"

"We are preparing to depart."

Addington frowned. "Why?" she said. "My lady, it is only fair to tell me what is wrong. What have we done?"

Lista knew she should tell her. Addington was right – it was only fair. Therefore, she struggled to delicately phrase it.

"You've done nothing," she said. "You have been so incredibly gracious and the last thing I would want to do is offend you or your brother or mother, but we must face facts. My mother and aunt are not appropriate guests for your mother's table."

Addington's eyes glittered in understanding. "So you are planning to take them away?"

Lista nodded. "I was going to come and tell you myself, I promise," she said. "I wanted to make sure the escort was ready before I did. We should have never accepted your invitation to sup. My mother and aunt simply do not belong around polite, civilized people."

"So you thought to spare us the shame of it?"

"I thought to preserve your mother's memory of a friend from long ago."

Addington smiled faintly. "That is noble of you," she said. "But unnecessary. Do you not know about the de Velts?"

Lista wasn't sure what she meant. "I… I know you are a great family," she said. "Your father was a great warlord."

Addington sighed faintly, taking Lista by the hand and pulling her over to a small bench that was pushed up against the wall of the stables. She sat down, taking Lista with her.

"Ask any man in Northumberland over the age of fifty years and they will all tell you the same thing about Ajax de Velt," she said quietly. "My father was a warlord of the most brutal sort. Years ago, he conquered portions of the Welsh and Scottish Marches. He confiscated several castles. He would not only defeat armies, but he would take his prisoners and ram poles through them and then prop the poles up so that there was a sea of macabre scarecrows all over the land. Kings feared my father.

There are those who still spit upon the name de Velt, so although I am flattered that you think we are a noble family, the truth is that we have a very dark past."

Lista knew that, sort of. Amaury had mentioned it earlier that day and she'd known from living in Northumberland that de Velt was a name to fear, but not much beyond that.

"But your father went on to make a good name for himself, didn't he?" she said. "He raised a kind and noble family."

"Why do you say that?"

Lista smiled faintly. "Even if I knew nothing at all about your father, I do not need to know anything about him at all because you and your brother and mother have been kind and generous. That tells me all I need to know about Ajax de Velt. He has a good family."

Addington was still holding her hand, now squeezing it. "That is sweet of you to say that," she said. "But the fact remains that Julian thinks you ran from him and I told him I would get to the bottom of the situation. You didn't run from him, did you?"

Lista shook her head firmly. "Nay," she said. "He was very polite and helpful."

Addington cleared her throat softly. "That's not what I mean," she said. "I meant... you did not run from *him*? From the way he is?"

"How is he?"

Addington could see that Lista had no clue what she meant. "Nay, I didn't think so," she said, relieved. "But he's had people run from him before and those who do not run will comment cruelly."

"Comment cruelly about what?"

Addington pointed to her eyes. "From this," she said quietly. "We all have our father's eyes in some fashion, but Julian's condition is more pronounced because his eyes are two different colors. He is self-conscious about it but please do not tell him that I told you. That would embarrass him."

Lista looked at her curiously. "I saw his eyes," she said. "I thought they were marvelous, like the rest of him."

Her cheeks suddenly turned bright red when she realized what she said and she lowered her gaze as Addington laughed. "You think so, do you?" she said. "He will be happy to hear that."

Lista shook her head firmly. "Nay, please do not tell him," she said. "I should not have said what I did, but…"

"Did you mean it?"

"Please do not tell him."

"Did you *mean* it?"

Lista wouldn't look at her, but she couldn't keep the smile off her lips as she nodded, once. "I suppose so," she said as it was practically forced out of her. "But if you tell him, I will call you a terrible liar."

Addington burst out laughing. "This is wonderful, truly," she said. "My lady, you have no idea that… well, it would mean a great deal to my brother if he knew. May I please tell him?"

Lista couldn't keep the smile off her face, but she was resolute. "He would think you were mad," she said. "He would think I was mad. I scolded him when we first met and shamed him in front of his men, yet I think he is handsome? He would not believe it."

"He would!"

Lista shook her head, squeezing Addington's hands. "Nay, my lady, please do not tell him," she said, growing serious. "I am not of his social station. Nothing could ever come of it, so there is no point in telling him. It would embarrass me and probably mortify him, so please do not say anything. Promise me."

Addington's smile faded. "What is this nonsense?" she said. "What do you mean you are not of the same social station?"

Lista shrugged. "I live with my mother and aunt in a quiet corner of Northumberland," she said simply. "My father was not a great warlord. We had no real friends or allies. Truly, we are nothing compared to the House of de Velt. When your brother marries, it should be to a woman who can bring him great status and honor. Not a woman with a drunkard for a mother. He deserves far better than what I have to offer."

By the time she was finished, Addington was looking at her with shock. There was also some sorrow in her expression were one to look closely enough.

"I cannot believe that," she said. "Are you destitute? Do you live in a cave?"

The question was somewhat sarcastic, but Addington was trying to make a point. Lista shook her head in response.

"We have a fine castle," she said. "We have rich lands and I am my father's heiress, so we are far from destitute. But we have nothing to offer beyond that. *I* have nothing to offer beyond that."

Addington wasn't convinced. "You are being silly," she said. "It sounds as if any man would be most honored to marry you."

"They would be wealthy and titled, but it comes with a price."

"Your mother?"

"Exactly. And that price is far too high for your brother. I would not wish it upon someone so kind."

Addington eyed the woman, but there was something going

on behind those magnificent eyes.

The thoughts were churning.

"I will not tell Julian any of this under one condition," she finally said. "I want you to return to the hall with me. Eat and drink and warm yourself. Please, Lista. May I call you Lista? It is such a pretty name."

Lista nodded, her resolve being broken down by a kind and understanding young woman. "You may, of course," she said. "And I suppose it would be nice to eat and drink and be warm. But I must sit with my mother and aunt and when I am finished, we will leave."

Addington shook her head. "You will not leave," she said. "There is a chamber in the apartments next to the gatehouse that I have prepared for you myself. You will hurt my feelings if you do not stay the night."

"I would not want to hurt your feelings."

Addington's smile was back. She pulled Lista off the bench and told the grooms to unsaddle the horses. Holding Lista's hand tightly, she pulled her out into the misty, cold night.

CHAPTER FOUR

"WHAT IS THE matter with them?"

Cole was sitting at the dais of the smoky and crowded great hall, hearing the soft question come from his wife. He took a drink of his fine wine.

"I do not know," he said. "They were acting strangely in town today, as well. If I did not know better, I would say they were drunk."

Corisande de Bourne de Velt looked over at the women in question. The great hall was packed with people on this cold, wet night, so it was standing room only on the fringes of the room. But over in one corner, Lady Felkington and her sister were entertaining a group of soldiers with elaborate stories and loud songs. The louder they'd sing, the more the men would laugh and cheer. Copious amounts of wine were being poured into their cups, which they would drain quickly. It had been going on since their arrival.

Corisande wasn't quite sure what to make of it.

"Where is the third woman?" she asked. "Lady Felkington's daughter?"

Cole delved into the pork and beans in his trencher. "Apparently, she was soaking wet when she arrived, having given her mother her cloak," he said. "Addie is taking care of her."

"Is she a drunkard, too?"

Cole shook his head. "Nay," he said. "She seems bright and articulate. She nearly came to blows with Julian because one of the soldiers shoved her mother."

Corisande looked at him in surprise. "One of the soldiers shoved her mother?" she asked, bordering on outrage. "Was he sufficiently punished?"

Cole put up a hand to ease her, fighting off a grin. "Julian dealt with the man but not before Lady Felkington's daughter dealt with Julian," he said. "I assure you, it was simply a misunderstanding."

Corisande eyed him. "She had every right to be angry if her mother was pushed, Cole," she said. "Your mother was there, was she not? I will ask her what she knows."

That was usual in the de Velt household. Sometimes, it wasn't sufficient what Cole knew. Corisande often went to Kellington for advice and information, and the two of them occasionally colluded for the greater good of the family. Cole, like everyone, just went along with it. He didn't really mind, however. He loved his wife more than words could express, just as he loved his mother, and he trusted them both implicitly.

It wasn't as if he could put up a fight, anyway.

"Where *is* my mother?" he asked, mouth full.

"With the children," Corisande said. "She is giving me a few moments of respite from that gang of unruly animals you like to call your children."

Cole grinned. "Atlas and Ajax are *not* animals," he said, referring to his two oldest sons. "They are cunning and bright. Ophelia is an angel, but I suppose Silas is a bit like an animal.

He has too much of my father in him, even at two years of age."

"And the baby?"

Cole leaned over and kissed her cheek. "Vivienne is as beautiful as you are," he said sweetly. "You have given me the most beautiful and brilliant children. I have no complaints."

Corisande fought off a smile. "Flattery will get you everywhere."

"It has gotten me five children."

Corisande started to laugh. "I suppose it has," she said, but then her smile suddenly faded and she began to look around the room. "Where did your mother's guests go?"

Cole looked over to the corner where he'd last see Lady Felkington and Lady d'Orbec. They were gone and the men who had been clustered around them had vanished.

He shook his head.

"I do not know," he said. "Mayhap to their chamber for the evening?"

Corisande continued to search the room for the missing guests. Unlike her husband, something told her they had not retired for the evening.

It was just a feeling she had.

"I FOUND LADY Lista," Addington said. "She is in my chamber changing out of that damp dress she was wearing. It is starting to smell, so I have ordered a bath for her."

Julian was in the chamber he shared with Ashton. He hadn't gone into the great hall after his conversation with Lista, instead choosing to eat in his chamber and retire early. He saw no reason to go into the great hall at this point.

He just wanted this evening to be over with.

"So you convinced her to stay?" he said. "That is good of you."

"I want you to come to the hall, too."

Julian shook his head. "Nay."

"Why not?"

He was growing irritated. "Because I will not," he said. "Stop asking me. Go back and enjoy yourself."

Addington knew why he wouldn't go to the hall. He was afraid of seeing Lista, afraid of feeling humiliated all over again. Therefore, she had to be careful in what she said to him. Beneath that hard exterior, Julian was quite sensitive.

"You did not offend her, you know," she said quietly.

He rolled his eyes. "Of course I did not," he said. "I've hardly spoken to her. How can I offend her?"

Addington eyed her brother. Julian, with the weight of the world on his shoulders, was the brother who still bore the burden of guilt about their father's death. Cole had Berwick and he was creating his own empire while Julian remained at Pelinom, ever the good son, serving Pelinom and his mother in his father's stead. Only it wasn't enough; it had never been enough nor would it ever be because Julian had yet to find peace within himself. Not only had he not prevented his father's death those years ago, but old insecurities had him firmly within their grasp. He was an unattractive freak, a man with nothing to offer any woman.

He'd learned that long ago.

Addington knew her brother was interested in women and possibly marriage because there had been at least two women that she knew of who had caught his eye. One had been a local girl who had flirted with him a little until another knight who had more of a stake in her had ridiculed and belittled Julian in front of her. That was the last time he'd ever seen her. Then, there had been a woman from Carlisle, a merchant's daughter, who had seemed interested enough until her father had married her off to a distant cousin. Perhaps she had never ridiculed Julian, but her father certainly had. He had ridiculed the man for being a de Velt, however, and not because of his unique appearance. Still, the end result had been the same.

After that, Julian threw his attention into Pelinom and his duties there.

That didn't leave room for anything else.

But now...

"Julian, I am going to tell you something very important," Addington said. "Are you listening to me?"

Julian lay back on his bed, hands folded over his head as he stared at the ceiling. "How can I help but hear you?" he said. "You are right next to me."

"I didn't say hear me. I said *listen*."

"I'm listening. Say what you're going to say."

Addington could see that his defenses were up. Julian had the strongest sense of self-preservation of anyone she'd ever known. It was going to be difficult to get through to him that way but she was going to try.

"I spoke to Lady Lista," she said. "You did not offend her. Do you know why she left so quickly?"

"I suppose you are going to tell me."

"I am, but I swore that I would not, so I am breaking a promise."

"What promise?"

"I promised not to tell you that Lista thinks you are handsome."

He continued to stare at the ceiling. After a moment, he blinked slowly. "Get out of here," he grumbled. "You're not funny in the least."

Addington slapped him on the leg. "I am not trying to be funny," she said, rather angrily. "I am breaking a confidence to tell you this and all you can do is tell me to get out? Stop feeling sorry for yourself and listen to me or you will lose this opportunity."

He frowned. "What opportunity?" he said. Before she could answer, he went on. "Addie, I appreciate that you are trying to cheer me up, but you know as well as I do why she ran. It's why they all run. I do not need you telling me otherwise. It is no great loss, as she can go on with her life and I can go on with mine. No harm has been done."

"Even if I swear on Papa's grave that it is the truth?"

That had some weight with him. He looked at her; *really* looked at her. A heavy gaze that was trying to determine just how serious she was. He had been dismissing her until this moment but they both knew that Addington would not have referenced Jax lightly.

He sighed heavily.

"What are you talking about?" he finally hissed. "Addie, I do not want to hear this."

She cocked an eyebrow. "Why not?" she said. "How difficult is it for you to believe a woman finds you attractive? You are, you know, and I say that without guile because I am your sister and I do not need to resort to trickery or empty flattery. But if I see something – or someone – that might make you happy, I am going to tell you. What you do with that information is up to you."

His gaze lingered on her for a moment before finally putting his hands over his face. "Then tell me," he said, muffled. "Tell me and get it over with."

Addington watched him rub his hands over his face, wearily. "Do you know why Lista ran from you?" she asked.

"Why?"

"Because she thinks you are handsome and she further believes that she is far below your social station," Addington said. "It's pathetic, really. She's much like you, Julian – she doesn't believe she's worthy of happiness. In her case, it's because of her mother. She says no man would want her because of her mother."

His hands came away from his face. "That is ridiculous."

"Do you think so?"

"I do."

"Do you think she's pretty?"

"She's marvelous."

"She said the same thing about you."

His head popped up. "She said... she *what*?"

Addington fought off a grin. "She said that she thought your eyes were marvelous, just like the rest of you."

That caused him to sit up, looking at his sister quite incredulously. But there was also great suspicion there. "Addie, tell me that you did not say... anything about... *me*. Please."

She knew what he meant and she wasn't going to admit that she had indeed mentioned his eye color. That was something the entire family knew but never spoke of. For Julian's sake, they'd learned not to. Therefore, she didn't want to embarrass the man. In this case, her honesty only went so far.

"Why would I do that?" she said. "She did notice our eye color, however, and I told her that our father had the same eyes.

I told her we all had similarly colored eyes. But that is all I said about it."

Julian studied her for a moment as if trying to determine just how much truth she was telling him. "*And?*"

"And she said that she had seen your eyes and they were marvelous, like the rest of you."

He didn't say anything right away. He just stared at her, almost suspiciously. "Did she really say that?"

"I swear to you on Papa's grave that she said it. I would not lie, Julian."

He thought about it. The suspicion in his expression died away, replaced by disbelief and then a hint of delight. The corners of his mouth twitched as he lay back down and covered his face with his hands.

"Surprising," he said.

Addington jumped to her feet and slapped him on the leg again.

"Is that all you have to say?" she demanded. "Julian, there is a woman who thinks you are marvelous within the walls of Berwick. What are you going to do about it?"

He didn't answer fast enough and she spanked him again, causing him to finally grab her hands so she couldn't hit him again.

"Whatever I do, I will not be pushed into it by you," he said. "Stop hitting me or I'll toss you into the wardrobe and lock the doors."

Addington tussled with him. "I'm hitting you because you are an idiot," she said. "You deserve to be hit if you do not do something about this. I am putting a woman in your hands and all you can say is 'surprising'?"

"What do you want me to say?"

"I want you to say 'marvelous'!"

"Marvelous!"

Addington yanked her hands from his grip. "Then get your shoes on and go to the hall," she said. "If you are not there when I arrive with Lista, I will tell Mother what I have told you and let the winds blow where they may."

Julian grunted. "They will blow right into this room and Mother along with them," he said. "Leave her out of it."

"I won't."

He knew she wouldn't. Sharply, he sighed. "Then I will agree to go to the hall under one condition."

"What?"

"That you not tell Lady Lista that you have told me all of this. Swear it to me, Addie."

"I swear."

He swept his hands at her. "Then go," he said. "Out of my sight, you little goat. Get out or I shall tell Ash that you are in love with someone else and then you can explain that to him."

Addington gasped. "You wouldn't!"

His eyes narrowed and he hissed at her. "*Go.*"

Addington complied, but not before she stuck her tongue out at him. He threw a shoe at her, but she was too fast. The door slammed and the shoe hit the wall and clattered to the ground. As Julian went to pick up the shoe, the grin he'd been trying so hard to fight off broke through.

Addington was a lot of things, but a liar wasn't among them. At least, not where it mattered. He knew his sister well enough to know that. What he did not believe, however, was her denial that she had perhaps prodded Lista into some sort of confession. Addington's heart was in the right place but she was relentless in her pursuit of her goals. Effington and Addington together had been merciless, like the most merciless warlords he'd ever faced, and with Effington on the Welsh Marches with her husband, Addington was going it alone as the *tour de force* of the House of de Velt.

Even to help her brother who couldn't seem to help himself. *Marvelous.*

Somehow, that word had new meaning to him now.

"I DO NOT see my mother and aunt anywhere," Lista said as she took a seat at the end of the dais as Addington had indicated. "Do you know where they have gone?"

Addington shook her head as she sat down next to Lista. "I do not know," she said. "I know they were here earlier. Would you like me to send someone to find them?"

Lista wasn't sure. She was looking around for Amaury, too, but he was nowhere to be found, either. Lista knew that Amaury was probably with them, as he was diligent about such things. She knew he wouldn't let them wander alone.

But she was still nervous when they were out of her sight.

"I suppose not," she said. "I am sure our knight is with them. If they do not return to the hall in a short while, then mayhap we can send someone out to find them."

Addington smiled, pleased that Lista was choosing to remain in the great hall and not running after her errant mother and aunt. Now, if she could only get her stubborn, skittish brother into the hall as well, perhaps something could really happen. Servants came around with trenchers of pork, peas, beans, and bread that had been baked with honey and rose-water. Addington dug in with gusto, pointing as she chewed.

"That's my brother, Cole, sitting with his wife, Corisande," she said. "You met Cole earlier today, but I do not think you have met Cori. She's terribly sweet."

Lista took a bite of her food and quickly realized she was famished. She hadn't eaten all day. "Nay, I have not met her yet," she said. "Julian said he had a brother and three sisters."

"Correct."

"Where are your other sisters?"

Addington broke apart the bread. "My oldest sister, Allaston, is on the Welsh Marches with her husband," she said. "Effington is also on the Welsh Marches, only to the south, towards Gloucester. Her husband is a garrison commander for the de Llion family."

"Welsh?"

"Aye."

"Have you ever been to the Welsh Marches?"

Addington shook her head. "Regretfully, I have not," she said. "Have you?"

Lista shook her head. "Nay," she said. "But I would like to go someday."

"So would I."

"Mayhap we can go together? It would be a better trip with someone to enjoy it with."

Addington's features lit up. "I would like that," she said. Then, something caught her attention and she quickly smoothed at her hair before wiping at her mouth to make sure there were no crumbs. "One of my brother's knights is approaching. Have you met him?"

Lista looked up to see a handsome young knight bearing down on them. He was well-proportioned and muscular, and he smiled when he saw Addington.

She smiled back.

"Good eve, Lady Addington," the knight said. "I was hoping to see you tonight."

Addington beamed. "It is agreeable to see you also, my lord," she said. "Have you met my friend, Lady Lista de la Mere?"

The knight shifted his focus to Lista. With the same rather devilish smile, he took Lista's hand and kissed it sweetly.

"Anteaus de Bourne at your service, my lady," he said. "Welcome to Berwick."

He seemed rather suave and full of himself. Lista took back her hand. "Thank you, my lord," she said. "It is an honor to meet you."

Somehow, Anteaus took that as an invitation to sit down and he did, eagerly. He took a seat on Addington's left hand because Lista was on her right. More food was brought in as Anteaus told stories about his home, a castle known as The Keld. He had two older brothers who came out looking like terrible bullies in his stories, but they were quite humorous. Lista chuckled at the antics of the de Bourne brothers but it was clear during the course of the conversation that Anteaus was paying special attention to Addington. He wasn't being rude to Lista in the least, but it was clear that he was focused on her. There was romance in the air.

Smiling at the subtle flirting, Lista went back to her food.

"May I sit, my lady?"

Lista heard the words, having no idea they were meant for her until she caught sight of a big body on her right hand. Startled, she looked up to see Julian standing beside her, indicating the chair.

Cheeks flushing madly, she nodded.

"Please," she said.

Julian sat down as servants rushed forward to bring him food and drink, but he wasn't looking at his food.

He was looking at Lista.

"I see you are wearing the dark blue garment," he said. "It suits you."

Lista looked at herself, dressed in the dark blue dress with the silver embroidery. "Thank you," she said. "Your sister was very kind to lend it to me."

"And the food? Is the food to your liking?"

Lista nodded. "It is very good," she said. "Do you always eat so well at Berwick?"

Julian wriggled his eyebrows, or at least the one eyebrow Lista could see. "Cori sets a fine table," he said. "The finest in the north. There will be more courses after this, so do not eat too much. There is more to come."

"Ah," Lista said. "I will have to be careful that I do not break the seams of your sister's dress with all of my gluttony."

Julian's glittering gaze lingered on her a moment before returning to his food. "You would be in good company, I assure you," he said. Silence settled between them for a moment because he was staring at her so much, so he hastened to find something to talk about, fearful that it was about to become awkward. "Do you come to Berwick often, my lady? To the market, I mean."

Lista shrugged. "Often enough," she said. "My mother likes to visit the apothecaries every month or two. And will you do something for me?"

"Anything, my lady."

"Will you please call me Lista? Addressing me as 'my lady'

sounds so formal and we are friends now, aren't we?"

He looked at her, surprised. "Are we?"

"I hope so," Lista said. "Unless my insults to you earlier have ruined any chance we have of a friendship and we are now mortal enemies."

His lips twitched with a grin. "We are not enemies," he said. "And your insults were hardly anything at all."

"I think you are being kind again, but thank you. Then we are friends?"

"I would be honored."

"Excellent," Lista said. "Then you will do something else for me, please."

"What is that?"

"If I insult you, or you are concerned with my behavior, will you come to speak to me directly and not send your sister as an emissary?"

Julian nearly choked on the food in his mouth in the face of her blunt and honest request. He knew exactly what she meant and, for a moment, thought to deny it. He was so unpracticed with women that his awkwardness was apparent, but looking at Lista, he realized he didn't want to deny it.

He didn't want to lie to her, not even for something as benign as this.

"I did not send her, I swear this to you," he said after a moment. "Addie took matters into her own hands when I told her that I feared I had somehow offended you. You ran away from me so quickly earlier... I did not know what I had done."

He was looking at her with the hair hanging over his right eye as he always did. Lista found herself looking into the man's beautiful face, for truly, he was a specimen to behold. She saw absolutely no reason why he needed to hide his eyes from her and after what Addington had told her, somehow, she didn't like that he was. She'd seen his full face and it was exquisite. Boldly, she reached up and gently moved the hair away from the right side of his face, exposing both eyes.

He didn't move.

For a moment, Lista simply looked at both eyes, smiling as she did so. Julian sat like stone, watching her like a hawk. Her smile grew as she tucked the hair back a little.

"You look like a young squire with your hair the way it is," she said. "You have a handsome face, Sir Julian. You should not cover it up."

Julian was starting to tremble. He had no idea why, but something in Lista's touch was like a hot knife against butter – and he was the butter. Her touch had been so light, so gentle, but perhaps one of the more impacting things that had ever happened to him in his adult life and he had no idea why.

But her words...

He couldn't decide if he was terribly embarrassed or terribly encouraged. Sweet words that he hadn't expected, unsolicited and sympathetic. The way she had said it told him that Addington had indeed told her about his self-consciousness when it came to his eye color, but he didn't care.

Her kind words meant a great deal to him.

"If I am to call you Lista, then surely you should call me Julian," he managed to say, feeling giddy and awkward. "You do not think we are being too... forward?"

Lista dropped her hand from his hair. "Probably," she said. "But you and I have had quite a day so it seems to me that if we have not killed each other by the end of it, then we should be fast and friendly companions. Agreed?"

"Agreed."

"Tell me where you fostered, Julian."

He did. Julian had never spoken so much about himself in his entire life. He drank, he ate, and he spoke of his younger years at Carlisle Castle before going to Northwood Castle for a time. His training had been difficult and strenuous and he'd spent his entire life in the north. He'd fought off countless Scots raids and he'd even fought against King John when the man was rousting warlords in the north towards the end of his reign. In all, he projected the image of a competent, highly trained knight who didn't have the time or inclination for anything other than his vocation.

At least, that was the impression Lista got.

But she wasn't going to feel bad this time. She wasn't going to run from him. She was going to enjoy the evening with a handsome young knight she would probably never see again, but it was worth it to her. It was incredibly rare for her to have any conversational companion other than her mother and aunt, so this was a rare treat and she was grateful for it.

In her world, she had to accept the pleasant moments and not yearn for more.

"My lady?"

Torn from Julian's tale of a particular Scotsman he'd had trouble with in one of the numerous battles he'd been part of, Lista found herself looking up at a very pretty woman with blonde hair, pinned to the nape of her neck. She had seen the woman sitting with Cole and Addington had indicated she was Cole's wife, so Lista immediately rose to her feet to greet her hostess. The woman, however, put out her hands.

"Please sit," she said. "I did not mean to disturb you, but Julian has been taking all of your time so I thought I should introduce myself. I am Lady de Velt, Cole's wife."

Lista regained her seat. "It is a great honor to know you, Lady de Velt," she said. "The meal has been delicious. Thank you for your hospitality to my mother and my aunt and me. We are very grateful."

Corisande smiled. She was a very lovely woman. "It is our pleasure," she said. "My husband's mother is with our children right now, but I was going to relieve her of the duty so she could come down here and speak with your mother, only your mother and aunt seemed to have disappeared."

It was difficult for Lista to keep the smile on her face. "I realize that," she said. "If you are going to send Lady de Velt down to the hall, then I shall locate my mother immediately and bring her back."

Corisande nodded. "I am sure my husband's mother would like that very much," she said. Then, she paused before continuing hesitantly. "Your mother and aunt... when I saw them earlier, they were quite lively."

Lista tried to keep a brave front. "They are lively anywhere they go," she said. "I am sorry if they were disruptive."

Corisande shook her head, sitting down when Julian stood up and brought her a chair. "They were not disruptive at all," she said. "You must have a happy home."

Lista cocked her head curiously because she wasn't sure what she meant. "My lady?"

"Because they seem so happy."

Lista wasn't going to ruin the woman's opinion of her mother if that was what she truly thought, but there was absolutely no truth to what she said. "I am glad they seem happy to you, my lady," she said. "At home, it is much different."

"Oh?"

Lista nodded. "My mother is still grieving the loss of my father and my brother," she said. "But I thank you for saying she seems happy. Certainly, she has been happy to visit Berwick."

Corisande smiled. "You must return and visit again sometime."

"How long have you lived at Berwick?"

Corisande's brow furrowed thoughtfully. "Since I married my husband several years ago," she said. "I have always lived in Northumberland, however. My childhood home is not too terribly far from here. My older brothers visit often, as does my father. They have several children to play with here, which does my father good. He dotes on my children."

She was trying to make Lista feel more comfortable and it worked. Lista smiled at the idea of a loving grandfather. "That is wonderful," she said. "It is lovely for your children to know their grandfather so well."

"I think so."

Lista was prevented from replying when she caught sight of Amaury entering the great hall and he was quite alone. The mood of the warm conversation vanished as Lista stood up, her concerned focus on Amaury.

"My apologies, my lady," she said. "I see our knight and my mother does not seem to be with him. Will you please excuse me?"

Corisande waved her on as Julian stood up, watching Lista all but run to Amaury. He was still standing, watching, as she exchanged several words with the knight. Several frantic-looking words, it seemed to him, because Lista was growing animated. Suddenly, she was ducking out of the hall with Amaury on her heels.

"Julian?" Addington said. "Why don't you go and help her? She does not know Berwick if she is to search for her mother. You might be of assistance."

Julian didn't say a word, but he was leaving the dais before Addington was even finished speaking. Anteaus, who was still sitting next to Addington, stood up as well and followed Julian purely out of duty because Berwick was his post. He knew it better than Julian did. Corisande and Addington watched them head for the hall exit together.

"She seems like a nice woman," Corisande said. "She seems very concerned for her mother, however."

Addington nodded. "She is," she said. "And she thinks Julian is handsome."

Corisande looked at her in surprise. "She does?" she said. "Does he know?"

"He does."

Corisande cast Addington a long look. "Are you playing matchmaker, Addie?"

Addington grinned. "I do hope so."

Corisande caught on and she, too, was grinning. But she also knew her mother-in-law was waiting for her, so she excused herself just as Ashton made his way to the dais. He'd been on the other side of the hall, watching Anteaus and not wanting to get near the dais because Julian had told him not to be confrontational with Anteaus. That had frustrated him to no end, but Julian had been serious and he knew it. However, with Anteaus following Julian somewhere, Ashton could make his move.

And he did.

Oblivious to what was transpiring in the hall, Lista was on the hunt for her mother and aunt. Amaury had lost them, somewhere, and had searched for almost a half-hour before seeking help. The misty night was now so dense that it was difficult to see a few feet in front of her, so locating her mother and aunt wasn't going to be a simple thing. She didn't know Berwick Castle and had no idea where to start looking, but every second those two were on their own, her anxiety was building.

"Where did you last see them?" she asked.

Amaury was trying to get his bearings. "Over near the apartment where your chamber is located," he said. "They went into the chamber, I fear, for some of the things they bought at the apothecary's stall. I think they were burning hemp because I could smell it from the window. Then, they came out and I lost them in the mist."

Lista sighed heavily. "Damnation," she grumbled. "I am going to find everything they bought at the apothecary's and throw it in the fire. They have been nothing but trouble since we arrived."

"If you give the stuff to me, I'll do it."

Lista nodded firmly, disgusted by her mother and aunt's behavior. "They are going to embarrass themselves and me in front of these kind people," she said. "I like them. Lady Addington and Sir Julian have been very kind and I could throttle my mother for behaving so poorly."

"My lady?"

A voice came from the mist and Lista whirled around to see Julian and another knight emerging from the fog. When their gazes met, Julian smiled timidly.

"Do you require assistance?" he continued. "We saw you abruptly leave, so we came to see if there is something we can do to help."

Lista didn't want to drag Julian into her mother's folly, but she did indeed need help at the unfamiliar castle. She had no idea where to even start looking and her anxiety was on the rise.

"I am sorry to trouble you," she said. "It seems that my mother and aunt have disappeared. If you could…"

They were interrupted by a howling sound. It was more like a baying, like animals crying at the moon, and there were two of them. Two decidedly female voices that then started laughing.

Lista clapped her hand to her forehead.

"God's Bones," she said. "Where are they?"

Everyone started looking around. "Is that your mother, my lady?" Julian asked.

Lista nodded, exasperated. "It must be unless you know of anyone else who would bay like a wolf and then laugh," she said. "It has to be them. It sounds as if they are in that direction."

She was pointing off to her right as more howling sounds filled the mist. The knights turned in that direction, listening carefully.

"The gatehouse," Julian said. "It sounds as if they are on the wall."

He started to move, with Anteaus and Amaury and Lista following close behind. Having no idea where she was going, all Lista could do was stay close to Julian as Berwick's great gatehouse came into view. There were stairs on the outside of the structure, slick with the wet but also well-lit with torches, and Julian headed up the stairs with the knights right behind him. Lista took the stairs more slowly because they were slippery and she didn't want to fall. She was about midway up when a body was suddenly in front of her and she looked up to see Julian standing there, extending his hand to her.

For a moment, their eyes met and Lista realized his hair wasn't hanging in front of his right eye like it usually was. She'd tucked it back and he'd left it there. Gratefully, she took it and he steadied her up the rest of the way. Even when they reached the wall walk, he didn't let go of her hand.

He held it tightly.

Lista would have been giddy with delight had more howling not caught their attention. More howling, more laughing.

Lista's anxiety had turned to anger.

"There," she said, pointing off to the right. "It sounds as if it is coming from that direction."

They were all looking to the west, towards the river, and Anteaus led the way with Amaury, Julian, and Lista following. Julian was still holding on to Lista because the wall walk didn't have any railings on this side because they were being repaired. The wooden railings had rotted away and Cole was in the process of having everything replaced with stone, so there were only partial stone barriers as high as a man's ankle. Not being able to see the fifteen-foot drop from the wall because of the mist, Lista was very glad for Julian's steadying hand.

Truth be told, she was almost glad for her mother getting lost.

Almost.

More howling. They were nearing a tower when Amaury suddenly spoke up.

"Lady Felkington?" he said sharply. "Lady d'Orbec? Cease this foolishness. You've caused enough trouble this night."

Lista could see her mother and aunt come into view. They were sitting on the edge of the wall, their legs hanging over the side. She gasped because of the dangerous position and she felt Julian squeeze her hand reassuringly. She was so startled by the squeeze that she was caught off guard when he released her and went towards her mother, slowly and carefully.

"My lady," he said in that steady, raspy voice. "I am going to help you to your feet, but you must be very careful not to slip. It is a long drop to the ground and I do not want you to injure yourself."

Meadow looked up at the knight, having no idea of the danger she was in. "It is a lovely night," she said. "We were just commenting on how lovely the night is. So dark and close. This is a time when witches walk the earth. Did you know that?"

Julian shook his head. "I did not, my lady."

Meadow smiled at him before catching sight of her daughter a few feet behind him. "Ah," she said, extending her hand to Lista. "My daughter has come. Have you met my daughter, Knight? She is a good and obedient lass."

Clearly, she didn't recognize Julian from earlier in the day and he didn't remind her. He simply held out his hand to her.

"Let me help you rise, my lady," he said, ignoring her question. "Take my hand."

Meadow looked at the hand but made no move to take it. "I think not," she said. "We are enjoying the night. I think we will remain here a little longer."

Listening to her mother, Lista knew she was drunk, but she was probably also under the influence of any number of weeds or potions that she'd bought at the apothecary. She managed to get around Julian and came up between her mother and aunt.

"Stop it, both of you," she hissed. "You are shaming yourselves and worst of all, you are shaming me. You are making a mockery of Lady de Velt's invitation to sup, so get up and behave yourselves."

Meadow and Flora looked at Lista, shocked by the tone she

took. "You cannot speak to me that way," Flora said. "I will do as I please."

"Shut up," Lista snapped, her patience gone. "You are a foolish, ridiculous woman and you have lured my mother into your foolish and ridiculous world. I'll see no more of this, do you hear me? My mother is going with me but I do not care if you fall off this wall and break your stupid neck. Do whatever you wish but leave my mother out of it."

With that, she grasped her mother under both arms and pulled her away from the ledge. Then, she helped her mother to her feet as Flora hurled insults at her.

"Ungrateful child!" she said. "Ungrateful and unruly child. Leave your mother alone. You cannot command her!"

Lista ignored her. She had her mother on her feet and that was all she cared about. Julian was there, once again offering his help. Lista had her hands on her mother, helping the woman walk, but when she looked up at Julian, all she could see was that handsome face in the weak torchlight. When their gazes met, she smiled.

He smiled back.

Meadow grabbed his outstretched hand and Julian led her and Lista back down the wall walk towards the tower. That left Flora sitting on the edge, grumbling and insulting her niece, as Amaury went to the woman and held his hand out to her. Flora turned her nose up at him, but he did what he'd done a hundred times before. He grabbed her by the arm to pull her to her feet but instead of being compliant, as she usually was when it came to Amaury, she violently pulled away from him. That momentum caused Amaury to lose his balance and with the slick stone, he wasn't able to recover. He pitched right over the side, disappearing in the mist as Flora screamed.

Startled, Lista and Meadow came to a halt just in time to hear Amaury hit the ground below. It was a sickening, loud noise. Flora was still screaming and men down below were shouting, and Lista broke away from her mother, running for the tower with the stairs that led below. She could hear Julian calling after her, telling her to slow down, but she didn't listen. She took the tower stairs too fast and ended up slipping at the bottom, falling to her knees in the mud of the bailey. But she was on her feet in an instant, running over to the area where Amaury had gone down.

Men were gathered around a crumpled form on the ground and Lista pushed through, only to be confronted by a man who had fallen on his face into the mud. At least, that's what it looked like. Amaury's neck was bent at a sharp angle and she fell to her knees beside him.

"My God," she gasped in horror, putting her hands on the man to turn him over. "Amaury, can you hear me?"

Julian and Anteaus were beside her, helping her roll Amaury over, but it was abundantly clear that the man was dead. His neck was broken and when he rolled onto his back, one eye was shut and mashed with mud while the other eye was open, staring into nothingness.

One look and Lista knew he was beyond help.

CHAPTER FIVE

I T WAS DAWN on a morning that, given the mist from the
night before, had cleared up rapidly. The sun was bright
overhead and the sky was a brilliant blue with the scent of the
sea heavy upon the air. In the bailey of Berwick Castle, which
smelled heavily of smoke from the morning fires, gulls cried
overhead as the de la Mere escort prepared to depart.

Amaury's body was strapped to a wagon loaned to them by
Cole, tightly wrapped in oiled canvas and secured for the
journey home. They had six soldiers with them and an old
sergeant who was now the commander of their escort. Even so,
the old soldier had four high-caliber de Velt knights helping
him with his very small escort, making sure the body was
secured, making sure the ladies' palfreys were ready, and any
number of smaller details. All these things, that one or two men
could have easily secured, still had Julian, Cole, Anteaus, and
Ashton going over to assist the escort.

Flora and Meadow stood with Kellington, looking forlorn
and pale. While Flora wept into her kerchief, Meadow and
Kellington spoke softly between them, even holding hands at
one point. Addington stood with Lista, who was watching the

preparations grimly. She'd spent a sleepless night with the impact of what had happened haunting her dreams, the death of a man she'd known more than half her life. Part of that sleepless night involved taking everything her mother and Flora had purchased from the apothecary and burning it. Every single thing they'd procured was in ashes. When Flora slapped her for her actions, Lista slapped her aunt hard enough to send the woman to her knees.

She utterly, completely blamed Flora for Amaury's death.

And Flora knew it.

Therefore, there was trouble brewing on this morning as well, with Flora's mood and Lista's morose countenance. It wouldn't take much for things to explode between them, another reason why they were standing so far apart. Lista wouldn't even look at her aunt and she would barely look at her mother while Addington kept silent vigil with her new friend.

A friendship, Lista was sure, would be over the moment they left the gates of Berwick.

"I did not yet thank you for the loan of your beautiful blue dress," Lista said, simply to make conversation. "You have many beautiful garments with such lovely embroidery. Did you do that?"

Addington looked at her, sliding her hand through the crook of her elbow because it was the first time all morning that Lista had spoken more than two words.

Addington took it as an invitation.

"Some of it," she said. "I've always liked to embroider, but what you saw is my mother and sister's handiwork. They sew beautifully."

Lista smiled weakly. "It's very beautiful," she said. "You were very kind to let me have my pick."

Addington looked her up and down, as she was now back in the rather plain dress she'd come to Berwick in. "You could have worn it home," she said. "In fact…"

She trailed off, turning to her mother and calling to the woman. It seemed to be some kind of secret signal between them because Kellington broke away from Meadow, making her way to her daughter.

"Mama?" Addington said. "Mayhap you should tell Lady Lista what we have decided."

Kellington turned to Lista, a smile on her face. "My lady," she said quietly. "Since you have lost your knight, Julian and Ashton have volunteered to escort you home. Addington would like to accompany you also if you are agreeable. They thought it would make the trip easier for you during this troubling time. Will you allow us to assist since it was our fault that you lost your knight?"

Lista looked at her in surprise. "Your fault, my lady?"

Kellington nodded. "The railing was removed because it was rotted," she said. "Had it not been removed, there would have been something there to prevent your knight from falling to his death, so truly, you must let us help you. We feel responsible."

Lista had to admit that she was floored by the request. She looked between Addington and her mother, at a loss for words. They were both gazing back at her, so very kindly. So very warmly. These people whom she'd only just met were people who treated her as if she were an old and dear friend. She'd never met such selfless and open individuals.

Finally, she shook her head in awe.

"Since the moment we have met, everything has been disastrous on our part," she said. "We have had trouble and tragedy and I have found myself making excuses because of it. You must think we are pathetic, indeed, but I promise you that we are not usually."

Kellington smiled. "I believe you," she said. "Trust me when I say we have all had our problematic events but it is never so unfortunate than in front of someone who does not know you well."

Lista sighed, hoping that she really meant it. "Thank you for understanding, my lady," she said. "I feel as if I have done nothing but make excuses since I have known you, but when my mother is involved... you can understand that I must take care of her, even if it is to protect your fond memories of her."

Kellington's smile grew and she touched Lista's cheek gently. "You are a kind and loving daughter," she said. "Your mother is very fortunate to have you. I will come and visit in a few weeks to see how your mother is faring. I did not have a chance to speak with her while she was here, so I will speak to her another time. It may help her to speak to another woman who has suffered the same loss as she has."

Lista was so overwhelmed by the kindness that tears stung her eyes. "You are so very kind, my lady, thank you," she said. "And... and if you are sure it is not too much trouble, I will accept your offer of an escort. Felkington is not too terribly far, but it will be reassuring to have knights to protect us on our journey."

"And me," Addington said, squeezing her arm. "I will be on your journey, too."

Lista giggled. "And you," she said. "Can you use a sword?"

Addington laughed. "I cannot," she said. "But I can tell stories to entertain you."

"I would like that," Lista said. "Felkington is truly no more than a half-day's ride from here, so you can stay the night if you wish and return on the morrow."

Addington's face fell. "I was hoping to stay longer than that," she said. "I like to visit new places. Can I stay longer than just the night?"

Lista was overjoyed at the thought of someone other than her mother and aunt to speak to. A young woman, the same age, someone who very much wanted to be her friend. She should have been guarded, at least a little, because the madness that those at Berwick had seen from Meadow and Flora was just the beginning. It would be worse at home. But Lista didn't have the heart to refuse Addington a visit because, in truth, Addington had been very friendly since nearly the moment they met and for a lonely young woman like Lista, that was almost too good to believe.

"I would be honored," she said after a moment. "But you should know that my days are full of work. I am chatelaine of Felkington, so there is much to do on a daily basis. There is not much time for much else."

Addington's smile was back. "I don't care," she said. "I am sure we can find lots of things to do when you are not busy."

With that, she dashed off to collect the satchel she'd packed, rushing towards the keep in a rush of swishing fabric and dark hair. As Lista watched her run off, Kellington spoke softly.

"She has an older sister to whom she is very close," she said. "My middle daughter, Effington, was married a few years ago and Addie has missed her terribly. Do not be surprised if she has elected you to be her new sister and confidante."

Lista looked at her, smiling. "Is that why she has been so terribly friendly?"

Kellington nodded. "Exactly."

"So it was not my charm that convinced her that she wanted to be my friend?"

Kellington laughed softly. "I'm sure that has a great deal to do with it," she said. "But she misses Effie so very much. I hope you do not mind that she has invited herself to travel home with you."

Lista shook her head. "Not in the least," she said. "I… I do not have any friends, not since my brother died and my mother became… grieved. My mother has taken all of my time."

Kellington's gaze moved to Meadow and Flora, who were standing rather pale and dejected as the last of the escort was prepared.

"I will see what I can do," she said softly. "I know what it is to mourn the great love of your life. I know what it is to lose a son when… well, suffice it to say that I understand her sorrow. Mayhap I can help."

There was something painful in the way she spoke about the loss of a love that had Lista taking a second look. Lady de Velt was beautiful and kind, with genuine warmth in her eyes, but as she spoke of a lost love… something dimmed in those brown eyes. Something that spoke of unbearable grief. But she quickly recovered, smiling at Lista when she realized the woman was looking at her.

Lista smiled back.

"I know my mother would love to see you again," she said. "Truthfully, you will be a much better influence than my aunt. My mother needs the companionship and my aunt is a terrible influence. The excessive drink, the fungi, the potions…"

Kellington nodded in understanding. "Your aunt must be very lonely, too."

"She is, but instead of doing something constructive or

benevolent, she tries to destroy herself and my mother along with her."

"And you try your best to prevent that from happening."

Embarrassed, Lista nodded. "You must think that I complain terribly," she said. "It seems that all I have done is tell you of our problems. I did not mean to, I swear it, but I thought you deserved an explanation as to why things are the way they are."

Kellington patted her on the arm. "Not every family is perfect," she said. "You do not need to explain. But I do hope things get better."

"Thank you, my lady."

The flash of armor caught her attention and she turned to see Julian and Ashton as they came riding up on their warhorses. Julian looked exactly the way he did when Lista had met him the day before – enormous, built for war. He was a de Velt, after all, and even if she knew very little about the family itself, she knew enough to know that if there was a battle, they were in the middle of it.

That included Julian.

Lista was so involved in watching the man that she failed to see the carriage that had been brought forth from the stables. It was a small carriage with a small cab, with wooden sides fortified with strips of iron, a door on one side of it, and small windows that looked out from either side.

Kellington grasped Lista by the hand.

"Come, my lady," she said. "I thought it might be more comfortable for you to ride in my carriage. It really is quite comfortable – there are two cushioned benches, enough for four women to ride quite happily together. It will also be much safer."

She had reached the carriage by that time, pulling open the

iron latch on the door and revealing an extremely comfortable cab inside. The walls were lined with brocade and there were two small, cushioned couches facing one another. Awed, Lista stuck her head in to get a good look at it.

"It's beautiful," she said. "I have never seen anything like it."

Kellington grinned. "Get in," she said. "I will bring your mother and aunt."

Lista did. She climbed into the carriage and sat down on the couch facing forward. There was a small window next to her, enough for ventilation but not enough for anyone to climb inside should there be trouble. She sat down but as she did so, an enormous hand reached in and took the satchel she'd been carrying. Startled, she looked up to see Julian standing in the doorway.

"Where did you come from?" she said. "The last I saw, you were on your horse."

She couldn't see his face because his helm was on. "I still am," he told her, heaving the satchel onto the top of the carriage, which contained a big, locked box that was bolted to the top of the cab. "You do not see me."

He was jesting with her and Lista fought off a grin. "A pity," she said. "I thought it was my friend, Julian, but I suppose I am mistaken. Mayhap you shall be my new friend instead."

The helmed head turned to her. "No one but me shall be your new friend," he said. "Remember that."

"I thought you weren't Julian?"

His helm was on but it wasn't secured yet, so he bent over and pulled it off, revealing his handsome face set within his hauberk.

And his hair wasn't covering his right eye.

"There," he said. "*Now* do you recognize me?"

Lista started laughing. "I do," she said. "I've not had the chance to bid you a good morn."

He smiled, his dimples deep. "Good morn, my lady," he said. "Are you feeling... better this morning?"

He meant after such a horrific night and Lista struggled to maintain her smile. "I do not know yet," she said. "But I will tell you a secret."

"What is it?"

"Knowing you are escorting us home makes me feel better already."

He was still smiling, though her gentle flirt had him shifting nervously. "Did you think I would simply let you go and not do what I could to assist you?"

"I did not think that, but I am glad we are traveling together," she said. "Your sister will be my guest for a few days, it seems. You are also welcome to stay if you wish. I am sure Addington will need an escort home when she decides to return, so you may as well stay unless you have pressing duties elsewhere."

It was an unexpected, but not unwelcome, invitation and his cheeks flushed in the slightest. Mostly because he very much wanted to accept. He'd spent his life being shunned one way or another, so an invitation from a lovely young woman had his heart fluttering.

"I do not have pressing duties elsewhere, at least not for the moment," he said. "I accept your invitation."

Lista grinned at him and he grinned back, but it was an embarrassed sort of grin and quite charming. But Lista was precluded from saying anything further when Kellington arrived at the carriage with her mother and aunt. They climbed in, lethargically, and sat on the couch facing backwards in the cab. Neither one of them were happy, with aching heads and bellies from everything they'd ingested the day before.

"Do not forget, Meadow," Kellington said. "I will see you in a few days for a nice, long visit. I am looking forward to it."

Meadow smiled weakly. "As am I," she said. "I am so glad to have seen you again, Kelli. I hope this means we shall not lose touch again."

"We won't, I promise," Kellington said, reaching out to squeeze her hand. Just as she did so, she was buffeted by Addington, who had just arrived. She shoved her satchel at Julian and climbed into the cab, pushing past her mother as she sat next to Lista. "Ah, Addie is here. Safe journey to you all, ladies. I shall see you soon."

Addington waved at her mother, excited to be going on a new adventure, as Kellington stepped back and Julian shut the door and bolted it. They could hear the knights outside the carriage, mostly Julian, shouting orders to the escort and Lista realized that not only were the knights accompanying them home, but there were evidently about forty de Velt soldiers coming as well.

It made for quite a secure escort.

The carriage lurched forward and the rocking motion had Meadow and Flora sleeping before they'd even left the village of Berwick. As the pair snored away, Addington pulled out a deck of painted cards and she and Lista settled down to a card game where each player had to come up with card combinations totaling the number ten and setting those cards aside until there were no more cards left.

Lista had never played it before and it was a lovely way to pass the hours until they reached Felkington Castle on a rather clear and blustery day, but no matter how focused they were on the game and their conversation, Lista kept her ears open for a certain young knight who seemed to be riding directly next to the carriage. Every time she looked up from her card came and to the window behind Addington, she could see Julian there.

In spite of the cargo they carried, it turned out to be one of the more enjoyable trips home.

CHAPTER SIX

Felkington Castle

"**D**ID YOU SEE how those knights looked at her?" Flora asked. "Did you see how the one with the strange eyes looked at her? The de Velt son?"

Meadow and Flora were burning hemp in the tower room where they always burned such things. It was high enough above the castle that the smell of the smoke, a sickly sweet smell, floated skyward and didn't fill the castle below. The two of them would pile the dried leaves from the *henep*, or hemp plant, into a brazier and light them on fire. The smoke would fill the tower chamber and they would inhale deeply, bringing about a sense of calm and relaxation to them both. Sometimes, they'd spend days in the tower room, simply inhaling the smoke.

Like today.

Two days after their return from Berwick, they were holed up in the tower room inhaling smoke and had been ever since they'd buried Amaury at St. Paul's Church, the tiny parish church in Felkington where Meadow's husband and son were both buried. Once Amaury was put in a crypt in the corner, a stone box that had been emptied of the lord who had once been buried there, Meadow and Flora retreated to the tower room and sat in a haze of blue smoke.

After two days of burning the weeds, they were down to the last of the hemp. The food that the servants had been bringing to them on an hourly basis during the day was mostly gone as they awaited the morning influx of sustenance, but Flora, who hadn't spoken much since their return, now seemed to have something to say.

That sweet-smelling smoke had her thinking.

At times, that could be dangerous.

"Did you hear me?" she said to her sister. "Wake up and listen to me."

"I am awake," Meadow said, her eyes half-lidded. "I did not notice anyone paying Lista attention. What did you see?"

Flora was laying on a cushioned pallet, staring at the ceiling. Her mind was so much mush but, in a sense, it was also heightened. The smoke from the hemp was potent and gave her thoughts that were often profound and enlightening. At least, she thought they were.

Most of the time, however, they were nonsense.

"Lista is meant to help us," she mumbled. "The Wu has spoken to me, Meadow. He tells me that our opportunity has come. Lista *is* our opportunity."

Meadow was staring into the room, dazed, but her sister's words had her turning to the woman questioningly.

"What do you mean?" she said. "What opportunity?"

Flora sat up, unsteadily, and leaned over the brazier, inhaling the smoke deeply. Since it would soon be gone, she wanted to inhale all she could.

"There was a time when we were in the top social circles," she said. "Our mother's father was an earl and connected to King Henry, and Papa was a great knight. We spent our youth at court with Henry and his mistresses, and then with John when Richard was absent. Do you remember those days, Meadow?"

Meadow closed her eyes, nodding faintly. "I remember."

"Do you remember when we were powerful and beautiful?"

"We were never that powerful, Flora," Meadow said. "We simply followed the crowd and did as we were told. We carried food, we mopped piss at times, and if a nobleman wanted to put his hand up our skirts, we let him. We were nothing."

That had been the reality of court life for them but Flora refused to acknowledge the truth. In her muddled haze, she only remembered the moments that made her feel powerful and bold.

"We *were* powerful and we can be again," she insisted. "Marry Lista to a knight with ties to the king and we can regain those days of our youth. Don't you see?"

Meadow's eyes opened. "Is that what you wish?" she said, incredulous. "To marry my Lista to a man for power?"

Flora focused her bloodshot eyes on her sister. "The de Velt knight is interested," she said. "The de Velts are very powerful. They are a major family in the north and not only do they have ties to the Earl of Northumberland, but also to William Marshal. The name de Velt opens doors all over England. Should Lista marry into the family, we would have influence over her and, consequently, over her husband, a de Velt heir. Do you understand that?"

Meadow nodded. "For what purpose?"

Flora's gaze was intense. "What do you think, stupid?" she

hissed. "We could return to court again. Young Henry is upon the throne, but surely his wife would appreciate our experience and guidance since we knew court in the old days. No longer would we be useless here at Fuckington. I hate this place and these gray, dreary walls. We could regain that which we deserve – power and prestige. We could be on top again!"

Meadow was following her sister for the most part. Flora had always had ambition, so this was nothing new, but she hadn't seen her ambitious streak in quite some time. With a knight from a prestigious family paying attention to Lista, that had apparently changed.

"We have never been on top," she finally said. "We were the lowliest ladies-in-waiting in court."

That wasn't what Flora remembered. "Men gave us coinage," she growled. "Men kissed us and gave us coinage. I took a few to my bed, powerful lords, and received more money because of it."

"And then you married one of those men you took to your bed and that was the end of it."

Flora was teetering on a rage. "It does not have to be," she said. "Meadow, think on it – we can be back where we used to be. Mayhap there are men looking for wives for companionship, not foolish young things who want home and hearth."

Meadow didn't want to hear anything about a new husband. She wasn't over the death of the only man she'd ever loved and the son she mourned daily. "Cease," she hissed, putting up a hand. "You have dreams of grandeur and now you are involving my daughter. Lista has been of marriageable age for some time but you have never spoken of an advantageous marriage for her before."

Flora lay back down on her makeshift bed. "Because no

man has looked at her before," she said. "Lista is pretty enough. She could be beautiful with the right clothing. She does not even have a maid to help her most of the time. She needs a proper lady's maid and more beautiful clothing if we are to entice the de Velt knight."

"All of this so you can regain your position at court?"

"Lista must marry. Why not a knight who can do us all some good?"

She had a point. Meadow thought on her daughter, so responsible when she herself was not. Lista fostered at Richmond Castle and then at Bamburgh Castle, and she'd learned from the finest tutors. She was quite intelligent, but she seemed to be more focused on taking care of Felkington, her ancestral home, than in finding a husband. Or friends for that matter. Meadow hadn't even concerned herself with that until now. Her daughter wasn't the frivolous type who dreamed of something better. As far as Meadow knew, Lista had no dreams at all, which was sad for a woman her age.

Perhaps Flora was right. Perhaps the introduction of the de Velt knight might change that.

It couldn't hurt to have her daughter married to a powerful knight.

"The de Velt son is here," she said after a moment. "He escorted us home. What if I tell Lista to go into Berwick and find a seamstress? She can have the knight escort her and they can spend that time together."

Flora waved her off. "Berwick?" she said. "Pah! Tell her to go to Newcastle."

Meadow looked at her in surprise. "But it is two days there and two days back."

"Exactly," Flora said firmly. "Four days with the de Velt

knight. That means two nights or more. Mayhap he will seduce her and then he *must* marry her, so it is a perfect plan."

Meadow wasn't convinced. "Do you think so?"

"The Wu declares the plan to be perfect," Flora said, closing her eyes and imaging the emperor from the Far East speaking to her in dreams. "Lista *must* marry, Meadow. And we must find ourselves a respected part of the nobility again. You will tell your daughter tonight that she is to depart for Newcastle on the morrow and insist the de Velt knight take her."

Meadow wouldn't argue with her sister. Flora was the only one who understood her grief and turmoil, so she didn't want to disappoint her. Flora often saw things that Meadow didn't and being related to the de Velt family and privy to their political and social station was indeed something that shouldn't be overlooked. Lista was indeed of marriageable age, so it was time to do something about it.

But perhaps it wouldn't take a journey to Newcastle.

Perhaps it would be as simple as speaking to Kellington, who promised to visit soon. From one mother to another, perhaps she could convince Kellington that Lista would be a perfect wife for the woman's son. She didn't even know his name but she would remedy that.

Meadow was going to find her daughter a de Velt husband.

CHAPTER SEVEN

A S JULIAN QUICKLY discovered, Felkington was a most remarkable castle.

So was its chatelaine.

Tucked away in a remote area of Northumberland, or at least a not very well-traveled area, Felkington had been built two hundred years before to protect a convergence of roads. The road leading west ended in Carlisle while the one leading east went into Berwick. The road north led past Northwood Castle and into Scotland while the road leading south went down into the heart of Northumbria.

Once, Felkington had been very important. But as the years passed, bigger roads were built, cities grew, and travel moved away from this remote area. Felkington, however, remained big and strong, as it had been when it was an important outpost. It was built in a square shape, with impenetrable walls on the outside and no windows until the third floor. There wasn't a keep, but simply many rooms built against the walls so the castle was essentially one building with a courtyard in the center. There were passages and guard rooms and stables and an enormous hall on the third floor, with lancet windows overlooking the land below.

The castle, in fact, was perfectly defensible.

Julian was greatly impressed with it. One of the biggest things he was impressed with was the courtyard itself, carved out in the middle of this enormous, square structure. There were several doorways that opened onto the courtyard, including a passageway that was the main castle entrance. There was a gigantic portcullis on the outside, protected by fortified gates, but if one happened to make it through those gates and the portcullis, there was another portcullis and a set of gates on the interior where it opened into the bailey.

Each door leading into the courtyard also had its own portcullis and iron gates, so even if an enemy made it into the courtyard after all of the defenses in the passage, there was no way to make it into one of the doorways. Overhead, looking into the courtyard, were dozens of windows from which an army could fire arrows down into an invading army.

Like shooting fish in a barrel.

Above the courtyards and gates and portcullises, the castle reached five stories into the sky on all sides, plus the roof as the sixth floor. The grounds outside of the castle were protected by a wall and a moat, but they were just for show. They were weak compared to the structure itself. The wall protected an area of more stables and a garden and even a vineyard, but given how some walls were on contemporary castles – massive and tall – the relatively short walls of Felkington were really just meant to keep out marauders or animals or thieves. An army could easily get over them, but once they ran into the castle itself, the gesture would be futile.

It was little wonder that Felkington hadn't seen a siege in over one hundred years.

Lista had been right about one thing – Felkington lived in its own little world, a bucolic paradise in a remote area of Northumberland. No one really bothered them, so it was quite idyllic. Julian and Addington followed Lista around, listening to her talk about her ancestors who had built the place, of the fortification features, of the bake house and the brew house and a dozen other self-sufficient trades they had. Everything about them was completely self-sufficient and after the tour of the castle itself, which took most of the day, they ended up outside in the vineyard.

Felkington was built on the top of a hill overlooking a green and placid valley. As they emerged from the main entrance and headed out towards the vineyard, they were joined by Ashton. Julian had kept the man purposely busy for most of the day making sure the warhorses had their shoes adjusted because he'd made up an excuse about his beast's odd gait and wanted it checked. That meant checking every shoe of the horse who wasn't particularly cooperative, which took time. Then he forced Ashton to check his own horse's shoes.

In truth, it was simply to keep him away from Addington because Ashton and Anteaus had shown some aggression towards one another back at Berwick. The aggression had been mostly sidelong glances and stiff expressions, but Julian didn't want Ashton overwhelming Addington at the moment. She was here to visit with Lista, so Julian was trying to keep Ashton away from her.

But that hadn't worked for long.

"I thought I saw you coming out here," Ashton said, following them from the gatehouse. "May I join you?"

Lista and Addington came to a halt, turning to the smiling knight as he caught up to them. Julian was already a few paces ahead, trying to think up another excuse to keep Ashton away. But the more he thought about it, the more he was thinking he might have done the wrong thing. If Ashton had Addington's attention, that meant he could have Lista's.

Aye... perhaps he'd been wrong all along.

Sometimes, his consideration for others was at his own expense.

"Lady Lista was going to show us the vineyard," he said as he watched Ashton go straight to Addington like a moth to a flame. "We just had the tour of the castle and I must say that I am quite impressed. This is far more of a fortress than I had imagined."

Hearing the comment, Lista turned to Julian just as Ashton and Addington came together.

"It is a magical place," she said, smiling at him. "We are hiding here from the world."

"And for good reason," Julian said. She was so close that he boldly held out an elbow to her, inviting her to take it and holding his breath while she considered it. "This must have been a wonderful place to grow up."

Lista only considered his silent invitation for a brief second before she slid her hand into the crook of his elbow. Beneath her fingers, through the fabric, she could feel his big muscles and it was enough to make her heart pound against her ribs. Her hand, touching him, seemed the most natural of things.

She could easily become used to it.

"It was," she said, hoping she didn't sound as breathless as she felt. "Honestly, I can count the times we've known trouble on one hand."

"Who from?"

She shrugged as they headed down the slope towards the

vineyard. "Scots, mostly," she said. "Sometimes they come down to raid our garden and steal our grapes, but we have large dogs that we turn into the garden at night and they are an excellent deterrent."

Julian looked out over the stunning green landscape. "How many men do you have?"

"Around two hundred."

He looked at her in surprise. "For a fortress this large?"

She nodded. "Look at it," she said, gesturing to the obvious. "Once we close the passageway to the courtyard, it is impenetrable. They can get over the walls if they try and damage the garden and the stable yard, but they cannot make it into the castle no matter how hard they try."

Julian looked back over his shoulder at the castle behind him. "That is true," he said. "I do not think I've ever seen such a tall fortress."

"The Scots had a name for it, many years ago."

"What's that?"

"*Meuran gu nèamh.*"

Julian had lived on the borders his entire life and he was fairly fluent in Gaelic. "Fingers to heaven?"

Lista nodded. "Doesn't it look like the corner towers are stretching to heaven?"

"It does," he agreed. His gaze was still on the structure, looking at the southwest corner in particular. He came to a halt, gesturing to the very top of the corner tower. "Is that smoke I see?"

Lista already knew what he meant before she looked. Therefore, her glance was brief. "Aye," she said. "That room is used exclusively by my mother and aunt."

"Are they burning something up there?"

Lista nodded, her humor completely gone. She released his elbow and began to head towards the vineyard. "They are burning dried hemp leaves," she said.

His brow furrowed, but he started to follow her. "For what purpose?"

Lista sighed heavily and she came to a halt. "Julian, in case you have not yet realized it, my mother and aunt have a… problem," she said. "They drink to excess, they eat or snort or inhale anything they can find that will alter their state of consciousness. In short, they are addicted to anything that makes them feel happy or sad or giddy or mad. My mother has not been sober in two long years, so they go to the tower room and burn hemp leaves because the smoke intoxicates them. Even now, they are inhaling it as deeply as they can because they will soon be out of dried leaves and will want for more. But at least while they are in that room, things at Felkington are quiet and lovely. Look around you and see our paradise. But this paradise hides a troubling secret."

He was looking at her intently, the wind lifting the hair that usually covered up his right eye. "I knew it from the start," he said. "I knew it when your mother came out of the apothecary's stall and plowed into one of my soldiers and then slapped him for being in her way. All things considered, it is not such a terrible secret. I've seen families with worse. But it must be a burden upon you to have to manage your mother and your aunt constantly."

Lista lifted an ironic eyebrow. "Burden, indeed," she said. "She's my mother. She is supposed to be the responsible one, yet she cannot manage it, so the duty must fall to me. All of the duty must fall to me while she behaves like a woman who is trying to force herself into an early grave."

"And this makes you bitter?"

"It makes me frustrated."

He folded his massive arms across his chest, those bulging muscles at Lista's eye level. "Why does she do this?" he asked. "You said it has only been for two years? What happened two years ago that caused her to take this path?"

"A little over two years ago, my father died and my brother was murdered shortly thereafter," she said. "That did something to my mother. What she does, she does to forget. Or mayhap she simply wishes to join them. I really don't know because she will not speak to me of it at all. My mother and I are not close these days because she locks herself away with my aunt and they do all they can to intoxicate themselves. That leaves me to make sure Felkington survives."

He nodded in understanding. "I see," he said. "I'm glad you told me. I know a little something about having great responsibility thrust upon you. It can be… heavy."

Off to their left, Addington let out a yelp as she tripped over something in the vineyard. She and Ashton had strolled down to the neat rows of grapes and had been picking them straight off the vine, at least those that hadn't already been harvested. When Addington tripped, Ashton was there to catch her and they giggled together.

Lista found herself watching the pair.

"She likes him a great deal," she said softly.

Julian was watching, as well. "That has been going on between them for a few years now," he said. "He will not commit and she will not let him catch her, so on it goes. She's rather old to still be a maiden, so I hope she stops running from him soon. It is time for Addie to have a family and grow up."

Lista turned to him, watching his expression as he observed

Addington and Ashton in the distance. "Are all of your siblings married?" she asked.

He nodded. "Cole, Allaston, and Effington are," he said. "Addington is not and it is time for her, so I can stop worrying about her. Let her be Ashton's problem from now on."

Lista smiled faintly. "You do not mean that."

"Of course I do," he said, looking at her. "With all of my sisters married, I will not have to worry any longer."

Lista frowned. "Why is it your worry?" she said. "What does your mother say? She should be the one to worry."

He turned for the vineyard, reaching out to take her hand as he went. "After my father's death, I have more or less assumed his mantle," he said. "My mother is strong, but it is my duty to help her any way I can."

Lista was starting to feel giddy again as he held her hand. "What about your brother?" she said. "He is the eldest, is he not?"

"He is," Julian said. "But Cole has Berwick and his own family to worry about. He has five small children, a wife, and a very strategic castle. He manages Berwick and I manage Pelinom, our family home."

"Is that what you meant by understanding great responsibility thrust upon you?"

He glanced at her. "You were listening, were you?"

She grinned as they came to a halt because they were at the vineyard now, which was tiered because of the slope of the hill. Julian let go of her hand and reached out, grasping her around the waist and lifting her down to the next tier. Once he set her on her feet, he didn't let her go. Lista found herself gazing up at him, feeling warmth and interest radiating from his eyes.

There was no mistake.

"I have listened to every word you have spoken since we first met," she said sincerely. "Even when I was angry with you, I still listened to you because I think you are a man with a good deal to say, Julian. I would always like to listen to you if you will let me, so in answer to your question, I heard you. You spoke those words as if there were something more behind them, but I will not ask. If you want me to know, you will tell me."

He looked at her, a smile playing on his lips, digesting every word. "You are much different from any woman I have ever known," he finally said. "At least, any young women. You seem much wiser than your years."

Lista cocked an eyebrow. "Is that a bad thing?"

He shook his head. "Not at all," he said. "In fact, I rather like it. May I be perfectly honest with you?"

"Of course. As my friend, I would expect you to be."

His smile broke through. "I admire you a great deal," he said. "You have shouldered a difficult situation with your mother and aunt but you've not let it crush you. That is something to be applauded."

"Thank you."

"May I say something else?"

"You may."

"You need to learn to laugh."

She looked at him, surprised. "Why do you say that?"

"Because I've not seen you truly laugh out loud since I've known you."

That was probably true. Lista paused to think about his statement. "I suppose I am so focused on what needs to be done to keep Felkington running smoothly and my mother placated that I've not found the time to laugh," she said. "Unrestrained laughter is for people who do not have too much on their minds."

Julian fought off a grin as they both heard Addington squealing with laughter when Ashton stole something from her and she ran after him.

"Addie will teach you how to laugh freely and often," he said. "Spend time with her. Learn from her. She may not have your responsibilities, but she's not as foolish as she seems."

Lista cocked her head. "You will not teach me to laugh?"

He chuckled softly. "I am in need of lessons myself."

"Can we not learn together?"

He looked at her, his dual-colored eyes glimmering. "I would like nothing better."

Lista grinned at him. Then she reached up and pushed the hair away from his eyes again. "I think we can learn to do it," she said quietly. "Because over the past day, you have learned to look me in the eyes. When I first met you, you would not do it. Therefore, if you have learned to look me in the eyes, I know you can learn to laugh, too."

He was still smiling, but it was difficult. The mention of his eyes had him faltering. In fact, he immediately lowered his gaze but she grasped him by the chin and forced his head up.

"Look at me," she said softly but firmly. He did, but it was guarded, and she smiled openly. "That's better. You have the most beautiful eyes, Julian. I know you do not think so, but I do. The colors are magnificent."

He sighed, a long and drawn-out sound. "You should know that it is not something I speak of," he said. "No one does."

"Why not?"

He searched for an answer. "Because we do not," he said simply. "*I* do not. All of my siblings have unusual eye color, just like my father did. We do not speak of the obvious."

Lista leaned forward, getting closer to his face and looking at him dead-on in the eyes. "If you expect me to learn to laugh, then I expect you to learn to look me in the eyes, always," she said. "If you do not wish to speak of it, then I will not, but know my expectations. And know I think your eyes are as beautiful as the rest of you, so you do not have to hide them from me. I will be disappointed if you do."

With that, she dropped her hand and turned away, heading off into the vineyard and leaving Julian standing there with his heart in his throat. *Thump, thump... thump, thump.* He could hardly breathe because of her words.

Didn't she realize how freakish he looked?

Didn't she realize how odd he was?

Clearly, she didn't care but he couldn't figure out why a woman as magnificent as she was didn't care. He was trying to think of an underlying motive, but he couldn't. That only led him to the next conclusion.

That she was being truthful.

After all of these years, and the disappointments he had suffered, he could hardly believe it. With a smile on his lips, he followed her into the vineyard where Addington and Ashton had ended up throwing grapes at one another and having a marvelous time.

But Julian only had eyes for Lista.

CHAPTER EIGHT

"IT IS TIME for sup, Mama," Lista said from her position in the doorway of her mother's tower chamber. "Pull yourself together and come down to the hall. The men will more than likely want to celebrate Amaury's life and you should be part of it."

The smoke in the chamber had cleared away for the most part, leaving a sickly sweet smell behind that permeated everything – the walls, clothing, the floor. *Everything.* It stank and Lista resisted the urge to sneeze as her aunt stirred on the floor and her mother sat up from the small bed she'd been lying on.

Lethargic and pale, they looked as if they'd been sleeping for fifty years.

"I think not, Lista dear," Meadow said. "We are weary from our travel."

Lista had no sympathy for either of them. "You mean you are full of that intoxicating smoke," she snapped softly. "You are full of that horrible weed and anything else you have ingested. Well? What else have you eaten, sniffed, or inhaled since we came home?"

Her sharp tone had Flora stirring more than usual. "Shut up, Girl," she said, throwing her arm over her eyes as she lay there. "Shut up and go away."

Lista had never had much of a liking for her aunt, but that was never more evident than it was at this moment.

"I would watch myself if I were you," she said slowly. "You have caused enough trouble."

That brought Flora off the floor. "What trouble?" she demanded angrily.

Lista's jaw ticked. "The death of a man who was far better than you could ever hope to be," she said. When Flora opened her mouth to retort, Lista nearly shouted at her. "You heard me, Flora. You caused the death of a good man with your sickening behavior and if you do not watch yourself, I will have you thrown out of Felkington and you can fend for yourself."

Flora's face began to turn red. "How dare you speak to me like that?" she hissed. "Meadow? Are you going to allow her to speak to me that way?"

Meadow, the weak one, didn't want to get between her loud-mouthed sister and her strong daughter. That was a situation she could not win, so she simply put her hand up in surrender and shook her head. Seeing that her mother wasn't going to interfere pleased Lista immensely.

"Of course she is going to allow me to do as I please because whatever I say or do, you deserve it," she said. "You are a worthless cow, Flora d'Orbec, and you have cost a good man his life and that is something I shall never forgive."

"It was not my fault!"

"If I tell the men in the hall that you caused Amaury's death, they will happily throw you out of Felkington," Lista fired back. "In fact, you'll be fortunate if that is all they do. Be thankful that

I've not yet told them, but if you do not behave yourself, I shall show no such restraint."

Flora wasn't used to being challenged, although she and Lista had never had a cordial relationship. Lista tolerated the woman and that was about it, but they had been known to butt heads from time to time. When a rash, entitled woman met a stubborn, rational woman, things were bound to happen.

Like now.

Picking up the bowl that contained the ashes of the burned leaves, Flora threw it at Lista as hard as she could. The bowl only flew about two feet in the air before landing heavily, ashes scattered everywhere.

"To hell with you," Flora snarled. "You have no power over me."

Lista lifted an eyebrow. "That is where you are wrong," she said. "Do you care to test that theory?"

Flora was infuriated but, even in her current state, she wasn't stupid. She eyed her niece for a moment before turning back to her bed upon the floor.

"You need a husband," she grumbled. "A man to hold power over you. Then we'll see how bold you really are."

Lista shook her head at her ridiculous aunt. "A husband will have no bearing on how bold I am," she said. "Especially when I am right. You will remain in this room until I decide what to do with you. Meanwhile, Mama, you will come down to the hall."

Meadow had been watching the situation between her daughter and sister unfold with apprehension. When the focus was back on her, she looked at her daughter fearfully.

"You should not speak so to your aunt," she said, scolding her as much as she dared. "Please, Lista. Be kind."

Lista's patience was gone. "Mama, I know you believe she

has helped you since Papa and Simon's deaths, but all she has done is ruin you. She is mean and cowardly and cruel, and she as much as murdered Amaury. I was there; I saw it. I know what she's done."

Meadow reached out her hands, pleadingly. "It was an accident."

"It was her stupidity!" Lista was back to shouting again. Her mother's blind spot when it came to her sister always enraged her. "Mama, she has done nothing but harm you and harm me and now she's killed Amaury. I want her gone. You can tell her to leave or I will, but either way, she will be gone by the end of the week."

Meadow was stricken. "But… but where shall she go? *This* is her home!"

"This is *not* her home," Lista said firmly, looking over at Flora, who was glaring at her. "She has her manse in Scarborough and she can return to it. She does not belong here, Mama. I have tolerated her because I know she brought you comfort, but she has only succeeded in ruining you and killing Amaury. I do not care where she goes, only that she does go. If you do not support me in this decision, then I shall tell the soldiers what really happened to Amaury and let nature take its course. Felkington used to mean something before she came and tried to ruin it. It will mean something again after she has gone."

With that, she quit the chamber, slamming the door behind her. There was a deafening silence in her wake as Meadow struggled to show some backbone when it came to her sister. Perhaps she knew that everything her daughter said was true, but the weak woman in her needed her sister's presence. She needed the woman to help her find relief from the crushing grief she experienced every hour of every day.

But perhaps she knew, deep down, that Flora was indeed destructive.

She simply couldn't bring herself to admit it.

"Do you hear her?" Flora finally said, hissing angrily. "She is trying to take Fuckington away from you, Meadow. She will do it, too, if you do not marry her off quickly. I told you to speak with the de Velt son. You must do it now!"

Meadow couldn't bring herself to look at her sister. "She will see reason, in time," she said. "The death of Amaury has upset her. She did not mean what she said."

"She meant all of it," Flora snapped back. "She means to throw me to the wolves and you must do something about it or the next person she throws to the wolves will be you. Thrown from your own castle! Marry her off immediately, I say. She needs a husband to control her!"

Meadow knew her daughter needed to marry, but Flora was using marriage like a punishment, anything to subdue Lista and her intention to remove Flora from Felkington. But it wasn't like Flora was destitute – she wasn't. She had money and a small manse near Scarborough called *The Filey*. Her husband had bought it years ago because it faced the sea, but it was damp and cold and Flora didn't like it.

She wanted to be in the enormous castle with an unlimited supply of weeds, herbs, and alcohol and her sister paying for everything.

Deep down, Meadow knew that.

But she still couldn't give her sister up.

"I will speak to the de Velt son," she finally said, sounding defeated. "Tomorrow, I will do it."

Satisfied she'd manipulated her sister yet again, Flora lay

back down to sleep off the effects of the smoke she'd been inhaling for the past few days. But she slept with the confidence of knowing that her niece would not have the last word in all of this. Above all, Meadow was the Lady of Felkington and as Lady Felkington, her commands would be obeyed above her daughter's.

That was the hope she would cling to.

It would be a harsh reality for Lista de la Mere.

CHAPTER NINE

A ND THE RAINS came.

The frolicking in the vineyard was cut short by a storm that had blown in from the east. The wind had picked up and gray clouds blew in towards sunset, dotting the land with fat droplets. But that was just a harbinger of things to come – in little time, darker clouds blew in that unleashed a torrent that sent Lista, Julian, Addington, and Ashton running back into the castle. By the time they entered the courtyard, they were soaked.

With laughter and chatter, they made their way up the spiral stairs that led to the living levels three stories above the ground. Here, there were many chambers, including guest lodgings. Julian had a room to himself, as did Ashton, but Addington was on the level above with Lista. There was a small adjoining chamber to Lista's larger chamber and Addington had settled into that quite comfortably.

As Julian and Ashton dried out before the evening meal, Lista and Addington were doing the same. Their dresses had soaked up a goodly amount of the rain, but both chambers were warm and cozy from the enormous hearths that were blazing. Servants had put water on to boil in both hearths and the maid that usually helped Lista had brought in big pieces of drying cloths.

Thunder crashed and lightning lit up the sky as the maid helped the women peel off the wet clothing and into something warm and dry. A servant brought warmed wine and they imbibed generously, listening to the inclement weather outside and chatting amiably. Addington ended up sitting in front of the hearth, wrapped up in a heavy robe as Lista brushed out her dark hair, which went all the way down to her knees.

"When I get back to Pelinom, I'm going to tell Mama that we need to plant a vineyard like yours," Addington said, sipping on her wine. "We already have orchards of apples and cherries, so we can plant grapevines, too."

Lista continued to brush Addington's straight, silky hair even as her own hair dried with a kink to it. "Grapes take work," she said. "We have a man who tends our gardens and he is forever tending the grapes."

Addington thought on that. "Then mayhap he can teach Julian how to tend grapes," she said. "It will give him something to do when he is finished with his knightly duties. A man should have something to occupy his time."

"And Julian has nothing?"

"Nothing but horses and his books," Addington said. "Did he tell you that he likes to read?"

Lista shook her head. "He did not," she said. "He has not spoken much of himself, to be truthful."

Addington was watching the lightning flash on the other side of the oiled cloth that covered the window. "I saw you two speaking earlier," she said. "What was he saying?"

Lista shrugged. "Nothing, really," she said. "Cursory things. We spoke of my mother and why she is the way she is. He said I behaved like someone who had a good deal of responsibility thrust upon them and that he understood how that feels."

Addington hesitated before speaking. "He *does* understand," she said. "I know I tease Julian quite a bit, but the truth is that I love the big dolt. You would never know what a tender heart he has."

"Does he?"

Addington nodded. "Has he spoken of our father?"

"Briefly."

"Did he speak on his death?"

"Nay. Why?"

Addington sighed. "Because he blames himself for Papa's death," she said. "He was there when it happened. It was during a battle and he tried to force Papa to go into the keep because bolts were flying over the wall, but Papa wouldn't move. He was struck by the bolts. I do not think Julian has ever forgiven himself for not preventing it."

Lista slowed her brushing. "He did not tell me that," she said. "I heard your father died in battle against King John."

"He did," Addington said. "I was there. Julian was always Papa's shadow, you see. I have three brothers – Cole, the eldest, was always his own man. Strong and steady. Cassian, the youngest, went away at a young age and disappeared shortly after my father died. He was the baby and everyone doted on him. But Julian… he's the middle brother and I think he was always overlooked. He is quiet and never makes a fuss, and he followed my father about like a loyal dog. More than any of us, save Mama, I do not think he's ever gotten over the loss of our father and when I saw him speaking to you today, I was hoping he was beginning to feel a little happiness. He hasn't had much."

Lista stopped brushing and came around the front of Addington, planting herself on a small three-legged stool next to the hearth.

"He said he needed to learn to laugh," she said seriously. "That was after he told me that I needed to learn to laugh. I will be truthful with you, Addie – he seems guarded and he seems sad. Like a man who has seen much sorrow."

Addington nodded. "He has," she said. "He has seen more than most. Lista... it is clear to me that he likes you. As I said, Julian has known so little happiness, so if you do not like him in a romantic sense, then please do not tease him. Do not let him think there could be something between you two if there is no chance for it. I do not think he could take it because women have been cruel to him before."

Lista's eyes took on a warm glimmer. "I would never be cruel to him, nor would I give him hope where there is none," she said. "I like Julian very much. He is sweet and thoughtful. But I told you... he is far above my social station. Addie, we have discussed this."

Addington sighed sharply. "He is *not* above your social station," she said flatly. "You are perfect for him. You think he is kind and handsome and his different eyes do not bother you in the least. You are what Julian has been waiting for his entire life. Would... would you consider him for your husband?"

Lista's eyes widened. "Me?" she said, surprised. "Would *I* consider him? I would consider no one else. Although I've only known the man a few days, sometimes you do not need to know someone for months or years to know that you could spend a lifetime with them and it would never be enough. But Julian is a de Velt... it means he should marry a wife who can bring him prestige."

"You would bring him happiness and that is far more valuable," Addington said, grasping her hand and squeezing it. "And look at this magnificent castle. You underestimate yourself, Lista. Any man would be proud to have you and Felkington. Please let me tell Julian that you are agreeable to a courtship. If I do not tell him, he will be too afraid to ask. You would both go to your grave feeling something for each other because Julian would never have the courage to bring it up."

Lista frowned. "The man fights battles and he has no courage for something as simple as that?"

Addington chuckled. "He is the bravest man you have ever seen on the battlefield," she said. "He has that de Velt beast in him, something my father had, something that turns a man into a monster when he smells the first blood. You've seen how big Julian is and he uses that strength in a fight, believe me. But he has been badly hurt by cruel women he thought were fond of him. Do you know how it is with a horse when you raise your hand and the horse shies away because he's afraid of being hit? That is Julian. He is hand shy. He has been hurt before and he will not put himself in that position again."

Lista thought on the handsome, quiet knight she was quickly becoming very fond of. It was true that she once believed she was unworthy of him, not of his station, but she was coming to think that she may have been mistaken. Addington certainly thought so and that was enough to give her hope.

"It is very sweet of you to be so concerned for your brother's happiness," Lista said. "If I had a sister, I wish she would be as concerned for me as you are for Julian."

Addington smiled. "Everyone else has left home," she said. "It is just Julian and I left with Mama. I want to make sure he finds the right woman."

"And you think that is me?"

"I do. I truly do."

"After only having known me a short amount of time?"

Addington chuckled. "As you said, when you meet people, sometimes you just know," she said. "You just know if they are good in their heart. I knew that you were good within the first few hours of knowing you. I think that I would very much like for you to be my sister."

Lista grinned broadly. "It would be like a dream for me to have a sister like you," she said. "And to have a husband like Julian... it is too good to be true. Addie, I have told you about my mother and aunt. How they are."

Addington waved her off. "Julian has the patience of Job," she said. "And you said your mother became grieved following the death of your brother, did you not?"

"That is true."

"Mayhap, in a small way, Julian can replace him," she said. "Mayhap she would not be so sad to have a new son in her life."

Lista hadn't thought of it that way. "It's very possible," she said. "But before we get too far ahead of ourselves, don't you think Julian should decide if I am someone he wishes to court?"

Addington beamed. "Not to worry," she said. "I shall ask him."

Lista was a bit leery. "You're sweet to want to play matchmaker, but don't you think that's something that Julian and I should work out between us?"

Addington took the brush from Lista's hand and began brushing her hair with it. "You cannot ask him because it would be unseemly," she said frankly. "And Julian will never have the courage to ask you, so you need my help. Trust me on this, Lista. I will be subtle, I promise."

As Lista watched the young woman brush her hair, some-how, she didn't think subtlety was one of Addington's great virtues. She had many, but that more than likely wasn't one of them.

Subtle as a garlic pie, Lista thought.

Little did she know.

"LISTA IS AGREEABLE to having you court her," Addington said. "Well? What are you going to do about it?"

Julian nearly choked on his wine. In fact, he did choke and it all went spraying onto the floor of Felkington's enormous hall. He was sitting with Ashton and they had been indulging in some very good wine that a servant had brought up from the cellars when Addington had entered the hall, dressed in a lovely gown that flattered her figure. Ashton certainly thought so. But words of courtship were the first thing out of her mouth when she saw her brother and Julian wiped away the wine he'd just sprayed on his hand.

"My God, Addie," he said, wiping it from his lips. "You have the diplomacy of a dog fart. What do you mean by that question?"

Addington looked at him with little patience. "What do you think I mean?" she said. "I have interrogated Lista and although she feels she is not of your social station, I have convinced her otherwise. Julian, she thinks you are marvelous. Remember? That has not changed. Better still, I do believe she is falling for you. Are you going to let this perfect woman get away from you?"

Julian was staring at her as if she'd grown two heads, horrified and intrigued and, most of all, thrilled. But he couldn't decide which emotion was stronger. He knew Addington meant well, but the woman was indeed as subtle as a farting dog sometimes. She was clubbing him over the head with his romantic future.

He set his wine cup down.

"Addie, I appreciate that you are trying to help me. But in this case, I do not need your help," he said. "This is between Lista and me."

"That's what she said," Addington said. "I disagree. I know that women have been... unkind to you in the past and I wanted you to know that Lista is not that sort. She is kind and compassionate and understanding. She is far too good for you, but she is agreeable to a courtship if you will only have the courage to ask her."

"Did she ask you to tell me that?"

Addington frowned. "Of course not," she said. "I am doing it of my own accord. I am doing it because it is important. Don't you like her?"

Julian could hear Ashton snickering next to him, laughing at Addington's pushiness. He was growing annoyed with them both.

"That is none of your business," he said, eyeing her. "But, if you must know, I like her very much."

Addington gasped in delight. "I knew it," she said. "I could tell. Will you ask to court her tonight? You must not wait, Julian. A delay could ruin everything."

He waved a hand at her, trying to force her to back off a little. "In my own time," he said. "And I swear if you push me or push her, I will spank you and I do not care if you tell

Mother. Some things you must let me do on my own and this is one of them."

"But…!"

He cut her off. "Nay, Addie," he said firmly. "Let me do this myself. I do not want your help. Please."

He was serious and Addington knew it. Sighing heavily, she nodded reluctantly, seeing Ashton grinning at her and patting the seat beside him. Pushing aside her stubborn brother, she went to sit next to Ashton, leaving Julian the least bit dazed at the swift turn of subject. He was still trying to process everything, but the conversation wasn't over between them.

Not yet, at any rate.

"Where is Lista?" he said, turning to his sister.

Addington had already taken her seat next to Ashton as he poured her some wine. "She went to see to her mother and aunt," she said. "She'll be down directly."

That meant he had a little time to prepare. Turning away from Addington and Ashton as they engaged in conversation, Julian lost himself to thoughts of a courtship with Lista de la Mere.

Truthfully, he was more than delighted at the prospect. That beautiful, smart, and sweet woman was interested in him. In *him*. Sometimes, Addington was annoying, but there were instances when she used that annoying trait for good. She did the hard work he should have done but, in this case, she was right – it probably would have taken him days or weeks or even months to work up the courage. He'd worked up his courage twice before in his life and had been slapped back for his efforts, so that kind of bravery didn't come easily to him. Romantic intentions were the only conflicts he ran from.

But Addington had given him hope.

He'd never tell her that, though.

As Julian sat there and pondered his next move, Lista entered the great hall. The hall actually had two big entrances – one from the south, one from the north, and she entered from the southern side. The hall was full of de la Mere soldiers who had been drinking to Amaury since they'd entered, about one hundred of them filling up the room and filling up the chamber with their singing and praise for their dead captain.

It was a meal that had turned into a wake.

When they saw Lista, they cheered her loudly, as the daughter of their mistress, and she was polite as she made her way through the men who wanted to tell her how much they loved Amaury and how much they would miss them. As far as Julian knew, no one knew how the man had died, only that he had. It was probably best considering the cause of his death was their mistress' sister. They probably would not have reacted well to that.

Julian watched Lista as she approached the dais. She was clad in a dark green, simple garment, avoiding the things that the ladies usually wore these days – kirtles and surcoats and other complicated vestments. Lista's garment was one piece, or it seemed to be, for simplicity, but there was nothing simple the way it clung to her figure. She had a full figure of big breasts, a narrow waist, and flaring hips, something Julian found quite alluring. Very, *very* alluring. He was still looking at her hips when she finally reached the table.

"Good eve," she said. "I hope I did not keep you waiting too long."

Embarrassed that he'd been caught looking at her body, Julian looked her in the face and smiled. "Of course not," he said. "I've had Ash and Addie to keep me company, but I am thankful for your opportune arrival. Will your mother be joining us?"

The smile on Lista's lips wavered. "Nay," she said. "Travel does not agree with her, so she is... resting. I do not expect her to join us, though I have asked her to."

Julian could never fault the woman for being perfectly truthful, even when the truth was less than pleasant. As the soldiers at one of the tables pulled out a citole and began to sing a song of tribute to Amaury, Lista sat down next to Julian.

"They've been mourning your knight since I arrived," Julian said, pouring her a measure of wine himself. "It seems the man was well-liked."

Lista looked over the group in the hall, all seasoned soldiers who lived a rather easy life at a peaceful castle. "He was," she said. "I am sorry you did not come to know him a little. Amaury had been with Felkington since my father was a young man, so he was a legacy here. The place will not be the same without him."

Julian watched her face as she spoke, the grief she was trying to conceal. "I'm sorry," he said quietly. "Had that damnable rail been in place, his death might not have happened. I know Cole feels quite badly about it."

Lista shook her head. "It is not his fault," she said. "I told him that. It was *not* his fault. It was my aunt's fault for being such a... well, suffice it to say that it was not your brother's fault at all. I do not hold him responsible."

Julian knew she meant it, but he still felt guilty. "You are kind," he said. "But know how sorry we are for it."

Lista nodded, smiling timidly at him because it was a sensitive subject. "That is because you are men of honor," she said. "I appreciate that. But let us speak no more of Amaury. I want to talk about you."

"Me?"

Lista's smile turned real. "You speak very little about yourself," she said. "A little bird told me that you like books."

He fought off a smile as he averted his gaze as if embarrassed. "Was this bird named Addie?"

Lista laughed softly. "Are you angry?" she said. "Please do not be. I find it quite fascinating that a knight should like to read. I've heard that many can't or won't."

Julian shrugged. "It takes an intellect," he said. "Some knights are simply trained to fight and that is what they are focused on. They have scribes to write their missives for them, because they never took the time to learn. Fighting was more important. But do not think poorly of them."

"I don't," she said. "My father loved to read, too. He has an entire wall of shelves that contain books, some from places far to the east. They are quite rare."

That had Julian's interest. "Many books were brought back by the crusading armies who had gone to The Levant with King Richard," he said. "I have a few myself. I would like to see your father's books, if I am permitted."

"Of course," Lista said. "I will be happy to show you."

"Good."

The conversation died, but it wasn't uncomfortable. Julian's eyes glittered at her over the top of his wine cup and Lista smiled coyly, looking away. It was a sweet and flirtatious game. Julian took a drink of his wine and set the cup down.

"That same bird told me something, too," he said.

Lista looked at him curiously before realizing what he meant. "The same bird that told me about you and your books?"

"Aye."

"What did the bird say?"

"That you would be agreeable to letting me court you."

Lista's face immediately turned several shades of red and she leaned forward, elbows on the table as she covered her face with her hands.

"She didn't," she said, muffled.

Julian was enjoying her chagrin. "She did," he said. "Do not be angry."

"I am not angry."

"Then why are you covering your face?"

"Because I am ashamed she told you that I was agreeable."

"Why? You're not agreeable?"

Lista looked at him through splayed fingers. "A woman is not supposed to say that first," she said. "I am very sorry she told you. If you are not agreeable, we shall speak no more about it. I am content to remain your friend."

"But I'm not content to remain yours."

Her hands came away from her face and she suddenly looked quite serious. "I'm sorry," she said. "I've driven you away with my foolishness. I understand."

He lifted his eyebrows. "You do?" he said. "I am not sure that I understand what you just said because you certainly have not driven me away. Lista, I... I would like nothing better than to court you. If you really are agreeable."

Her serious expression faded into something of surprise and delight. "I am," she said. "Are you *really* agreeable?"

"I am, really."

"Even knowing... about my mother and my aunt?"

He smiled. Reaching out, he took one of her hands and lifted it to his lips for a gentle kiss. "That means nothing to me," he said. "I was agreeable within the first five minutes of knowing you, or didn't you realize that?"

Lista watched his lips as he kissed her hand again, shocked to the bone. But also thrilled beyond measure. "But I insulted you so," she said. "Julian, I was terrible to you!"

He laughed softly, still holding her hand. "I've had worse," he said. "You were strong and beautiful and you defended your mother and aunt. It was very admirable. In fact, had you not told that little bird that you were agreeable, I would have asked to court you myself at some point. After I'd worked up the courage. A woman like you is far too magnificent for a man like me."

Lista found herself holding his hand, that enormous warm appendage that was so strong, yet so tender. "You are mad," she said softly. "But... are you *sure* about this?"

He laughed softly. "I am sure," he said. "Are *you* sure?"

"Never more about anything in my life."

"That brings me joy like you cannot imagine."

"And me," she said, reaching out to take his other hand, which he clutched tightly. "But what of your mother? Will she approve?"

He nodded, now kissing both hands. "She likes you a great deal," he said. "She will be positively thrilled."

It was decided. Lista was so happy she thought she might literally burst. All she could manage to do was look at the man, the man who would one day be her husband, and shake her head in wonder.

"Oh... Julian," she breathed. "Is this real? Is this really happening?"

He grinned. "I am asking myself that same question," he said. "That a woman like you should be interested in a man like me… this kind of thing only happens in my dreams."

"And in mine."

"Then let us dream together."

Lista smiled broadly. Then, she nodded her head, so firmly and eagerly that she started to laugh. Julian joined her. Soon, they were both laughing and he kissed her fingers again, finally reaching out a big hand to gently cup her face. Her skin against his was like velvet against steel. It was all kinds of joy and excitement, delight that neither one of them could have ever imagined. They were so busy staring at each other that it took Addington twice before they finally looked at her.

"Julian?" she said. "*Julian!*"

Julian heard her, barely, and tore his gaze away from Lista. He was immediately frowning at her. "What?" he said, testy.

Addington laughed at her gruff brother. "Do you have something happy you wish to tell me?"

"Nay," Julian barked. But he softened when he saw Lista giggling. "At least, not until after I speak with the lady's mother. Until then, keep out of my business or I'll beat you with a wet rope."

Addington knew exactly what was going on and she was delighted. She started laughing, which made Lista laugh, which made Julian and finally Ashton laugh. They were all laughing but only Ashton had no idea why. Julian was still holding Lista's fingers with one hand while drinking with the other until the food began to come in great trenchers and he was forced to let her go so he could eat. He'd barely taken a bite of his boiled beef when a wet, panicked soldier entered the hall and headed straight for the dais.

"My lady," he said breathlessly, focused on Lista. "Scots climbing the walls. They're raiding, my lady."

The mood of the table vanished and Lista stood up, followed quickly by Julian and Ashton. "Where?" she demanded.

The soldier pointed in the general southerly direction. "Near the vineyard," he said. "They've killed two of the dogs. There must be a hundred or more of them, from what we can see. They came through the trees with torches against the rain."

Julian looked at Lista, who seemed to be holding herself admirably. When she caught his eye, she shook her head with great regret. "As I said, the Scots have raided us on occasion," she said. "But never in the midst of terrible weather and never with more than a few handfuls. Hundreds of men... that is concerning."

Julian could see, in those first few moments, that she wasn't sure what to do. Amaury had always taken charge of the defenses and she simply followed his lead, so his knightly training kicked in.

This is what he was born to do.

"I know you do not have a commander any longer," he said quietly but steadily. "Would you like me to take charge, Lista?"

She looked at him, the first real glimmer of fear in her eyes. "You are a guest. I cannot ask that of you."

Julian waved her off. He also took it as permission. He pointed to Ashton. "Get to the courtyard and make sure the entire thing is secure," he said. Then, he looked to Lista again. "Tell your men I have command. Hurry, sweetheart. There is no time to waste."

Lista looked at him in surprise. Not because of the request but because of what he had called her.

Sweetheart.

After a moment of shock, she swung into action.

"Sir Julian will be in command," she told the breathless

soldier. Then, she climbed onto the table with Julian's help and shouted to the men in the hall. "We have Scots raiding the vineyard and gardens and God knows what else. Since Amaury is no longer with us, Sir Julian shall be in command. He is from Pelinom Castle, a de Velt. You know the name. You know that the de Velts are great battle lords, so you will respect his judgment and obey his command!"

The entire room of soldiers were on their feet, now looking at Julian as Ashton rushed from the hall. Julian didn't delay; he began shouting orders to the room.

"Do all of you have battle posts?" Heads were bobbing an affirmative so he continued. "Get to your posts, then. Who is the senior sergeant? I need a senior man!"

Julian could bellow orders loud enough for the Scots to hear him. Even Lista was startled by the volume of his voice but, in the same breath, she'd never heard anything so steady and commanding and comforting in her entire life. Surely nothing terrible could happen with Julian in command. As she climbed off the table, Julian was already huddling with three older soldiers in the middle of the hall, men she had known her entire life, and those three men had the room moving as Julian filtered out with them.

In little time, the entire hall was cleared and around Fel-kington, a horn could be heard. *The battle horn.* Lista hadn't heard it in a very long time.

"What do we do?" Addington asked.

Lista turned to her friend, reaching out to clutch the woman's hands. "We make sure the stairwells are secure," she said. "We make sure that all of the doors with stairs leading into the courtyard are secure and then we start preparing for wounded, if any. Will you help me?"

Addington nodded firmly. "Of course I will," she said. "I am a de Velt, too, and this is not my first battle."

She smiled and Lista smiled in return. "Then you are a seasoned veteran," she said. "Come along – we must hurry."

Gathering their skirts, the women flew out of the hall to prepare the stairwells while the soldiers were moving frantically below. They presumed it was just another raid until lightning lit up the sky and hundreds of Scots could be seen on the approach to Felkington.

It was starting to look more like a siege.

The night would be a long one.

CHAPTER TEN

I T TOOK JULIAN about ten minutes to assess what was happening.

Along with Ashton and the three senior sergeants, one of whom had been part of the escort from Berwick, Julian assumed that the Scots had come to raid the vineyard and the gardens for stores.

His stores.

When he married Lista, all of this would become his, so already he was protective over it. Mostly, he was protective over Lista. These Scots bastards who had come down from the border, bypassed Northwood Castle, which was a massive castle along the River Tweed and quite accustomed to border raids, had come straight down to Felkington nestled in her little valley. They'd deliberately avoided Northwood and her enormous army.

That made Julian particularly angry.

Given that he had just been in that vineyard in the afternoon, he didn't want the Scots ruining it or the gardens that had a variety of vegetables and flowers. It was all so tranquil and beautiful and to think about the Scots damaging that infuriated him. The Scots seemed to be focused on raiding anything contained within that ten-foot wall and weren't particularly focused on the castle itself, which gave Julian time to form an army. Never one to simply stay idle while there was an attack going on around him, Julian took one hundred and fifty men with him and left the safety of the castle, leaving Ashton to seal it up behind him.

Out into the field he went.

When the Scots saw the Felkington army coming, they moved to meet them. But Julian noticed something particularly strange going on in the middle of the road that led to the gatehouse. There was a mounted knight, all by himself, fighting off a gang of Scots that were clearly trying to dismount him and steal his horse. Julian was mounted, of course, and charged towards the English knight who was ably keeping the Scots at bay, but once Julian joined the fight and cut off a couple of heads, the Scots fled in terror.

Julian and the other knight went after them.

They were swarming the garden and the vineyard. Since the gate was closed, Julian couldn't get his horse through, but he pulled the animal alongside the wall and climbed over it. Fully armed, wearing armor that weighed more than a ten-year-old child, he began plowing through the Scots as they stole vegetables and ripped young trees out by the roots in order to steal what fruit they were bearing.

Julian wasn't even trying to chase them away. He was out to kill them and the Scots realized that very early on. He had a massive sword, serrated on one side, that could slice through a man's neck as easily as a hot knife through butter. When he started leaving headless bodies amidst the carrots and apples, the Scots couldn't get back over the wall fast enough. Worse still was the other English knight who had followed him, a big knight who was beating men with crushing blows. He didn't seem to be killing like Julian was, but he was definitely thrashing men as they tried to flee.

On it went into the night.

The storm, which had been lighting up the sky overhead, had eased up by midnight. There were still Scots around, men who were hiding out and then trying to steal goats and chickens, but Julian found them and the body count piled up. The other English knight was rooting out any who might be hiding and driving them straight to Julian. In truth, they made a very efficient team, as men often did who had experienced a great deal of battle in their lifetimes. There was intuitive behavior and tactics that helped them work well together, teamwork that continued until dawn.

When the sun finally began to rise and the storm clouds cleared out over a wet and verdant land, Julian found himself out of the garden, standing by the open portcullis leading into the courtyard of Felkington. There were many soldiers in the garden and vineyard, cleaning up, taking inventory of what had been damaged or lost. Julian thought that the English knight had departed sometime towards the dawn because he hadn't seen the man in the last hour, when he suddenly emerged from the garden leading a scruffy Scotsman by the neck.

He came right up to Julian and tossed the man on the ground.

"I thought you might like to find out where the Scots came from," he said in a smooth baritone voice. "You can also send this fool back with a message to his clan as a warning to those who try to raid this castle again. What castle is this, by the way?"

Julian pulled off his helm, handing it to a nearby soldier. His hair fell over his right eye as it always did, especially when facing someone he'd never met before.

"Felkington Castle," he said. "I am Julian de Velt and my comrade is Ashton de Royans. Who are you?"

The knight pulled off his helm, revealing a younger knight with dark eyes and black hair, sweaty against his pale skin. He grinned.

"Louis de Rhos," he said. "I was traveling through the valley and saw the lights of Felkington, so I thought to get out of the storm. I was just coming up the road when I saw the Scots and they attacked me, so I had little choice but to engage them."

A succinct explanation of what had happened. Julian smiled faintly. "Your assistance was most welcome," he said. "You have my thanks. Where are you from, de Rhos?"

The knight threw a thumb in a southwardly direction. "Herrington Castle."

Ashton, listening to the conversation, cocked his head thoughtfully. "That's near Sunderland, isn't it?"

Louis nodded. "Aye," he said. "My father is the Earl of Sunderland."

"Ah," Ashton said. "So we have the high nobility among us. Your father may be the Earl of Sunderland, but Julian's father was Ajax de Velt. The Dark Lord of legend. Surely you've heard of him."

Louis looked at Julian with some surprise. "Of course I have," he said. "Your father is indeed legend. I heard he was killed a few years ago."

"He was," Julian said.

"You have my deepest sympathies," Louis said. "John, wasn't it?"

"Unfortunately."

Louis grunted in disgust. "An unworthy man against your father's greatness," he said. "My father never liked John, either."

"Your father is a man with good taste."

Louis grinned. "I think so," he said. "Speaking of taste, would it be too much to ask for a meal and a bed for a few hours? I've not eaten since early yesterday."

Julian motioned to him. "It would be my honor to eat with you," he said. "Ash, deal with this prisoner. Find out what he knows and send him back with a message that further raids at Felkington will not be tolerated. I will take our guest inside."

As Ashton nodded and grabbed the prisoner by the hair, Julian escorted Louis through the long entry passageway and emerged into the courtyard in the center of the castle, with the tall walls all around. In fact, he had to pause because Louis had come to a halt. The man was looking at the walls around him with awe.

"God's Bones," he muttered. "This place is enormous. How is it I have never even heard of Felkington Castle?"

Julian smiled weakly. "Impressive, is it not?" he said. "Evidently, it used to be quite important about a hundred years ago, but now the main road takes travelers away from it. It did not, however, take you away from it. Where are you coming from?"

Louis finished his inspection and started walking again. "I was in Berwick on business for my father and continuing on to Kelso, but the storm threw me off track. Which road am I supposed to be on to reach Kelso?"

Julian's grin widened. "North, about three miles," he said. "You must have taken the wrong road to end up on this one. If you continue on, it should take you south to Wooler."

"I do *not* want to go to Wooler."

"No one does."

They shared a laugh as they entered the main entry of the castle. Before them was a large mural stairwell that led to the upper floors and Louis followed Julian up two flights before reaching a common room that had a fire burning. The door to the chamber, which had been so recently bolted, was wide open and the fire was inviting. Louis immediately went to the fire and began removing his gloves and helm.

"I'll find the lady of the keep," Julian said. "Meanwhile, I'll have servants bring you some wine. After a night like that, I'm sure you can use it."

Louis was holding his hands out to the fire. "Will you join me?"

Julian nodded. "Certainly," he said. "But first let me…"

He wasn't able to finish before Lista was rushing through the door, plowing into him in her haste. "Julian!" she gasped. "I heard your voice! Are you well?"

She'd hit him in the arm, teetering him sideways. He reached out to steady her, to steady them both, as he chuckled.

"I was fine until that moment," he said. "Now I think I am gravely wounded, all thanks to you."

Lista laughed, her hands on him as if to make sure he was indeed all in one piece. "Stop whining like a woman," she teased. "A big man like you? It would take a building to fall on you to hurt you."

He grabbed her by the shoulders, planting a kiss on her cheek. It was a sweet gesture, and a bold one, but Lista didn't seem to mind. She put her soft, warm hands on his face, looking at him before tucking the hair back over his right eye so she could see both eyes. She inspected him closely.

"Swear to me that you are well," she said suspiciously.

He grinned lazily. "I am perfect," he said. "With you, I could be nothing else. But I have brought a visitor so that is the most you will get out of me at the moment."

Lista had been so focused on Julian that she hadn't seen the knight next to the hearth that was taller than he was. Julian had her by the hand, leading her over to the handsome, black-haired knight.

"Sir Louis, this is Lady Lista de la Mere," Julian said. "She is the mistress of this castle. Lista, this is Louis de Rhos, whose father is the Earl of Sunderland. Louis was fortuitously traveling last night when he encountered our Scots. He helped chase them away, so we should show him all manner of gratitude."

Lista smiled at the handsome knight. "You have my thanks, Sir Louis," she said. "May I provide you with food and drink?"

"And a bed," Julian said before Louis could respond. "The man needs to sleep a little, too."

Louis grinned, focusing intently on Lista. "Food, drink, and a bed would be much appreciated, my lady."

Lista's smile turned bright. "Gladly, my lord," she said. "Please come with me. You, too, Julian."

Julian didn't even have to be told. He was already following her. Louis brought up the rear, following them through a large antechamber before entering the great hall, which had a few wounded near one of the hearths. Lista directed the knights to the dais, where they sat heavily. Gloves, helms, and other possessions went on the table as Lista sent the servants running for food and drink.

It wasn't long in coming.

Mostly everything that had been served the night before ended up on the table again, warmed over and sauced. There was boiled beef with a gravy of wild mushrooms, an egg and cheese pie, and also a hot pottage comprised of green beans, cabbage, wine, beef, and barley. It was a veritable feast and the knights dug in as Lista stood next to Julian, watching the pair eat ravenously.

"I am afraid to ask how bad the damage is in the garden," she said. "Some of the servants are out there now, but you've seen it. Is it terrible?"

Julian's mouth was full of the egg pie. "It could have been worse," he said. "I think some of the young trees were torn out, and many of the vegetables were uprooted, but we'll go out in a bit and assess the damage. I'm afraid there might not be any grapes left."

Lista sighed heavily and sat down next to him. "They'll grow back," she said. "As long as the vines were not damaged."

"I do not think so, but I did not look closely."

"Is this kind of thing regular?" Louis asked, chewing. "The raids, I mean. Is it a regular happening here?"

Lista shrugged. "Not too often," she said. "They seem to leave us alone for the most part but, from time to time, they come around. It is nearing winter, so they are looking for food. Were there many of them?"

Louis nodded. "I'd say a couple of hundred, if not more," he said, glancing at Julian. "What do you think?"

Julian cocked his head thoughtfully. "At least that many," he said. "But there are a lot of dead bodies in the garden right now."

"You mean headless bodies," Louis said, a smile playing on his lips.

Julian sensed the humor, but he was unapologetic. "If one chooses to tangle with a de Velt, one must pay the price."

"I will keep that in mind."

They chuckled at one another, shoveling more food into their mouths. Julian buttered a piece of white bread, handing it to Lista, who took it gratefully. She dipped it into the gravy on his trencher and took a big bite.

"Where were you traveling to when you got caught in the battle, Sir Louis?" she asked.

Louis glanced up from his food. "Please call me Louis," he said. "I never liked formal titles. They seem so... oh, I don't know. So cold. But in answer to your question, I was traveling from Berwick to Kelso and was driven off course by the storm. I never even knew Felkington was here, but from what I've seen, it's a magnificent castle. How long has your family lived here?"

"Since the Duke of Normandy came to these shores," Lista said, eating more food off Julian's trencher. "Felkington was one of the first stone castles in this entire area."

"And you have lived here your entire life?"

"My entire life."

"Where did you foster?"

"Richmond Castle and Bamburgh Castle. Do you know them?"

Louis nodded. "I do," he said. "My father is allied with Richmond. He's also allied with Northwood Castle, not far from here. My older brother married the earl's daughter."

That realization struck Julian. He hadn't even made the connection until this moment. His older brother, Cole, was supposed to marry Audrie de Longley, the Earl of Teviot's daughter, but the woman broke their engagement to marry the heir of Sunderland. He felt stupid for not even thinking of that before now. Not knowing if Louis would have known that, he didn't bring it up. He didn't see a need since Cole had been rather relieved by the broken engagement.

"We are close allies of Northwood Castle," Julian said. "And when I say 'we', I mean the de Velt properties. Pelinom and Berwick Castle included."

"Oh?" Louis said, interested. "I thought Berwick was a royal property?"

Julian nodded. "It is," he said. "But it was entrusted to my father to manage since our family home is so near to it. My eldest brother is the garrison commander."

Louis nodded in understanding. "Then the next time I am in Berwick, I shall pay my respects to a son of de Velt," he said. "Who is your brother?"

"Cole de Velt."

Louis paused in his eating. "I have heard that name," he said. "But where?"

He didn't seem clear on the answer to the question, but Julian had a feeling he might figure it out so he simply told him.

"It's possible you heard it because my brother was betrothed to Audrie de Longley before your brother married her," he said. "But do not fear – there were no hard feelings. My brother is happily married to a good woman and we enjoy a strong alliance with Northwood, still."

Louis lifted his eyebrows as if realizing the same thing Julian had. "Ah," he said. "That's where I've heard it. Audie's former betrothed. I remember my father was terrified of angering Jax de Velt when my brother and Audie declared their feelings for one another. I am glad to hear there are no lingering hard feelings."

Julian grinned. "Not at all," he said. "Be at ease. I hope Audie is well."

"Very well, thank you. I shall give her your greetings."

"Please do."

The conversation died a little, but only because their mouths were full. Lista was picking beef off of Julian's plate, contemplating getting her own food, when two lone figures entered the great hall. Glancing up, she found herself looking at her mother and aunt.

Immediately, Lista was on her feet.

"What are you doing here, Flora?" she asked, moving to intercept the woman. "There is nothing for you to see here. Kindly retreat to your chamber and if it is food you desire, I'll have it sent up to you."

Flora eyed her niece but her gaze moved to the two big knights in the hall. She moved around Lista, heading for the dais.

"Will you not introduce us to our guests?" she said loud enough for Julian and Louis to hear. "It seems we have some fighting men at our table."

Lista was greatly displeased that Flora had moved around her. She wasn't even paying attention to Meadow, who slipped past her and went to sit next to Julian. Since it would have been rude not to make introductions, she sighed heavily and tried not to sound unhappy as she spoke.

"Sir Louis, this is my mother's sister, Lady Flora d'Orbec," she said. "The woman who just sat down is my mother, Lady Felkington. Ladies, meet Sir Louis de Rhos, whose father is the Earl of Sunderland."

Flora's eyes glittered. She pulled away from Lista and went to sit between Louis and Julian.

"Welcome to Fucking... I mean, Felkington Castle, my lord," she said, fixed on Louis. "I have been to Sunderland, many times. It is a lovely village."

Louis didn't sense anything odd, but though the woman

looked quite haggard as she sat down. She'd also been rather vulgar with her greeting.

Perhaps all was not as it seemed with her.

"Thank you, my lady," he said steadily. "I agree with you. It is rather nice."

Servants started to bring food and drink, but Flora was fixed on the dark-eyed knight. "Your father is Henry de Rhos?" she said. "My mother was the daughter of the Earl of Malton and I do believe he was a friend of your grandfather, Warren. I miss the days when we would visit with our great allies of the north. I do remember Herrington Castle to be particularly nice."

Louis nodded. "It is comfortable."

"Do you live there?"

"I do, my lady."

"And you have brothers?"

"Three, my lady. I am a middle son."

"Like Julian," Lista piped up, wanting to pull Flora's attention off Louis. The older woman seemed particularly focused on him. "Julian is the middle son of Ajax de Velt."

Louis looked at Julian and lifted his cup. "Ours is the best of the birth order."

Julian chuckled, lifting his cup as well. "We are gods."

Louis laughed as he shoveled more pottage into his mouth, which Flora didn't see as a deterrent to a conversation. Servants set food and a cup of wine in front of her and all she did was go for the wine. She took a couple of healthy gulps, all the while her focus on Louis.

"Are you married, Sir Louis?" she asked.

Louis choked a little on his food, taking a sip of wine to wash it down. "Nay, my lady," he said. "Though my older brother is, I've not yet had the time."

"Pity," Flora said, turning to look at Julian. "And you are not married either, are you?"

"Flora," Lista hissed, cutting the woman off. "That is not an appropriate question for men you have just met."

Flora waved her off. "I was simply making conversation," she said, gulping at her wine again. "Forgive me. I did not mean anything by it."

She demanded more wine and Lista watched her with growing fury. Meadow, however, was eating pottage, her eyes darting around the table nervously. She was always nervous when Flora got to talking and Lista became irate.

There was no telling what could happen.

Julian sensed it, too, because his attention was moving between Louis and Flora and Lista. He could see that Lista was glaring at her aunt so he sat forward at the table, blocking her view.

"Where is Addie this morning?" he asked.

Lista turned her attention to him, seemingly gratefully so. "She was up most of the night so she is sleeping right now," she said. "Where is Ashton?"

"Outside supervising the clean-up," he said, mopping up the last of his bread and gravy. "I will sleep a few hours, too, while I am able. I find that I am wholly exhausted."

Lista smiled faintly. "Then you must rest," she said quietly. "I will take the watch."

He looked at her as if surprised by her words. But he realized it was one of the sweetest things he'd ever heard. He was weary and she was prepared to stay vigilant while he slept. Was that what it meant to have a woman's genuine concern? Her loyalty? God help him, he'd never had that before. He'd seen it between his parents, between Cole and Corisande, and even his sisters and their husbands, but it was something he never imagined he would have for himself.

Reaching out, he took her hand under the table, fondling her fingers.

"Show my new friend where he should rest," he said softly. "Then you will escort me to my chamber. I want your face to be the last one I see before I sleep."

Giving him a wink, Lista stood up from her seat, collecting the pitcher of wine on the table and topping off his cup. Then, she moved to Louis, completely ignoring her aunt and her empty cup.

"When you have had your fill of food and wine, I will be happy to show you to a comfortable chamber," she told him, pouring a little more wine into his cup. "You have had a busy night."

Louis grinned at the true statement. "Busier than I had hoped for," he said, taking a drink of the tart, red wine. "I am very grateful for your hospitality, Lady Lista."

Lista smiled at him and set the pitcher down, out of the reach of her aunt, who was growing frustrated that she was being denied more wine.

"And we are very grateful for your sword," she said. "I must check on the wounded on the other side of the hall, but fetch me when you are ready to lie down."

"I am ready now," he said, standing up wearily and collecting his things. "I do not wish to be any trouble, so if you point me in the right direction, I shall find a bed."

"Nonsense," Lista said. "I shall show you myself. Mayhap Julian would care to join us?"

Julian was already on his feet, moving around the table as he collected his own things. "I am so tired that I am not entirely sure I will be able to make it under my own power," he said. "You two may need to drag me."

Lista giggled as Louis answered. "I fear Lady Lista may be dragging us both," he said. "I could curl up on a rock and sleep like the dead."

"I have no rocks," Lista said as she came off the dais, heading for the southern door to the hall. "But I do have comfortable beds. That shall have to suffice."

Grinning, Louis and Julian followed.

Lista led them around to the front of the castle, near the great portcullises, where there were small guard rooms, three in a row. The first two had been used but the third one had a bed that had not been slept in. The linens were clean, the pillow soft, and there was a hearth that was stacked with kindling and not lit.

"Here you are," Lista said, moving to the single window facing south and reaching up to pull the oil cloth down to dim the chamber and cover the window. "If you need anything at all, there is usually a servant or soldier at the end of the corridor. They will be happy to help you."

As Louis dropped his things wearily, Julian set his down at the doorway and went to light the hearth. Using a flint and stone, he sparked the wood easily and a blaze came forth, filling the chamber with some warmth and light. Lista picked up the empty water pitcher and went to find the servant she spoke of, sending the man for fresh water. As he ran off, Julian finished with the fire and went to collect his things again.

"Thank you," Louis said, removing the belt around his tunic. "I feel as if I have made a good acquaintance today, Julian. I hope it will not be the last time we see one another."

Julian nodded his head. "As do I," he said. "I realize Pelinom and Berwick have not been great allies of Sunderland, but we can change that."

"I believe we can."

Julian's exposed left eye twinkled. "If I do not see you before you leave, then this parting was well made," he said. "Find me at Pelinom the next time you are in the north and I shall seek you at Herrington the next time I am further south."

"I hope you do."

"Good sleep to you, my lord."

Louis gave him a smile and Julian quit the chamber, running into Lista as she returned with the pitcher of water. She took it into Louis as Julian stood just outside the door, waiting until she emerged and shut the panel quietly behind her. Then she looked up at Julian and looped both hands through the crook of his elbow.

"Now," she said. "Off to bed with you, young man. You have had a busy night, too."

That was very true. Julian let her lead him back to his borrowed chamber, which was actually quite a large chamber and very comfortable. Far too big and comfortable to be for visitors. As they entered the room, Lista let go of him and went to the hearth, which was dead embers at this point. There had been a fire yesterday when Julian had arrived, but that had long since died out.

As Julian began to strip down, Lista swept away the ashes and neatly piled the kindling, lighting the fire with a flint and stone.

"This used to be my father's chamber," she said. "Normally, no one stays here, but I made an exception in your case."

Julian smiled faintly as he placed his belt upon the nearest table and bent over to begin stripping off the rest of his clothing.

"I am honored," he said. "Truthfully, I was wondering who this chamber belonged to, once. It is quite grand."

He pulled off his de Velt tunic as Lista glanced up at the enormous de la Mere standard that hung against one wall. "Grand, indeed," she said. "My father liked his comfort."

"Were you close to him?"

Lista blew on the fire, bringing forth a weak flame. "I was," she said. "Closer to him than to my mother. I miss him daily."

Julian put his tunic on the table and bent over to shimmy off his mail coat. "I am sorry," he said. "But I understand what it is like to miss your father. I miss mine daily, as well."

Lista fanned the flames a little more. "Were you close to him?"

"Very close."

She paused a moment. "What do you remember most about him, Julian?" she asked, then quickly added: "I do not mean to pry, but I wonder if it is the same thing I remember about my father. He has only been gone a little over two years and I awoke the other morning, terrified that I'd forgotten what he looked like. More than anything, I remember the sound of his voice. Do you remember that about your father?"

Julian's movements slowed as he set the mail across a chair to dry out, his thoughts moving to his father. He didn't often let that happen.

"I remember," he said, subdued. "Mostly, I remember the way he made me feel when I was in his presence."

"How was that?"

Julian's gaze drifted over to the de Velt tunic, like the one his father was wearing when he'd been killed. "Safe," he finally said. "My father made me feel... safe."

Lista pondered that. "I don't remember that about my father," she said. "Of course, we rarely had any trouble at Felkington. Last night was a rare occasion, indeed, so safety was never something I needed to feel. What I remember other than his voice is his hands. My father had very big hands. Odd, isn't it? What we remember about those we loved, I mean. It's the little things."

Julian didn't reply. He stripped off the rest of his clothing, leaving him naked from the waist up. There was a basin of cold water from the day before so he went to his saddlebags, pulling out a bar of white, lumpy soap that smelled of lavender. Using the cold water in the basin, he proceeded to lather it into a slick froth and ran it over his arms, neck, underarms, chest and, finally, his face.

But he'd gone silent for the most part and Lista was aware of that. She continued to blow on the fire, coaxing forth a healthy blaze.

"Did I bring up a subject you to not wish to speak of?" she asked. "If you do not ever wish to speak of your father, you only need tell me and I will never bring him up again. I am sorry if you thought I was prying. I wasn't, truly."

"I know," he said, overlapping her last word. "I know you were not prying. Since this is a time of discovery between us, you should know that it is not easy for me to speak of my father."

"You would prefer I did not speak of mine, too?"

He splashed water on his face and neck, rinsing the white froth off. "Nay, sweetheart," he said softly. "You may speak of your father as much as you wish. I would like to come to know him through your eyes. But my situation with my father is different. It is simply difficult for me to speak on him so do not press me if I won't. Agreed?"

Lista turned away from the fire about the time Julian pulled out a cloth from his saddlebags to dry off with. "Agreed," she said. But then she caught sight of his naked torso, illuminated in the weak light of the chamber, and her cheeks flamed. "Oh... goodness."

Quickly, she turned away because the sight of Julian's magnificent, naked torso had her heart thumping against her ribs. Naïvely, she hadn't expected him to strip down and wash up, so she abruptly found herself in a rather intimate position with a man she found quite beautiful.

More beautiful when his clothes were off.

She stood up.

"I will leave you to rest," she said, heading for the door and trying not to look at him. "I will be in the hall if you need me. Send a servant to fetch me and I will come."

Julian paused in his drying. He couldn't help but notice that she was moving rather rapidly for the door. "Wait," he said. "Where are you running off to? You do not need to leave right away."

Lista was at the door, her hand on the latch. "Aye, I do."

"But why?"

She wouldn't look at him, but she pointed a finger in his direction. "You are without clothing, sir," she said. "It is not proper for me to be here."

He grinned lazily. "I see," he said, tossing the drying cloth onto the table. "You think we are in a compromising position?"

She could hear the humor in his voice. "Do not tease me, Julian," she scolded. "You know it is not proper. You should have waited until I left before removing your clothing like that."

"Don't you like what you see?"

With a growl, she yanked the chamber door open and charged out, leaving him rushing after her. "Wait," he called. "Lista, I am sorry, truly. Come back!"

She was already halfway down the corridor, heading for the hall. "Nay!"

He started laughing. "Please?"

"You are incorrigible, Julian de Velt!"

He watched her disappear through a doorway and, still laughing, he went back inside the chamber and shut the door. He hadn't meant to chase her away but he had a feeling she'd run not because she was offended.

Because she was titillated.

It was just a feeling he had.

Going back to the basin, he stripped off his breeches and washed the rest of his body from the waist down with the lavender soap. It wasn't that he had a penchant for being inordinately clean but more that he couldn't stand the smell of a stinky body, especially his own. Once he was washed down and dried off, he climbed into the bed with the soft mattress, his thoughts lingering on the beautiful young woman with the sea-colored eyes.

Sleep claimed him before he realized it.

CHAPTER ELEVEN

"THIS SITUATION IS going to work in our favor astonishing well," Flora said. "Did you see how the earl's son looked at Lista? We have *two* knights to vie for her hand!"

They were back in their tower chamber. Having burned through the hemp, literally, they were now burning lavender and chamomile, which had a slightly calming effect. They also had at least three pitchers of wine and Flora had already drank her way through one of them. She was very drunk, inhaling the lavender and chamomile, as Meadow sat in the corner with her third cup of wine.

"Well?" Flora said. "Do you hear me?"

Meadow nodded. "I hear you."

"We must do something about it."

Meadow didn't think any of this was a good idea, but not because she didn't want to impose on her daughter. Lista's thoughts or opinions never had any bearing on what Meadow thought. It was more that Meadow simply didn't like making decisions. Her husband had always made the decisions and once he was gone, Simon had for a short time. Now, it was Flora and Flora was pushing her into doing what she wished.

There were two knights at Felkington.

Two knights, two potential husbands.

"What do you want to do about it?" Meadow finally asked. "You wanted Sir Julian for her and I am prepared to speak to him, but now you think I should not?"

Flora waved her off as if she were completely stupid. "Now we have an earl's son in our grasp," she said. "The House of de Velt is prestigious, but there is no earldom. We have Sunderland within our grasp, Meadow. That would be a much better marriage for Lista and a much better family for us. Sunderland is an advisor to the king and we can have everything we have dreamed of."

Meadow looked at her sister. "What *you* have dreamed of," she said. "Flora, I do not share your dreams. I am content to remain here and wait for death to claim me. There is nothing left for me, certainly not court life."

Flora frowned. "Then you remain here," she said, snappish. "Remain here and rot for all I care. But you must convince the earl's son that he should marry Lista."

Meadow shook her head and turned away, drinking heavily from her cup. "I am not going to force anyone."

Flora was on her feet, stalking her sister. She knew that yelling at her would do no good, nor would fear, so when dealing with Meadow it was better to cajole her in such a way that would make her want to do it. Meadow was a fool but, in this case, she was a fool who contained the key to Flora's future.

Their dreams seemed to be splitting.

"I want you to listen to me and listen carefully," Flora said. "Can you do this?"

Meadow could feel her nearby and she recoiled. "I always listen carefully."

Flora knelt down beside her, gripping her with her sharp-taloned fingers. "We must create a competition," she said. "We must make the knights vie for her hand."

"I thought you only wanted the earl's son?"

"I do," Flora said. "But he will have no incentive if he believes Lista is an easy target. But if there is competition, it will force de Rhos to move swiftly."

Meadow frowned and looked at her sister. "How do you know he is even interested in her?" she questioned. "I was in the great hall today, too. I did not see anything that would indicate he is interested in her."

Flora held up a finger. "We need a challenge."

"What challenge?"

Flora's drunken thoughts were gaining steam. "The knighthood is based on challenges," she said. "Men proving themselves stronger against their enemies. Men thrive on challenges and if the de Rhos son is challenged, he will fight. He will fight for Lista."

Meadow thought her sister was becoming mad. "Why should he?" she said. "He does not know Lista. He has no claim on her."

Flora knew that, but she was concocting a plan that, to her, made perfect sense. "But the de Velt son does," she said. "He is very fond of our Lista. Let him see her with de Rhos and then there will be a challenge. De Rhos will have to fight if de Velt challenges him."

Meadow shook her head, baffled. "And what if he does not?" she said. "What if he walks away, which is what any sane man would do. We are left with de Velt and you do not want him."

Flora looked at her. "He is acceptable," she said. "But de

Rhos is better. The man does not intend to remain here at Felkington; I heard him. He said he was traveling to Kelso, but we must delay that. We will send him to the vineyard and tell Lista that he wishes to speak to her. She will arrive and they will be puzzled, but then we will send de Velt to the vineyard. He will see them together, become insane with jealousy, and the challenge will be issued."

Meadow thought it was an extremely weak premise. "I think you are mad," she finally said. "They have only just met one another. What reason do they have to fight?"

"Because de Velt is fond of Lista," Flora said as if her sister were foolish. "I told you this – de Velt will be jealous and he will challenge de Rhos."

Meadow didn't think it was a good plan. In fact, she thought it was ridiculous. But Flora seemed convinced and she would not go against her sister. She never had. She went over to the big bowl in the center of the room, a pewter bowl that had turned black from all of the soot with the burning that took place in it, and she inhaled the smoke deeply.

"You risk much with this plan," she finally said. "Do you not see how weak it is?"

"It is not weak," Flora snapped. "*You* are weak. Weak and foolish."

Meadow ignored the comment for the most part, though it always hurt her when Flora took to insults to get her way. "If you do not see how weak this plan is, let me explain it to you," she said. "Both knights could become enraged at us and Felkington will suffer. We will have no husbands for Lista then because they will leave us and spread tales of the foolish women at Felkington. No man will want Lista then and your dreams of returning to court will be ruined."

Flora wasn't going to be refused. She was convinced she had the right scheme. "Trust me," she insisted. "Trust me that all will happen as it should. When you see de Rhos rise, you will send Lista out to the vineyard. Tell her that you want her to bring you some grapes. Tell her anything. But send her out to the vineyard. Then, you will tell de Rhos that Lista is in the vineyard and wishes to see him. That will send him to Lista."

Meadow was gazing at her, guarded. "And then what?"

Flora held up a finger as if the greatest idea was yet to come. "Then, we find de Velt and tell him that Lista wishes to see him," she said. "De Velt will go to the vineyard, see them together, and challenge de Rhos. Trust me, Meadow. All will happen as it should and, soon, we shall either have access to the great battle lords of de Velt or to the Sunderland riches."

Meadow sighed heavily. She knew Flora wouldn't be put off and if she tried, the woman would insult her and pester her until she gave in. It had happened before.

Therefore, she knew she had no choice.

She had to do it.

Summoning a servant, Meadow told the woman to inform her when de Rhos had risen. Six hours later, when the news came, she had a servant find Lista in the great hall with the wounded with a special request from her mother. Lista refused at first, but the servant was insistent, which sent Lista up to the tower room to demand to know why her mother needed her to bring her grapes, all of which had been stolen in the raid.

With Flora's silent prompting, Meadow drummed up tears and Lista unhappily surrendered. With her daughter heading out to the vineyard, Meadow went to find Louis to tell the man that Lista wanted to bid him a private farewell. He seemed reluctant at first, but that reluctance turned to curiosity. That was obvious.

With Louis on the move, the last piece of the puzzle was Julian.

Flora took care of that last detail herself.

CHAPTER TWELVE

L ISTA'S STRANGE AUNT had been at the door.

Pounding on it, really. Julian had been dead asleep when the rattling of the door had him bolting out of bed. He was a heavy sleeper, anyway, but he was also one of those men who was instantly awake, moving before he even realized he was moving. He was halfway to the door before he realized he was nude, so he had to take the time to put on a pair of linen braies, something he always carried with him.

It was enough to cover him up, anyway.

He went to the door and opened it.

"Sir Julian?"

He found himself looking at Lista's haggard aunt.

"My lady?" he asked politely.

Flora smiled, revealing yellowed and brittle teeth. "Lista has asked me to fetch you," she said. "She is in the vineyard and asked that you join her."

Julian rubbed his eyes, trying to wake up a little more. "Has something happened?"

Flora shook her head. "Happened?" she repeated. "Nay, nothing has happened. She has simply sent word for you to join her. You *will* join her, will you not?"

Julian nodded wearily. "If she wishes it."

"Good," Flora said, a bright smile looking oddly out of place on her face. "Hurry, now. There is no time to waste."

Julian simply nodded his head and shut the door. Yawning, he went to collect his clothing, which he had neatly laid out so it could air out. The braies came off and the leather breeches went on, followed by a clean tunic from his saddlebags. He pulled his boots on and secured them, debating about strapping on his broadsword but thinking better of it. He was fairly certain he wouldn't need it. He wanted to find out what Lista wanted and then perhaps return to the great hall for some food and drink with Lista by his side.

The thought of her made him smile.

Running his fingers through his hair as he headed to the door, he realized that he missed her. He'd been asleep for a few hours and, already, he missed the woman. He missed her smile, her wit, her tender heart. She had such a tender heart. He still couldn't believe a woman as magnificent as Lista de la Mere found something agreeable in him. Agreeable enough to let him court her.

He'd never looked forward so much to anything in his life.

He wasn't exactly familiar with Felkington, so he headed for the stairs he did know. He intended to go through the great hall to the mural stairs on the north side, but as he reached the south entrance, he caught sight of a spiral staircase in the wall that led to the lower level. He turned for the stairs just as he heard Addington's voice in the hall as she helped tend the wounded. Ashton was nowhere to be found so he assumed the man was sleeping, too.

He'd been up all night just like the rest of them.

With Addington's voice in the background, he headed down the spiral stairs and was fortunate enough to find an exit right away, one that dumped out into the big courtyard. It was full of men at this time of day, some of them lying along the wall, dozing, while still others were repairing equipment. A wheelwright was among them, fixing the wheel of a small wagon.

It was the usual bustle of a courtyard as he headed to the passageway that led to the exterior of the castle. Both portcullises were up, indicative of people outside the castle finishing the clean up after the battle, and he passed through, ending up on the road that ran alongside the castle walls. The gate to the gardens was open and he passed through, seeing the chopped-up gardens and broken trees, which were mostly cleaned up at this point. Servants were in the gardens, digging, replacing trees and fixing the wooden fences that kept the barn animals out.

The sun overhead was bright, beating down on a bright green world from the rains the night before. Julian came to a small stone wall that separated the fruit trees from the vegetable garden with the vineyard down the hill beyond. Shielding his eyes from the sun, he was on the lookout for Lista, but what he saw going on in the vineyard had him stopping in his tracks.

Stopped dead.

"MY LADY?"

Lista looked up from a grapevine to see Louis standing a few feet away. He was fully dressed, prepared for travel, and she stood up straight.

"You are leaving already?" she said. "I thought you'd at least sleep for the day."

Louis smiled weakly. "That is usually true, but I kept hearing my father in my ear," he said, lifting his hands as if to fend off a ghostly dream. "Get to Kelso, Louis! Stop lounging!"

Lista giggled. "God's Bones," she said. "You are not lounging. You are sleeping. You had a very busy night. Surely he would allow for that."

Louis cocked an eyebrow. "You think so?" he said, grinning. "You do not know my father, my lady. To him, idle hands are susceptible to the devil's work, so even as children, he made sure we were always busy."

Lista brushed off her hands. "I suppose there is something to be said for that," she said. "It's not as if you want a bunch of children languishing about, getting into trouble. Mayhap you were a troublemaker and he had good reason to pester you?"

Louis laughed. "I can see that someone has told you about me," he said. "Well? Who was it? Who has spilled all my secrets?"

Lista chuckled. "I will never tell," she said. "Ask all you wish, but I shall protect my source."

He shook his head at her. "You are cruel."

She nodded. "Now you know."

He laughed again but his smile soon faded. "Truly, I would not believe that about you," he said. "You have been an excellent hostess and although my acquaintance with Felkington was not ideal, the storm and the Scots brought me to your doorstep and I am grateful for your kind hospitality. I hope you will allow me to reciprocate. Someday, you must come to Herrington."

Lista smiled. "That is kind of you," she said. "It is far to the south, isn't it?"

He shrugged. "Not too terribly far," he said. "It is still north of York. Do you travel much?"

She shook her head. "Nay, not much," she said. "We can conduct business in Berwick or Alnwick or even Newcastle if we must, but we rarely go further south than that."

He nodded in understanding, his black eyes lingering on her. "I do not blame you," he said. "Why would you leave Felkington? It is a paradise."

Lista looked up at the soaring walls. "It is," she said. "It is my paradise and you are welcome back anytime to visit. It is the least we can do for a man who fought to protect us."

He lifted his eyebrows at the thought of the Scots. "They were surprisingly aggressive last night," he said. "Though I must admit, I do not see battle very often, so it was good to hone my skills. But de Velt... he is a man who needs no practice. His talents are beyond compare."

Lista tore her gaze away from her ancestral home and looked at him. "I do not know much about knights, but I do know that the de Velt men are warlords. We were fortunate he was here last night."

Louis nodded. "Indeed," he said. He eyed her for a moment before continuing. "May... may I ask a bold question, my lady?"

Lista lifted a hand, shielding her eyes from the sun as she looked at him. "Of course."

"Are you and de Velt betrothed?"

Lista's cheeks flushed a shade of pink and she lowered her gaze and her hand. "Nay," she said. "We have only just met, in fact, but he has asked to court me. What I mean is that he has asked *only* me – he's not yet asked my mother for permission."

"I see," Louis said. "Then your aunt's questions about my

being married make some sense. She was seeing if I might be interested."

Lista immediately lost her humor. "I am very sorry about Flora," she said. "She had no right to ask you such a thing. It is none of her affair."

Louis held up a hand. "I am not offended, I assure you," he said. "But it seems to me that she is trying to find you a husband. Or maybe a candidate or two?"

Lista could only shrug. "With Flora, one never knows," she said. "You should know that my aunt is a drunkard and so is my mother, so all is not as it seems here. It is a paradise to look at, but beneath the surface, we have our share of problems, just like everyone else. If my aunt ever says anything odd or offensive to you again, now you know why."

He shrugged, fidgeting with the mud beneath his feet. "As I said, I was not offended," he said. "May I say something else?"

"Speak freely, my lord."

He held up a hand. "First of all, call me Louis," he said. "I do not like being addressed formally. What I was going to say is that if you were not already spoken for, I might return to Felkington sooner than you think."

Lista smiled modestly. "That is flattering, thank you," she said. "Although I'm not spoken for I hope to be soon."

"I suspect you do not mean me."

Her grin broadened. "Nay."

"Then you clearly must mean de Velt."

"I do, indeed."

Louis' dark eyes twinkled. "That is what I need to hear," he said. "I will not interfere."

She smiled. "Thank you," she said. "You are a man of honor."

He grunted, looking up at the castle, the sky, the land. "Honor, aye," he said. "But unlucky in this case. Julian is a fortunate man."

"I feel as if I am the fortunate one."

He snorted. "*He* is the fortunate one," he insisted. "If anything happens and he runs away with a Scottish princess or a pirate queen, you will let me know, won't you?"

Lista laughed softly. "I will let you know so that you can defend my honor."

"That is *not* what I meant."

They both started laughing. "I know what you meant," Lista said. "As I said, I am deeply honored, but my heart is no longer mine to give. It belongs to another."

He shrugged. "For your sake, I am glad," he said. "Every young woman – and man – should give their heart away at some point. I've yet to have the privilege."

"You will someday, I am certain."

"Mayhap," he said. His gaze lingered on her for a moment longer before he gestured at the castle. "I really must go. Was there something you wanted?"

Lista cocked her head curiously. "Wanted?"

"Your aunt said you wished to speak to me. To bid me farewell, I assume."

Lista was greatly puzzled, but when it came to Flora, nothing was a mistake. She wasn't sure what was going on, or why her aunt had told Louis that she wanted to see him, but she suspected it was some kind of tactic to throw them together. She tried not to let her frustration show.

"Aye," she said, trying to maintain her smile. "I wanted to bid you a farewell and thank you for what you did last night. I shall walk back to the castle with you."

"I would be honored."

Greatly annoyed at Flora, Lista came around the grapevines but the moment she did so, she put her foot in a patch of slick mud and ended up falling heavily on her right hip. Louis wasn't close enough to grab her but as she sat up in the mud, he bent over her with great concern.

"Did you hurt yourself?" he asked.

Lista rubbed her sore hip. "Other than my pride, I do not think so," she said. "I am usually much more graceful than that."

"I believe you," Louis said, reaching down with both hands. "Let me help you."

He pulled Lista up easily but the moment she put weight on her foot, pain shot up her leg and she nearly went over again. Louis had a good grip on her as she winced.

"It seems I twisted my ankle," she said. "Do you mind helping me into the castle?"

Louis' response was to bend over and scoop her into his big arms. Lista gasped at the unexpected move as her arms went around his neck to support herself.

"You do not have to carry me," she insisted. "I can walk."

Louis turned for the castle. "I can move faster than you can."

"I *can* walk."

"Let a man be chivalrous, will you?"

He said it with humor, but he was mostly serious. Lista opened her mouth to say something but movement caught her eye. She lifted a hand to shield her eyes from the sun as she gazed up at the garden gate, the one that led to the road beyond.

"Strange," she muttered.

"What?"

"I thought I just saw Julian standing near the garden gate."

"He's still sleeping, isn't he?"

Lista gripped his neck again as he proceeded up the slippery slope. "The last I checked, he was," she said. "Mayhap it is the sun playing tricks."

Louis nearly slipped himself in the mud, gripping Lista tightly as he carried her out of the garden and through the gate. He was rather sorry he was going to have to put her down at some point, but he was enjoying it while it lasted.

Little did he know what the brief moment of pleasure was going to cost.

"ASHTON, WAKE UP."

Ashton had been dreaming about a trip he'd taken to London years ago, dreaming of the golden Thames at sunset and boats that were being pulled by swimming horses. It was a weird dream. But he opened his eyes to Julian's grim face.

"What's wrong?" he said, quickly sitting up. "Are the Scots back?"

Julian was dressed for battle. In full protection, his saddlebags slung over his shoulder, he was prepared.

"Nay," he said shortly. "I am leaving Felkington now. I want you to escort Addie home first thing in the morning."

Ashton rubbed his eyes. "You're leaving *now*?" he said, thinking he hadn't heard right. "Why?"

Julian's jaw was ticking faintly. "Because I am," he said. "Thank Lady Lista for her hospitality but bring Addie home tomorrow. Do not delay or I will send men for you."

Ashton frowned, becoming more lucid. "Julian, *what* is wrong?"

Julian's jaw was ticking so furiously now that he was about to break his teeth. "Do not ask me that," he said. "As long as you live, do not ask me more than you already have. If I want you to know, I will tell you."

Ashton was at a loss. Julian was serious about not asking any further questions, so he didn't. He watched Julian leave the chamber, not bothering to close the door, but then he quickly climbed out of bed and put his clothing on.

He had to find Addington.

"WHAT DO YOU mean that he is leaving?"

The question came from Addington. Sitting on the floor of the great hall, she had been bandaging a man who had taken an ax to the arm and the doctor had just cleaned the wound thoroughly. But the rather grim statement from Ashton had her pausing in her duties.

"Just what I said," Ashton said, quietly and seriously. "He just came to me and told me that he's leaving. When I asked him why, he said never to ask him that question again. I am afraid he will take my head off if I ask him again, so you must find him quickly. He must be in the stables gathering his horse, so you must hurry. Something is wrong, Addie."

Frowning with concern, Addington turned the bandaging over to a servant and let Ashton pull her to her feet. She was dressed in one of her nicer gowns, one she had brought to go visiting in, but over the gown was a coarse and dirty apron that had blood and dirt on it. She made a paradoxical sight, so nicely dressed, doing rather dirty work, but that was Addington. She grew up in a castle that had seen many battles, so she was used to such things. But she wasn't used to Ashton's tone where it pertained to Julian.

"I do not understand," she said as she began to remove the apron. "He just said this to you?"

"Aye."

"But nothing more?"

Ashton shook his head. "He had that look in his eyes that your father used to get when he was verging on tearing someone's head off," he said. "You know that look. I did not want to press him. But you can."

Addington pulled the apron off, tossing it aside as she headed out of the hall with Ashton on her heels.

"In the stables, you say?" she said.

Ashton was right behind her. "That is my assumption," he said. "Unless he is already gone. Julian moves like the wind when the mood strikes him. I would not be surprised if…"

"My lady!"

They were just at the stairwell, the spiral steps built into Felkington's thick walls when a shout caught their attention. Addington had her foot on the top step but paused to see Louis heading in their direction.

He seemed distressed.

"Sir Louis?" Addington said. "Is something amiss?"

Louis nodded. "I just brought Lady Lista inside," he said. "She has hurt her ankle. Will you see to her?"

Addington frowned. "How did she hurt her ankle?"

Louis threw a thumb in the direction of the vineyard. "We were near the ruined vineyard and she slipped in the mud," he said. "I picked her up and carried her inside because she could not walk. Will you come?"

Addington wanted to but she had more pressing things with Julian. "I will, but in a moment," she said. "You can help me in the meanwhile."

"Tell me what to do, my lady."

"Get a basin of cold water and some rags," Addington said. "Put the rags in the cold water and put them on her ankle. I will come as soon as I can."

Louis took the orders like a good knight and rushed off to carry them out. Addington continued down the stairs with Ashton still behind her, perhaps even hiding behind her because of Julian's mood. Given that he'd told Addington what had occurred, Julian might even be angry at him for it.

As he'd told her, he'd seen Julian like that before.

It never ended well.

They came off the stairs and headed out into the courtyard, which was crisp and cold at that hour with the sun's rays angled so that the courtyard was mostly in shadow. The ground was a little slick, a little wet, as Addington held her skirts up and quickly walked towards the stables, which was through a large, arched entry on the opposite side of the courtyard.

At that point, Ashton held back and waited just outside the entry as Addington went in. He didn't want Julian to see him, knowing he'd summoned Addington. He did, however, eavesdrop. His ears were open, listening for the conversation that was sure to come.

It didn't take long.

Addington spied Julian as he slung his saddlebags over the back of his saddle. He was securing them as she approached.

"Julian?" Addington said, sounding both concerned and

curious. "Where are you going?"

Julian was strapping the saddlebags to the saddle with leather strips. He glanced at her when he heard her voice.

"Ashton ran to you, did he?" he said.

Addington hesitated before shaking her head. "I saw you through the window," she lied, not wanting to get Ashton into any trouble. "Why are you leaving?"

Julian finished with one strap and started on the other. "I told Ashton to bring you home tomorrow," he said, avoiding her question. "Thank Lady Lista for a nice visit and come home."

Addington shook her head. "I do not want to go home yet," she said. "I did not think you did, either, so what has happened? Why are you leaving?"

He finished with the tie and looked at her. "I do not wish to speak of it," he said. "I will see you at home."

He moved to mount the charger but Addington put herself in front of the horse. "Tell me why you are leaving or I will not move," she said, more firmly. "You are going to have to go through me to get out of this stable block and if you try, I will tell Mother. Worse still, I will tell Cole and you will have a lot of explaining to do. Stop being so evasive and tell me what has happened."

He stopped short of climbing into the saddle because her threat was a real one. He knew she wouldn't move and he didn't want to hurt her, but given Addington's determined nature, he probably would have to plow through her to leave and he wasn't going to go that far. So he stood there for a moment, thinking on the answer he didn't want to give.

He snorted softly.

"I am a fool," he said simply. "Can we just leave it at that? I am a fool and I belong at Pelinom."

Addington didn't understand him in the least. "Why?" she begged softly. "Please tell me, Julian. You know you can trust me. I would not betray a confidence."

He knew that. He and Addington were inordinately close. Scratching his head, he looked at her. "It seems that Lady Lista has another suitor," he said. "I thought... well, it does not matter what I thought. I was wrong so I am going home."

Addington's face screwed up with confusion. "What suitor?" she demanded. "Who?"

Julian fumbled with the reins. "De Rhos," she said. Then, his control slipped. "I saw them, Addie. Their arms around each other. I trusted him... I trusted her... the worst part is that I genuinely liked de Rhos. Nay... that is not the worst part. The worst part is that I thought Lady Lista liked me. She certainly acted like it and even agreed to let me court her. But, yet again, Julian de Velt is made a fool of."

Addington genuinely had no idea what he was talking about. "Julian, you are not making any sense," she said. "You saw them with their arms around each other? Where?"

"In the vineyard," he said. "They were in quite a romantic embrace, so there is no point in me remaining. I will not be humiliated again."

Pieces of the puzzle were starting to come together for Addington, especially when he mentioned the vineyard. "I just saw Louis upstairs and he said that Lista had hurt herself in the vineyard," she said. "I am sure that is all you saw. Mayhap he was helping her?"

Julian cast her a look of disbelief before finally mounting his horse. "Helping her, indeed," he said. "Is that what he called it?"

Addington grabbed on to the reins so he couldn't get by

her. "Julian, *stop*," she commanded softly. "I do not know what you think you saw, but Lista likes you very much. She is quite agreeable to having you court her and she did not lie to you about that. Why in the world would she carry on with de Rhos? That does not seem like something she would do."

Julian pulled his helm out of a saddlebag. "How do you know?" he said. "She has us all fooled into thinking she is sweet and kind when the truth is that she is just like the rest of them."

"She is not," Addington insisted. "I do not know what has happened, but the least you could do is go and ask her."

He grunted. "Not me," he said. "I *know* what happened. Get out of the way because I am leaving now."

Addington held fast. "I am not getting out of the way because you are acting rashly," she said. "I know you are used to women treating you poorly, but Lista is not one of them. If I thought she was, I would have never agreed to come here. I came here because I wanted to play matchmaker between you two and I have. Why are you trying to ruin this?"

"I told you what happened. I will not tell you again."

"You told me what you saw. You did not tell me what happened."

"Do not be stupid, Addie."

"You are the one being stupid. You have so little faith that you will not even ask Lista?"

"Excuse me, my lady. I am sorry to trouble you."

It wasn't Julian who replied. It was Louis. He was suddenly in the entry of the stables and both Addington and Julian turned to see the man standing there, mostly looking at Addington, but having some confusion when he managed to look at Julian.

Addington smiled weakly.

"How can I help, Sir Louis?" she asked.

He gestured to the castle. "The physic said it would be better for Lady Lista to soak her foot," he said. "Since the servants seemed to be missing or occupied, I've come looking for a bucket. I thought there might be one out here."

Addington saw the opportunity to clarify the situation for Julian. "You mean for Lista's sore ankle?" she said. "The one she twisted when she slipped in the vineyard?"

It was a long way to get to the point, at least for Louis, and he nodded at the rather odd questions. "Aye," he said. "Is there one around here I can rinse out?"

Addington sighed heavily but, in truth, it was mostly in annoyance at Julian. The man was being irrational as far as she was concerned so if he was going to leave, then she figured he should have all the facts.

It was a risky move, but she was going to take it.

"Sir Louis," she said. "Can you please tell my brother what happened in the vineyard with Lista?"

Louis' gaze moved to Julian. He was confused, trying not to show it. "She slipped in the mud so I brought her back to the castle," he said. "Her ankle is swollen. She wrenched it when she fell."

Julian simply looked at him for a moment before dismounting. Addington held her breath, hoping that it would calm the evidently terrible misconceptions that Julian had. But Julian simply stood next to his horse, holding the reins, as he looked at Louis near the entry of the stables.

"I will accept that," he finally said. "But I have a question for you."

Louis could sense the hardness and, in fact, the rage. He wasn't exactly sure what was going on, but he could guess. "Ask what you will."

"What were you doing with her, alone, in the vineyard?"

"I was told she wished to bid me farewell," he said steadily. "I am leaving today, as evidently, you are also. I was unaware of that."

Julian was processing what he was being told but his body language hadn't changed. He was still stiff. "She wanted to bid you farewell in the vineyard?" he repeated as if to clarify it, as if there were something odd about it he still didn't believe.

Louis nodded. "Her mother told me that she wished to have a word with me, privately," he said. Then, his gaze moved between Addington and Julian. The man wasn't stupid. "Is that what the problem is here? That I was alone with Lista? Julian, nothing untoward happened. We only spoke. I swear it."

Instead of being eased, Julian's stiff stance only grew worse. "Her mother told you that she wanted to see you *privately*?"

Louis nodded. "Aye, but I am sure that meant nothing," he said. "In fact, she seemed a little confused by my appearance, to tell you the truth. We spoke a few words, she thanked me again for my assistance against the Scots, and we were leaving the vineyard when she slipped. Since she could not walk, I carried her back to the castle."

Julian's gaze lingered on him a moment longer before he finally shook his head as if the entire situation was laced with great irony. It was clear that he didn't believe what he was told.

"I see," he said, showing some cracks in his composure for the first time. "Lista wants to see you privately before you leave and then she conveniently slips so that you must carry her into the castle. De Rhos, I sincerely hope you are not playing me for a fool because I will not be lied to, not by you and not by anyone. Either you are making this up or Lista is manipulating you and me. Personally, I do not care what it is because I will leave here and never see either of you again. I wish you good health and happiness, wherever you may find it."

With that, he swung onto his horse again, this time yanking the reins away from Addington. But Louis was greatly puzzled and just the least bit offended by what he said.

"No man will accuse me of being a liar, my lord," he said, reverting to a formal stance. "I have not, nor will I ever, lie to you. I went to the vineyard because Lady Lista's mother told me to and for no other reason than that. In fact, the lady and I had a discussion about you and she told me that she was very much committed to you even though you'd not formally asked for her hand yet. That is not something I would ever violate, de Velt. I told you that once already."

Julian spurred his warhorse forward, brushing past Addington. "I know what I saw," he muttered as he moved past de Rhos. "No man, and no woman, will make a fool out of me, so save your breath. Good life to you."

With that, he trotted out into the courtyard, heading for the double-portcullis passage. Louis watched him go with great distress, as did Addington, who came to stand next to him. Together, they watched Julian disappear into the passage. When Louis turned to Addington, baffled, he could see the tears in her eyes.

"What happened?" he said, genuinely perplexed. "Why did he leave like that?"

Addington sniffled, flicking away the tears. "Because he is afraid," she said simply. "Julian has been hurt before, by men and women he trusted. He thinks the same thing is happening now."

Louis scratched his head. "Nothing is happening," he said.

"Nothing *happened*. Lady Lista slipped. I picked her up. What was I supposed to do? Leave her wallowing in the mud?"

Addington shook her head, looking to Louis. "Please do not be offended by what he said," she said. "Julian… he is a skilled knight and a wonderful brother, but he has always lacked great confidence when it comes to women."

Louis' eyebrows lifted. "Him?" he said, shocked. "The man is built like a god. Why does he lack faith in himself?"

Addington pointed to her eyes. "Did you notice his eyes?"

Louis shrugged. "I think so," he said. "I have looked at the man, so of course I have seen his eyes. What about them?"

"Did you notice they are two different colors?"

"What does that have to do with anything?"

Addington smiled in spite of herself. "Bless you for saying so," she said. "But he is very self-conscious of the fact that his eyes can scare people. He has been fond of a couple of women in the past only for them to taunt him because of his eye color and then leave him for someone else. He thinks that is happening again. He is simply trying to protect himself."

Now, it was all starting to make some sense to Louis. "And he thinks I am trying to steal Lady Lista away."

"Exactly."

Louis nodded as if it all became clear to him now. But that still didn't ease him. "It is unfair of him to think that I have been underhanded," he said. "It is unfair of him to judge me when he does not even know me. We stood side by side against the Scots and fought together, preserving one another's lives in the process. And he thinks that I would actually try to steal away the woman he wants?"

Addington nodded. "Do not be too hard on him," she said. "He has been betrayed before."

Louis' jaw ticked. "But not by me," he said. "I've never hurt the man. The fact that others have does not give him the right to assume the same from me."

He was building up a rage and Addington was feeling increasingly desperate for Julian. "He is a kind and compassionate man," she said. "I am sorry if he offended you, but you must understand the damage others have inflicted."

Louis looked at her. "In this case, he has brought it on himself," he said. "Lady Addington, I realize you are defending your brother and that is admirable, but he is a bitter fool to go around accusing people he does not know of betraying him. If he is going to do that, then mayhap I should have no such restraint when it comes to Lady Lista. A man like that does not deserve her."

Addington looked at him with some horror. "What do you mean?" she said. "Of course he deserves her. He is a good man."

Louis' jaw ticked. "A good man does not behave the way he just did," he said. "Good day to you, my lady."

With that, he headed out of the stables, moving for the stairwell that led to the great hall and leaving Addington with a bigger problem than ever. Feeling frustrated with Louis and hurt on Julian's behalf, she knew she needed to talk to Lista before Louis got to her and told her what had happened.

But she needed to find Ashton first.

He had to know what had happened.

A bad situation was about to get worse.

CHAPTER THIRTEEN

S HE JUST FELT silly.

Silly and clumsy.

Laying on her bed with her right ankle elevated on a pillow, and throbbing, Lista felt absolutely ridiculous for having twisted her ankle. With wounded in the hall, and guests visiting, it was a terrible time to be crippled with an injury.

Louis seemed to feel responsible, which was ridiculous in Lista's opinion. He was off trying to find someone to help her as she lay on that bed with her throbbing ankle, hoping it wasn't as bad as it felt. She had to laugh, an ironic sort of sound, when she realized she was thankful that Louis had been present because if he hadn't, she would have had to crawl on her hands and knees all the way back to the castle.

She would have made quite a sight.

At one point, she sat up and tried to stand up on the ankle, only to feel that same sharp pain shoot up her leg. Oddly, if she turned her foot slightly, the pain wasn't so bad, but it was still achy. Achy, she could live with. But that shooting pain was uncomfortable. As she stood there, leaning against the bed and trying to decide just how badly she was hurt, there was a knock on the chamber door. Before she could answer, it creaked open and Louis entered, carrying a bucket of hot water.

"My lady, you should be off that ankle," he said, lifting a dark eyebrow as he set the bucket next to a chair that was positioned near the hearth. "Standing on it will not help it."

Lista knew that, but she made a face at him, just because she didn't have a sharp answer for him. Once he set the bucket down, he came over to her and picked her up again, depositing her into the chair.

"Now," he said. "Get your foot into the bucket. While the water is hot."

Her shoe was already off, courtesy of Louis when he had set her on the bed earlier, so Lista lifted her leg and gingerly slid her foot into the water. It was hot and she hissed, but it felt good.

She sighed.

"Thank you for taking the trouble to do this," she said. "I fear that I have ruined your plans to leave early, but truly, you can go now. I will not detain you any longer and the servants will help me from here."

Louis didn't make any move towards the door. He acted as if he didn't hear her. Kneeling down, he moved the bucket slightly so her foot would fit more easily.

"Is that better?" he asked.

Lista nodded. "It is," she said. "Truly, Louis, you can leave. I hate that I have detained you."

"You have not detained me."

"But you said you needed to be in Kelso today. You must leave soon."

He was still kneeling, still looking at her foot in the bucket. "I am more concerned that you have injured yourself," he said.

"Had my reflexes been faster when you slipped, we would not be in this predicament."

She shook her head. "That is nonsense," she said. "You are not to blame. I am, for being clumsy."

He didn't say anything. Instead, he was peering intently at her ankle, which was rather scandalous. Naked feet and ankles were off limits as objects of study for unmarried men and women.

"I am not particularly accustomed to modes of healing, unfortunately," he said after a moment. "I am better with battlefield wounds. Most knights are, in truth. We all receive basic training in such things, but this... I wish I had some knowledge to utilize."

He seemed somewhat pensive and concerned, which Lista thought was sweet. She'd told him that if there had never been a Julian, she might very well allow Louis to court her. She could see that he was a kind individual and she didn't sense that it was a pretense.

But he wasn't sweet enough for her to throw over Julian.

He had all of her attention.

"Truly, you needn't worry," she said. "I am a fast healer. I am certain I will be walking tomorrow with ease."

"I hope so."

"That is kind of you to say so."

He looked up at her as if he wanted to say something more. There was a glimmer in his eyes that was curious and intense. Lista lifted her eyebrows expectantly, prepared for something to come forth, when Addington suddenly entered the chamber.

Her focus was on Louis.

"You will leave us," she said.

It was a command. There was no mistake. Louis' gaze

moved to her and, obediently, he stood. But he was looking at Addington strangely. *Challenging.* As if he took her command as a challenge. Suddenly, there was something strange in the air, something tense. It was there for a moment, quickly gone as he left the chamber, as silent as the grave.

Lista looked at Addington curiously.

"Why did you order him out like that?" she said. "What is amiss?"

Addington went to the chamber door and shut it, throwing the bolt. When she turned to Lista, it was with a good deal of restraint, of contemplation, and of limited patience.

She was a woman with a good deal on her mind.

"Lista," she said. "I want you to tell me what happened in the vineyard."

Lista could tell by the tone of her voice that something was wrong. "I slipped in the mud," she said, pointing to her foot in the bucket of hot water. "I wrenched my ankle. Why?"

Addington listened carefully, still standing at the door. When Lista was finished, she came closer, her gaze intense.

"But why were you in the vineyard?" she asked.

"Because my mother said she wanted some grapes so I went to fetch them," she said. "Addie, *what* is wrong? Why the questions?"

Addington wasn't finished with her interrogation yet. "And why was Louis there?"

Lista was becoming the least bit perturbed that Addington seemed to be avoiding her questions. "He said my mother sent him to say farewell to me," she said. "Nay... that is not exactly what he said. He said my mother told him that I wanted to bid him farewell."

"And did you?"

"I am not answering another question until you tell me what is wrong."

It was a standoff. Lista was taking a stand against Addington, who was behaving most strangely. Addington could see that she wasn't going to go any further, but she was still brittle from her conversations with Julian and, subsequently, Louis. She didn't sense any evasiveness or deception on the part of Lista because the woman genuinely had no idea what she was talking about.

"Julian saw you in Louis' arms," she said simply. "He thinks you've been deceiving him the entire time."

Lista's eyebrows lifted. "Me?" she said. "Deceiving Julian? Why, that's ridiculous. I've never deceived him with any thought or action, not in the entire time I've known him."

Addington was starting to relax a little, realizing that her take on the situation had been right all along. Julian had simply seen something and took it out of context.

"That is what I told him," Addington said. "But somehow, he saw you in Louis' arms and he thought... he thought both you and Louis had made a fool of him."

Lista had gone from shocked to immediate concern. "Addie, that is simply not true," she insisted. "I would never hurt Julian, not while there was breath left in my body. When Louis and I were in the vineyard, for a brief moment, I thought I saw Julian in the garden gate but he was quickly gone. That must have been when he saw us."

Addington sighed heavily. "He most certainly saw you," she said. "He saw you in Louis' arms and thought the worst."

Lista took her foot out of the bucket. "But why?" she said, feeling a great deal of angst. "Why should he think such a thing? I have never given him any reason to think so poorly of me."

Addington could see that this was becoming a big mess. "I know," she said. "But I told you that other women have treated him poorly. I told you that Julian was hand shy. I'm afraid my brother thought he was about to be struck again. It has happened before and he knows that pain. That humiliation. The worst part is that I think he's liked you more than any other woman he's ever known, so he's hurt. Very hurt."

Lista gripped the chair she was sitting on as she stood up. "Where is he?" she said, trying to walk. "Take me to him immediately, Addie. I must explain things to him."

Addington reached out to stop her, trying to direct her back into the chair. "You cannot," she said. "Lista, he left. He gathered his things and left."

Lista came to a halt, teetering to one side because it hurt to put her weight on her right ankle. "Where has he gone?"

"Home. To Pelinom."

The realization hit Lista and she looked at Addington with shock. After a moment, she lowered herself back onto the chair.

"God's bones," she muttered, bewildered. "He simply left? He did not even ask me what he had seen?"

Addington was feeling a great deal of sorrow at the expression on Lista's face. "As I said, he's been hurt before," she said. "I know it is a weak excuse, but he told me he was not going to let you make a fool out of him. He already had words with Louis, which is why…"

Lista looked at her when she trailed off. "Why *what*?"

Addington took a deep breath, clearly reluctant to continue. "That is why I came up here," she said. "Louis was quite offended by it. From what I could gather, Louis must have asked if you and Julian were betrothed. He told Julian he would not pursue you, but when he saw how Julian would not believe the truth of what he saw, he said that Julian did not deserve you."

Lista stared at her a moment before averting her gaze. Addington couldn't help but see the tears forming as the reality of the situation began to settle.

"He did not ask me to explain, either," she said tightly. "He assumed the worst and fled."

"I know."

"That's *not* fair."

"I know, Lista," Addington said, trying to be of some comfort. "I am going to speak to Ashton and we will return to Pelinom and tell Julian that…"

Lista cut her off. "Nay," she said sharply. "You'll not tell him anything. He did not have the decency or courage to ask me to explain what he saw, and worse still, he simply assumed I was doing something deceptive and dishonorable. That is not something I would have ever assumed of him, in any situation, so I cannot understand why he did not give me the same courtesy. It was cowardly, Addie. Your brother is a coward."

Addington didn't like hearing that come from Lista, true though it might be. "Do not speak so unkindly of him," she said quietly. "He has been hurt many times before. He was trying to protect himself."

"I understand that, but it does not excuse his behavior," Lista snapped, more forcefully now. "Since the moment I met him, he has refused to look me in the eyes and I believed it was because he was self-conscious about his eye color. But now I think it is something more than that. Mayhap it is because he is shallow and weak. Mayhap it is better that I find out now rather than later. How dare he assume the worst of me?"

"He has never known anything else," Addington said. "His

reaction was natural, at least for him."

That didn't soothe Lista. The more she thought on it, the angrier she became. "I do not need a man who runs whenever he is faced with a challenge," she said. "I do not want a man who runs whenever he is confronted with something he does not understand, afraid he'll be hurt. Nay, that is not the kind of man I want. Julian can keep running for all I care."

The tears were starting to trickle but she flicked them away angrily as Addington struggled not to snap back at her.

"Lista, I know you are hurt," she said patiently. "I cannot explain Julian's reaction more than I have. What more do you want me to do?"

Lista stood up from the chair and hobbled over to her bed, climbing onto it. "I want you to stop defending him," she said, trying not to openly weep. "I thought Julian was different. I thought he was sweet and shy. He did not care about my mother and aunt and their escapades. He seemed to care for me, as a woman. He gave me hope. He took my heart and gave me hope in return and now I see that the hope he gave me wasn't strong enough to stand up to his foolish doubts."

Addington watched Lista have a breakdown, covering her face and sniffling softly. She felt as bad as she possibly could because nothing Lista said was untrue. None of it except for the fact that she believed Julian to be a coward, although perhaps he was when it came to his heart.

That was something he protected fiercely.

But she didn't like hearing Lista speak so poorly of him.

"Lista, please listen to me," she said. "I have a feeling that Louis will try to make his interest known now that Julian has fled. Will you please resist him? At least until I can speak with Julian. Please do not break my brother's heart more than it already is. He has made a mistake. Should he not have the chance to redeem himself?"

"Why?" Lista said. "Because he gave me a chance to redeem *myself* in his eyes. Nay, Addie. He believes I lied to him. He did not even give me the chance to defend myself."

"And you do not have the capacity to forgive him?"

Lista looked at her, her eyes flashing. "Do not act as if all of this is my fault," she said. "I have done nothing wrong, Lady Addington. If Julian must protect his heart, then so must I. You cannot expect me to do less."

Addington was feeling horrible about the situation. A misunderstanding and Julian was going to ruin his entire life. She could see, in Lista's eyes, that Julian was ruining her life, too. There was more than interest and affection there.

She could see the adoration.

Lista had been falling in love with Julian.

"All I am asking is that you not do anything rashly," Addington said. "Do not do anything that you may regret later."

Lista wiped at her eyes and looked away. "While I am very glad to have had your company, my lady, I think it is time for you to go," she said, sniffling. "Thank you for the conversation and the laughter. I shall remember it always. But you will go home now."

She was essentially cutting Addington off. Addington knew it wouldn't be any use to argue with her, especially with such emotions involved. Perhaps Lista had known Julian just a few days, but those had been magical days. Sometimes one didn't need weeks or months to make up one's mind about someone.

One simply knew.

Lista and Julian had a connection not often found and to see it broken was a genuine tragedy. Addington turned and left the chamber, leaving Lista crushed and weeping. She couldn't do anything about Lista any longer, but she could do something about Julian.

She had to find Ashton.

"LADY FELKINGTON, MAY I speak with you?"

Meadow was shocked to find Louis standing at her door. She was in the tower room with Flora because they'd found a stash of hemp leaf they'd forgotten about, so the sickly sweet smoke was beginning to fill the chamber again. That delirious wave of blue smoke was about to carry them away again. Before she could answer, however, Flora came up behind her.

"Sir Louis," Flora said. "We thought you were leaving."

Louis glanced at her. "I was, my lady," he said before returning his attention to Meadow. "However, I have decided to remain for a day or two, with your permission."

Meadow was surprised by the request but she nodded when Flora elbowed her in the back. "Of course, my lord," she said. "You are welcome at Felkington."

"Fuckington," Flora muttered, snorting at her usual vulgar joke.

Louis heard the crack but he ignored it. "Thank you, my lady," he said. "I will come right to the point of my request to remain. I would ask permission to speak to Lady Lista with the intention of courting her."

Flora stopped snorting, looking at Louis in delight and surprise, as Meadow's eyes widened. "You... you would like to court my daughter?" she asked in awe.

"Only if she is agreeable, my lady."

Meadow's mouth had popped open into a shocked "O" and she looked at Flora, who was nodding emphatically. Meadow had to take a breath and drink it all in even though they'd manipulated the situation for this very reason. The triangle between Lista and Julian and Louis had just come to its hoped-for conclusion and they could not be more thrilled. At least, Flora was thrilled. Meadow stood there in stunned silence as Flora pulled Louis into the chamber.

"Please, Sir Louis," she said. "Please come in and sit. It seems that your interest in Lista has come rather suddenly, but it is not unwelcome. We did not even know of you before the Scots' raid."

Louis allowed himself to be pulled into the strange-smelling, cluttered chamber. There was a chair, only one chair, and Flora directed him into it. He sat, but the chair was old and decrepit and groaned under his weight, so he wisely stood up again.

"I realize this seems sudden, my lady," he said. "Mayhap it is even rash, but I assure you, I am not a reckless man. I am sure you would agree that Lady Lista is an eligible young woman of unique talent and charm. Frankly, I am surprised that she is not married already."

Flora was looking at him eagerly. "She's simply not found the right man," she said. "Mayhap that is you, Sir Louis. We would be glad to know what you have to offer her, as a husband. Sunderland is quite wealthy and prestigious."

Louis thought the woman looked much like a predator and he wasn't sure he liked it. Certainly, he'd gathered that the pair of women were strange during the time he'd spent at Felkington, but Lady d'Orbec was looking at him… hungrily.

He'd seen that look before.

"I am the second eldest son of the earl, my father," he said evenly. "My brother will inherit the title but I will be his heir unless he has male children. Even so, my father has gifted me with lands and a title that is within his power to grant. I am Lord Penshaw and I have a small outpost not far from my father's seat of Herrington Castle. As my father believes that all of his male children must have a source of income, and work for it, I have two villages and several farms on my lands. I am fair in the taxes I impose. In fact, more than half of my income is derived from my herds of sheep. I export wool at a profit."

Flora was practically bursting with joy from what she was hearing. "Then it seems you are a man of means, my lord," she said. Then, she looked at her sister. "Don't you think so, Meadow? Is he not more than worthy to seek Lista's hand?"

Meadow had been listening to all of it, unsure what to say. Certainly he sounded quite suitable, but Meadow had a blind spot when it came to her only daughter. She cared about the woman's feelings and if this wasn't what Lista wanted, then Meadow didn't want it, either – no matter what Flora said. That was usually where she drew the line if she was strong enough.

The question was would she be strong enough now.

"You seem more than suitable, my lord," she finally said. "Have… have you spoken to my daughter yet?"

Louis shook his head. "I have not, my lady," he said. "I did not want to overstep my bounds. I thought it best to come to you directly."

"And so you have," Flora said, answering for Meadow. "I am sure my sister would be more than happy to have you court her daughter. As she said, you are suitable and…"

"And you will let me make that decision," Meadow interrupted in a surprising show of courage. Her gaze moved from her sister to the young knight. "My lord, you will give me some time to mull this over and speak with my daughter. This is a big decision and I will not make it lightly."

Louis was perhaps surprised by Lady Felkington's show of strength but he nodded respectfully. "Of course, my lady," he said. "I have asked permission to remain at Felkington for a few days already, but would it be too much trouble to remain until you have decided?"

"I cannot promise you that I will make a decision in a few days."

"I understand, my lady. But may I remain, anyway?"

"You may."

That seemed to please Louis a great deal. "Thank you, my lady," he said. "I promise that I shall be no trouble at all, but rather, I shall try to be an asset to Felkington."

Meadow wasn't even sure what to say to all of that. Flora was practically foaming at the mouth, but Meadow wasn't quite so eager.

Things were starting to change a little with her as far as Flora was concerned.

It was true that Flora had kept her from killing herself in those days following Simon's murder. Flora had always been in control, telling her what to do and when to do it, but now… now, it wasn't only Meadow that Flora was trying to control. It was Lista and that didn't sit well with Meadow. Flora was trying to control the entire destiny of the House of de la Mere.

She wasn't entirely sure she was willing to go along with it any longer.

With a brief nod, she turned away as Louis excused himself and headed from the chamber. When he was gone and the door shut softly, Flora turned to her sister.

"Why are you so stubborn about this?" she demanded. "This is exactly what we'd hoped for. He is perfect!"

Meadow held up a hand to silence her. "For whom?" she said. "You? You're trying so hard to regain your position in court that you are failing to realize Lista may not wish to be courted by him."

Flora was outraged. "You are her mother," she said. "*You* will tell her who to marry, Meadow. Lista should have no opinion in this matter."

Meadow shook her head wearily. "I have a feeling she will have a good deal to say on the matter."

"Not if you do not let her."

Meadow didn't reply. She wasn't prepared to get into a battle with her sister who was both her protector and her bully. Deep down, she knew that Flora was correct and that Louis de Rhos was truly a fine candidate for her daughter, but she simply didn't want to make that decision. Not yet. Instead, she went to the bowl in the center of the chamber where the hemp leaf was burning and inhaled deeply, inviting that blissful stupor that it provided. It was escape from her world, escape from things she didn't want to deal with – or couldn't deal with, Flora included.

Sleep came because of the sweet-smelling smoke, carrying her off into the land of no pain, no sorrows. She vaguely remembered Flora leaving the chamber but she didn't pay her any regard. She drifted off as Flora went to find Louis, telling the man that he had Meadow's permission to court Lista. Sometimes, Meadow didn't remember what she said or did when she was intoxicated with the smoke from the hemp, so Flora used that to her advantage. She wanted to return to court, now as a relation to an earl, and she was going to use Louis de

Rhos to get it.

To hell with her sister's reluctance.

As Meadow slept away the morning hours, Flora was wreaking havoc.

CHAPTER FOURTEEN

"WE SHOULD RETURN to Pelinom," Ashton said seriously. "From what you have said, Julian is about to ruin his life. The man ought to know what he's doing to himself."

In the mostly empty great hall of Felkington, with only a few wounded still crowded into one corner, Addington and Ashton were standing over by the big oriel window that overlooked the bailey. Down below, they could see men moving about their business, repairing weapons or saddles or a variety of other tasks. The world was going on around them, normal for this bright and sunny day, but all Addington could feel as she watched them was turmoil.

There was much turmoil happening as far as she was concerned.

Peace and tranquility were a lie.

"I thought that, too," Addington said, still looking from the window. "At first, I did. But after speaking with Louis and Lista, I am not sure it would do any good. They are so angry with Julian and for good reason, but they do not know the Julian that you and I know. They do not know how caring and compassionate he is and how attached he becomes to people. They do not understand that he has been hurt and that he tries very hard to protect himself."

Ashton grunted. "At the expense of himself," he muttered. "I suppose I do not blame him for thinking the worst when he saw Lista in Louis' arms, but a rational man would have asked for an explanation rather than run off."

Addington looked at him. "Then you blame him, too."

Ashton lifted his shoulders. "He acted irrationally, in my opinion."

Addington didn't want to hear that, not from Ashton. "Then I shall go wrap myself around Louis and let's see how you react," she said rather hotly. "There is no crime in Julian wanting to protect himself."

Ashton put up a hand to soothe her. "I know," he said. "Let's not you and I fall out over this. We must think of Julian and what's best for him. What do you want to do?"

Addington wasn't quite cooled down yet, but she tried. She knew Ashton didn't mean his comment as an insult against Julian, simply the truth as he saw it.

"I think we should return to Pelinom and tell my mother what happened," she said, returning her focus to the courtyard below. "If anyone has any hope of convincing Julian he was wrong, it's my mother."

Ashton couldn't disagree. "Your mother has a gift when it comes to counseling her children," he said, making his way over to the window, his gaze drifting over Addington's hair, her profile. His heart softened. "I am sorry this has upset you so. You are always so concerned when it comes to Julian. You always have been."

Addington nodded faintly, catching sight of Louis as he emerged from one of the many doors in the courtyard. "He deserves to be happy and I think he is afraid of it."

"Why should he be afraid?"

"Because the greater the happiness, the greater the grief," she said. Then, she cocked her head thoughtfully. "Mayhap it is mostly the grief he's afraid of. He's had so much of it in his life. Even before Papa died, I remember my father saying that he wondered if his sins had brought down some of the torment Julian had to face."

"What kind of torment?"

Addington shrugged as she thought back over the course of Julian's life. "When he fostered, he was greatly tormented by fellow pages and squires," she said. "Cole and Cassian were, too, to a certain extent, but Julian's eye color difference is much more pronounced. The squires used to tell him that he had the eyes of the devil. One boy burned him with a hot piece of wood, telling him he was going to burn the devil out of him."

Ashton sighed faintly. "Boys can be cruel at that age."

"Cruel and hurtful," Addington said. "Hurtful to a lad who never hurt anyone, who only wanted to be their friend. I remember when Papa was dying, he told Julian that he had greatness in him but he needed to find it for himself. I wonder if Julian even knows how."

Ashton shook his head. "I remember that moment," he said quietly. "The burden on Julian was so great, greater than any of us. The entire de Velt empire staggered at that moment and he was the one to take the brunt. I suppose that's why I've remained at Pelinom even after my brother, Tristan, went home. Something compels me to stay with Julian. I was there for the most terrible moment of his life and I want to make sure he finds that greatness his father spoke of."

Addington looked at him. "Do *you* think he knows how?"

Ashton sighed heavily. "I think he has a gift for making a situation difficult for himself," he said. "Do I think he'll ever find the greatness within himself? I do not know. But I already see it. I have for some time. In the battle against the Scots, I saw it. There is no one fiercer than Julian in battle. He truly has the de Velt gift."

Addington could see the concern, the friendship in Ashton's expression. She was already quite fond of the man but seeing his concern for Julian endeared him even more. Her gaze moved over him, briefly, studying the handsome, blond knight. She was fond of him, of course, but he was also her friend.

She cherished that about him.

"Is that the only reason you remain at Pelinom?" she asked quietly. "Because of Julian?"

Ashton looked at her, watching her smile and coyly look away. He fought off a grin. "God knows, it should be," he said. "I've chased you up one side of Northumberland and down the other and still, you run from me. Why should I remain at Pelinom for a wisp of a woman who flirts with other knights any chance she gets?"

Addington broke down into soft laughter. "How else am I to get your attention?"

"You already have it. You have always had it."

"I have no way of knowing," she said. "It is not as if you have asked to court me."

"Give me time."

Addington lifted an eyebrow. "I will *not*," she said flatly. "You've had two years, Ashton de Royans, and I swear I'll not wait one moment longer than I have to. In fact, I... now, look at that. Isn't that Lista's aunt?"

Something in the courtyard had distracted her. Ashton

turned to see what had her attention, seeing Louis standing near the stables and Lista's strange aunt speaking to him. The aunt seemed to be quite animated, gesturing with her hands, as Louis stood like a stone and listened.

Ashton peered closer.

"I wonder what that's all about?" he muttered.

Addington was right beside him, watching the situation as well. "I told you that Louis was angry at Julian for assuming the worst when he saw Louis and Lista in the vineyard," she said. "He said he'd had no intention of pursuing Lista because of Julian's claim, but he went on to say that he should reconsider that stance. Ash... do you suppose that conversation has something to do with Lista?"

Ashton shook his head. "It is difficult to say," he said. "It could be any number of things. But one thing is for certain – Julian has made it easy for de Rhos to pursue Lista if he wishes."

"By speaking with her aunt?"

"Who will speak with her mother, more than likely."

Addington shook her head sadly. "Poor Julian," she said. "Louis is going to steal Lista from him."

Ashton glanced at her before turning away from the window. "As I said earlier," he said. "We must return to Pelinom and prevent Julian from ruining his life. If he is truly fond of Lady Lista, then he will see reason. If he doesn't, then de Rhos will happily take his place."

Addington could hardly disagree, watching the conversation below become more animated. It spurred her sense of urgency. "We must go now," she said. "If we leave within the hour, will we make it home before evening?"

Ashton nodded. "Mayhap after the sun has set, but not long after," he said. "Do you want to leave now?"

Addington's gaze lingered on Louis and Lista's strange aunt, who abruptly broke away and ran back inside.

She sighed faintly.

"I think we should," she said. "For Julian's sake. And Lista's."

Ashton wriggled his eyebrows in agreement as he turned to leave. He hadn't taken two steps when he abruptly stopped.

"And another thing," he said. "I shall speak to your mother when I am good and ready and not before. You *will* wait until I am ready, Addington. No more flirting with Anteaus de Bourne or any other knight that captures your fancy because you think it makes me jealous."

Her eyes twinkled as she looked at him. "Does it?"

"Of course it does!"

She giggled, biting her lip when she saw that he was mostly serious. "Then you must be ready faster, Ashton."

His eyes narrowed. "You will not force me."

"I am not forcing you into anything. I am simply stating a fact."

He sighed sharply and glared at her, indicative of his displeasure, before heading off to prepare their horses for travel. Addington took a couple of steps, calling after him.

"I will not wait forever!"

He was nearly to the exit. "Aye, you will!" he shouted back at her.

He was gone, leaving Addington in gales of laughter.

CHAPTER FIFTEEN

IT HURT TO walk, but Lista wasn't going to let a twisted ankle keep her down.

Wrapped tightly by a servant, Lista favored the joint as she made her way down the stairs. Her destination was the great hall, mostly because she thought that might be where Addington was. She wanted to apologize to her for being so sharp and asking her to leave which, in hindsight, wasn't what she wanted at all. The entire situation with Julian had her unnerved and upset and rather than make an enemy of Addington, she'd rather have her as a friend.

And an ally.

Limping when she came off the stairs, Lista was nearing the south entrance to the hall when she heard someone call her name. Pausing, she saw Flora coming up the stairs.

The woman was smiling.

"I was coming to see you," Flora said. "May we speak privately?"

Lista had limited patience for her aunt. "There is no one around," she said. "Say what you will."

That didn't please Flora too terribly. She was hoping for

more respect than that, considering what she was about to say. The smile on her lips faded.

"This is about your future, Lista," she said, sounding less pleasant and more threatening. "You can show me the courtesy of allowing me to tell you in private."

Unlike Meadow, Lista didn't cower to her aunt. "I have hurt my ankle," she said, annoyed. "Walking is difficult and that is why I told you that you may speak freely here. I do not want to walk more than I must. What is so important that you cannot tell me here? No one is listening."

To prove her point, she stuck out her foot, showing where the servant had wrapped it. Flora grunted and rolled her eyes, as if an injured ankle were no injury at all. But she didn't press further.

"Very well," she said, frustrated. "I had hoped to tell you this in a manner which would convey my joy for you, but since you are being difficult, I will simply come out with it. Your mother has given permission to Louis de Rhos to court you."

That wasn't what Lista had been expecting to hear.

Her eyes widened.

"She *what*?" she hissed. "Without speaking to me first?"

Flora was unapologetic. "De Rhos is an excellent match," she said. "You should be grateful to your mother for having the wisdom and foresight to make this arrangement for you. You will be married into the Earl of Sunderland's family, Lista. Your husband could be the earl someday and that would make you the countess. Does this not please you?"

Lista was looking at her aunt in shock. The woman was essentially scolding her as she told her of the course her life was about to take and she could see the glee in the woman's eyes. Glee that Lista was in a situation beyond her control, something she did not wish to be part of.

That always made Flora happy.

"Nay!" Lista nearly shouted. "God... nay, it does *not* please me. I do not even know Louis!"

"Most women do not know their husbands before they marry them," Flora said with limited patience. "I did not know Lord d'Orbec before I married him, but we came to know one another. You will come to know your husband, in time. That is the way of things, Lista. You must accept that."

Lista was still looking at her aunt in shock, emotions now joined by disbelief and rage. "Why are you telling me this?" she said. "This is not your place. You are nothing to me. Where is my mother?"

She tried to turn away, to search for her mother, but Flora snatched her by the wrist. "Your mother is sleeping," she said, squeezing with her clawed fingers. "I am speaking on her behalf and you will listen. No more foolery, Lista. You are too old for most men, so be grateful you have one who is interested. It is your duty to marry and I will ensure you do your duty."

Lista could sense bitterness and malintent. When it came to Flora, that was usual. She fed off of power, like she was at the moment as she delivered Lista's fate. She liked having the upper hand and that delight oozed from every pore.

But Lista yanked her wrist from the woman's grip.

"You have no right to ensure anything," she said, her voice lowered into a growl. "I called you a worthless cow once and that opinion still stands. You are nothing to me or to Felkington. All you do is eat our food and spend my mother's money and if I had my way, you'd be out begging on the street. You are wholly unworthy of me and my mother, so don't push me, Woman. I will push back."

Infuriated, Flora reached up and slapped her. Without missing a beat, Lista swung her open palm at her aunt's face and slapped the woman so hard that she fell sideways. As Flora gasped and tried to catch her balance, Lista shoved her down by the shoulder so that she ended up on the floor.

A gloating aunt was one thing. A physical attack was quite another.

"I told you I would push back," she seethed. "Strike me again and I will make it so you cannot get up the next time. Am I making myself clear?"

Flora was frightened. For the first time in her life, she was frightened of Lista. She hadn't expected the girl to strike her back and now that she'd felt the force of Lista's hit, she didn't want to experience another one. This was the second time Lista had hit her back and she realized it would continue. She rolled onto her knees, away from Lista, and struggled to her feet.

"It does not change the fact that de Rhos has permission to court you," she said, straightening her dress as she moved out of arm's length. "If the man has any courage, he will beat you into submission. You never did understand your place in the world."

"Nor did you," Lista said, her eyes tracking her aunt like a cat tracking a mouse. "Get out of my sight, Flora. I shall speak with my mother about this and then I shall speak with Louis. I do not know how or why this came about, but I will get to the bottom of it."

"And I hear my name."

The de Rhos knight chose that moment to come off the stairwell, coming up from the courtyard below. Flora saw him and immediately scattered, leaving Lista alone. Quickly realizing she was with a man who had permission to court her, Lista simply looked at him, emotionlessly.

Louis smiled timidly.

"Greetings, my lady," he said. "I hope I have not interrupted something."

Lista was having a difficult time not viewing him as the enemy at the moment, the embodiment of something she very much didn't want to do. They'd only just discussed her fondness for Julian hours earlier and Louis had told her that he would not encroach on that. He'd made it seem as if he were bowing out, a man of honor. But perhaps she'd been wrong.

Perhaps he'd only told her what he thought she wanted to hear.

Lista pondered all of the things she could say to him, the roundabout flirting, the meaningless chatter, but all she could really come up with was the truth.

The unbridled truth.

She wanted answers.

"My aunt has just informed me that my mother gave you permission to court me," she said. "Is this true?"

Louis was standing at the top of the stairs, making no effort to come any closer to her. He nodded without hesitation.

"It is, my lady."

"Would you mind telling me how this came about?"

He sighed, faintly, perhaps knowing she would ask that question at some point but not thinking it would be so soon. Worse still, she didn't sound pleased, which wasn't a surprise. Louis knew of her fondness for Julian, but that didn't change his sense of determination. He still intended to court her, Julian or no Julian.

He was careful in his approach.

"Have you been told that Julian saw me carrying you back to the castle when you slipped in the vineyard?" he asked.

Lista nodded. "I have."

"And you were told that he assumed we were carrying on behind his back."

Lista's hard stance wavered. "I have."

Louis cleared his throat softly and leaned against the wall. "I saw him in the stables not long ago as he was preparing to leave," he said. "He was... angry. Truth be told, it was unreasonably so. You and I had done nothing wrong, yet he would not believe that. His sister, Lady Addington, was present and she explained to me that Julian has been humiliated before, by people he considered his friends. He thought that we were behaving dishonorably. He told me that he would not be made a fool of."

Lista's stiff stance broke with that disturbing and rather heartbreaking information. She hobbled over to the nearest wall, leaning against it to take the pressure off her ankle.

"Addington told me," she finally said. "Julian has terrible self-confidence because of his different eye colors. Truthfully, that never mattered to me. Julian is kind and witty, but also quiet and introspective. He's a remarkable man, but the fact that he would not allow you or me to explain what he had witnessed is greatly offensive. He is too quick to judge."

Louis shrugged. "Mayhap," he said. "I do not even know the man, but he was quite willing to believe I was dishonorable. You, too. In fact, I do not even understand how all of this happened. It all started when your mother told me that you wanted to bid me a private farewell and then..."

Lista's head came up. "My *mother* told you?" she said, interrupting him. "She told you that, exactly?" Although he had already told her that, it was finally sinking in.

Louis nodded. "You were in the vineyard," he said. "Your

mother told me that you were waiting for me there."

Lista's eyes took on a glimmer of realization. "She sent me to the vineyard because she wanted grapes," she said, almost to herself. Then, the truth of the situation hit her. "God's Bones... she sent me to the vineyard and then she sent you to the vineyard under false pretenses."

Louis wasn't quite following her. "Then you did not wish to bid me farewell?"

Lista shook her head, but then she quickly nodded. "Of course, I would bid you farewell and thank you for your sword against the Scots," she said. "But never did I tell my mother that I wished to bid you a private farewell. She lied about that."

Now, Louis was coming to understand. "To throw us together."

"Exactly."

"And Julian saw it."

Lista put both hands to her mouth in shock, realizing the manipulation that had gone on. "I'm sure they liked Julian well enough as a suitor until you came along, as an earl's son," she said. "They set the stage to chase Julian away, making the path clear for you."

Louis shook his head at the level of deceit going on in this quiet corner of Northumberland. "Well, it worked," he said, somewhat exasperated. "Julian is gone, he accused me of lying to him, and I played right into your mother's hands."

Lista's focus lingered on him for a moment. "Then how did the permission for courtship come along?"

"I asked."

Lista processed his reply, and the situation, thinking that it probably wasn't her mother's doing as much as it was Flora's. The woman was sinister and manipulative, and now apparently out to control Lista's life.

She sighed heavily.

"Surely you see that you were manipulated into it," she said. "Surely you can see that this was a controlled situation. Louis, I will not hold you to your request. You were forced into making it."

He lifted his eyebrows. "Is that what you think? That I was manipulated?"

"Weren't you?"

Louis shook his head. "It seems so, but that wasn't entirely why I asked to court you," he said. "It was something Julian said – he told me that he would not be made a fool of and accused you of manipulating the both of us. When I tried to explain, he refused to listen. It wasn't so much the words as the tone... so incapable of understanding and forgiveness. So unwilling to give others the benefit of the doubt. It occurred to me that a man like that would make a miserable husband. He would make you miserable with his distrust. You told me once that you were fond of Julian and I respect that, but what I do not respect is the way Julian treated you. The way he treated *both* of us. He does not deserve you, my lady, and that is what changed my mind."

Lista could see his logic. It made perfect sense and some small part of her agreed with him. If Julian was truly so mistrustful of everyone, she would go the rest of her life with him walking on eggshells, fearing a time when she would make him suspicious. She'd been furious at him for leaving and thinking the worst of her, but time had a way of easing that anger. She'd only known Julian a short amount of time, but in that time, he'd given her something she'd never had before – genuine interest.

But he'd also taken something from her, as well – her heart.

The realization stumped her for a moment. She never thought of her heart as something to give, as so many young women did, but that was because she'd never met a man she considered giving it to.

That had all changed.

"I understand your position," she finally said. "And I am unhappy with Julian, too. I told Addington so. But if I remained hard and unforgiving, I would be just as bad as he was."

Louis shook his head. "Nay," he said. "You would be sensible."

"I am sure you see it that way."

"He is not coming back, Lista."

He used her Christian name without her formal title, hoping to emphasize his point, but Lista saw it as a manipulative move. Louis wanted her to stop thinking of Julian.

It wasn't that simple.

"What would you think of me if I told you that I could forget Julian immediately and accept your suit?" she said. "You would think I was a fickle, ungrateful creature who could give her affections away too easily. Is that truly the kind of woman you want?"

Louis shook his head. "Of course not," he said. "I realize it will take time. I do not expect you to accept my suit tomorrow or next week or even next month, but I will tell you here and now that when you are ready, I shall be here. I will wait for you, Lista. I believe you are a lady worth waiting for."

"How can you know that when you have only just met me?"

"Because I know a woman of character when I see her."

Those were kind words, but Lista wasn't sure she wanted to hear them. They didn't give her any comfort. If anything, they made her feel hurt and confused because something in those words signified the finality of Julian's departure.

He's not coming back.

Perhaps he wasn't, but Lista didn't want anyone else. Louis was a fine knight, but she didn't even want him at the moment. Perhaps with time that would change, but right now, her heart was with another and she wasn't even sure she could get it back. Her only hope was that Julian would cool down enough to realize he'd been wrong and he'd come back to her. She could pray for that, but it would be difficult with Louis hanging around, trying to pull her into his world.

She only wanted to be in Julian's world.

"I appreciate your candor, Louis," she finally said. "But I will ask something of you."

"Anything, my lady."

"Please leave me. I must have time alone to think and I cannot do that if you are around."

Louis didn't want to hear that but the gracious knight in him had him acquiescing. "If that is your wish," he said. "May I at least remain at Felkington?"

Lista didn't want to be cruel, but she really didn't want his interference. "If you promise to leave me alone until such time as I am more comfortable with your presence," she said. "But if that time never comes, I want your vow that you shall leave Felkington if I ask it of you, with no questions."

Louis hesitated a moment before nodding. "I will always do as you wish, my lady," he said. "No questions."

Lista smiled weakly, suddenly feeling fatigued and muddled. Her ankle was hurting and she wanted to lie down and think about the events the day had brought. She also wanted to think about her mother and aunt, trying very hard to orchestrate the world around them. *Her* world.

There was much to ponder.

"Thank you," Lista said. "Now, if you will excuse me, I will return to my chamber. I suppose standing on this ankle is more painful than I realized."

Louis came away from the wall. "May I lend assistance, my lady?"

Lista almost denied him but the truth was that she needed someone to lean on. Purely for the sake of practicality because if she didn't accept his help, she'd be hopping and limping all the way back to her chamber. Therefore, she gave a reluctant nod and held out her hand. But Louis bypassed her hand and scooped her up into his big arms, carrying her all the way back to her chamber.

Lista was not happy about it.

Louis was.

Somehow, Lista knew Louis wasn't going to give up so easily now that Julian was gone.

CHAPTER SIXTEEN

Pelinom Castle

H E WAS AT peace.
At least, that's what he told himself. But the truth was that he felt anything *but* peace. Here he was, at his ancestral home, the fortress where he was born, and he expected a certain amount of comfort from the place.

You are home now. Be at peace.

Those words kept rolling through his mind, over and over, as he tried to convince himself that he was where he needed to be. Not out and about in Berwick, or at an unfamiliar castle like Felkington with people he thought were his friends, but here where his family lived. People who never lied to him or humiliated him.

He was never going to leave again.

His jaunt from Felkington earlier in the day had been rather fast because Felkington wasn't far from Pelinom. It was less than a half-day's ride, so he'd made excellent time. He'd been greeted by his mother and, surprisingly, his sister, Effington and her husband, Rod. Then he'd been attacked by three nephews when he walked in the door, Effington's young sons Reid and Rigg, the twins, and their younger brother, Ross. Julian had wrestled with lads he'd not seen since they were very little but they seemed to have no fear in trying to take him down, which they very nearly did when Ross threw himself into the back of Julian's knees.

He could still hear his sister laughing.

Truth be told, it had been a marvelous way to be welcomed home. It had taken his mind off his troubles, but only briefly. For even now as he stood beneath the light of a three-quarter moon and watched the landscape beyond the walls of Pelinom, he could only think of one thing.

Lista.

He was coming to regret fleeing Felkington without telling her what he thought of her and her games. That magnificent woman who had held his face in her hands and had told him she thought his eyes were beautiful. Like a fool, he'd believed her. He *wanted* to believe her. He wanted to believe that some woman, somewhere, would find him attractive with his oddly colored eyes and that name that still made some people whisper with fear.

De Velt.

The Dark Lord.

Mostly, he was angry at himself for letting his guard down, for believing the lies he shouldn't have believed. He was angry at himself for making a friend of Louis, who turned out not to be a friend at all. It seemed that all men were alike, liars or cads or both. The only men who weren't like that were family members and close friends, like Ashton and Anteaus. Never again would he trust anyone else.

Looking up in the night sky, he found himself speaking to

the heavens, as he so often did.

"Papa," he murmured. "Mama says you watch over us all and I'd like to believe that, but I'm embarrassed that you saw that I allowed myself to be made a fool of. I wish you were here to tell me what to do, to make me feel better about the situation. But the truth is that I'm not even sure you could work your magic this time."

A soft breeze blew across the land, up the walls of Pelinom, lifting the hair that draped down over his right eye. Julian leaned against the wall, looking out over the landscape below.

"I thought she was the one I would marry," he said. "She was a remarkable woman, Papa. Beautiful, kind, intelligent. At least, I thought she was remarkable. She told me that she liked my eyes and everything else about me. I let her lull me into a false sense of security. I trusted her and that trust was rewarded with betrayal."

"I was wondering why you came home from Felkington so soon. Now, I know."

Startled, Julian looked up to see his mother standing a few feet away. She'd come up the stairs and onto the wall walk and he never even heard her. Slightly embarrassed, he averted his gaze.

"I wasn't trying to be mysterious," he said. "I simply wasn't ready to speak on it."

Wrapped in a heavy shawl against the damp night, Kellington came close, her fair face illuminated by the torchlight dotting the wall.

"Yet you told your father," she pointed out. "Even if he cannot answer you, he is listening. He is always listening."

Julian nodded. "I know," he said. Then, he looked up into the sky again. "It's strange. I feel his presence more heavily here, on the wall. Mayhap it is because it is taller and closer to heaven, but I feel closer to him here. He was always willing to listen to my troubles."

Kellington's lips curved with the hint of a smile. "You had many troubles, Julian," she said. "From the moment you were born, you had troubles. You were born early, you know."

"I know."

"I had been chasing Cole around and your father insisted I rest, but I would not listen," she said. "Cole ran out into the kitchen yard and as I came through the door, I slipped in mud from the rain we'd had the night before. I did not fall, but I strained myself. I could feel pain in my belly but I did not think anything of it until the middle of the night when you were demanding to be born. Papa did not have time to summon the physic, you came so quickly, out into his waiting hands. Did you know that? He was the first person to hold you, Julian. Next to me, you were the last person to hold him in return. I find that poignant."

Julian looked at her, great sorrow in his eyes. "I had not thought of it that way," he said. Then he sighed heavily and hung his head. "I fear all I've done is make a mockery of myself, Mama. Papa had such profound words for me before he passed and I've not been able to do as he asked. I do not know why... mayhap I am unable to. I really do not know."

Kellington reached up, putting a gentle hand on her boy's head. "What did he ask of you, Julian?"

"To find the greatness within myself."

"Did you ever stop to think that greatness is not what you think it means?"

He turned his head, looking at her. "What do you mean?"

Kellington shrugged as she pulled her shawl more tightly

around her body. "Greatness can mean many things," she said. "It can mean perfection in battle or the love of your family. It can mean the love of a good woman or simply finding satisfaction with yourself. I think your papa meant that you needed to find *your* greatness... not anyone else's idea of it or their expectations of what it might mean, but yours alone. Does that make sense?"

Julian nodded as he thought on it. His mother always had a way of putting things so that he could understand. "It does."

She smiled faintly. "You have always put so much pressure on yourself to be perfect," she said. "I do not think you realized that, to your father, you *were* perfect. You just never saw it in yourself. That was why he told you that you must find your greatness when he really meant that you must find your happiness. You must find what makes you the happiest – no matter what anyone else thinks."

Julian sighed heavily, his gaze moving to the landscape below, the road that led to Pelinom's gatehouse. "I thought I had found it," he said. "I thought Lady Lista was perfect for me and that we would be happy together."

"What happened?"

His lips twisted into a wry expression. "She made a fool of me."

"How did she do this?"

He sighed sharply, starting to feel some angst. "Because there was another knight at Felkington," he said. "His name is Louis de Rhos and he is the son of the Earl of Sunderland."

"Sunderland?" Kellington repeated, recognizing the name. "Then his brother must be Ren de Rhos, the knight who married Audrie de Longley."

Julian nodded. "It is," he said. "Louis and I acknowledged

that we both knew his brother had married the woman intended for my brother. In fact, I liked Louis. I thought he was an honorable and witty man. I enjoyed speaking to him and thought I'd made a friend."

"Then what happened?"

Julian rolled his eyes and looked away. "I went to find Lista this morning, at the request of her mother, and I found her in Louis' arms."

Kellington nodded faintly, realizing the situation. Or, so she thought. "I see," she said. "Lista had fallen for de Rhos?"

Julian shrugged. "I suppose," he said. "I did not ask. I saw what I saw and I left. There was no longer any reason for me to remain at Felkington."

Kellington frowned. "You did not ask?"

Julian wouldn't look at her. "Why should I?" he said. "I know what I saw. Lista was in Louis' arms and that is all I needed to see."

The shouts from the sentries suddenly went up, piercing the night air. Julian looked to the road leading up to the gatehouse purely out of habit and could see two riders approaching, followed closely by at least forty men. He wasn't close enough to see who they were but those at the gatehouse evidently recognized them because men on horseback and with torches rode out to greet them. As they came closer, it occurred to Julian that one of the riders was a woman.

"I think that's Addie," he told his mother. "I told Ashton to bring her home immediately."

He moved away from the wall, heading towards the stairwell with his mother behind him.

"Did Addie see any of this?" Kellington asked. "Lista and de Rhos, I mean. Does she know?"

Julian took the first steps down the steep spiral stairs that led down to the bailey, but he held out his hand for his mother.

"She knows," Julian said, taking his mother's hand and steadying her down the stairs. "She came to me after it happened."

"What did she say?"

Julian didn't want to answer her. He'd spoken about the situation as much as he wanted to because the return of Addington and knowing how she tried to talk him out of leaving Felkington was weighing heavily on him. Truthfully, he didn't want to see his sister.

He didn't want to hear her version of events again.

"You'll have to ask her," he said as they reached the bottom and he let go of her hand. "I'm weary, Mama. I shall retire for the evening and see you on the morrow."

Kellington called after him but he kept walking just as Addington and Ashton rode in through the great gates of Pelinom, followed by their escort. Kellington watched her son as he headed for the keep before turning her attention to her daughter as the woman brought her steed to a halt and dismounted. Addington spied her mother and made her way toward her, but Kellington simply stood where Julian had left her, lost in thought. Perhaps the only other person who could tell her what had happened had just arrived and she was going to get to the bottom of the situation.

Something told her that all was not as it seemed.

"IT'S NOT TRUE, Mama," Addington said. "Julian thinks he

knows what he saw, but that's not what happened at all."

Kellington had the courtesy to wait until Addington came into the keep before pulling her into the old solar that had once belonged to Kellington's father, Keats. Jax had left his mark on it over the years, but it had become Kellington's retreat now that the males of the family had passed on. Now, she faced her youngest daughter with the simple question of what had transpired at Felkington.

What Addington said did not surprise her.

"Then tell me everything," she said.

Addington was reluctant to tattle on her brother, but she did as she was asked. She knew it was for his own good.

"This morning, Julian saw Lady Lista in the arms of another knight," she said. "His name is Louis de Rhos and he is the son of the Earl of Sunderland."

Kellington nodded. "I know," she said. "Julian told me of him."

"He seems like a good man, Mama," Addington insisted softly. "He helped Julian fend off a Scots raid and he was kind and polite. I do not think poorly of him at all. But Julian saw him with Lista in his arms this morning and when I asked Lista what happened, she told me that she had twisted her ankle in the mud and Louis was carrying her into the keep. Louis said the same thing – that Lista hurt herself and he was helping her. It was not a passionate embrace that Julian saw, but one of assistance. Still, he does not believe it. He refuses to."

Kellington digested the information, an expression of distress crossing her features. "I was afraid of that," she said, sinking into a chair that had once belonged to her husband. It dwarfed her as she sat in it. "Julian has never been one to stand up to something hurtful. He learned that as a young lad. He would simply walk away from the situation rather than confront it. Your father tried to convince him to stand up for himself and to fight those who would persecute him, but Julian never did. He felt that it was safer to ignore it, to walk away from it."

Addington went to her mother, kneeling down beside the chair. "Julian is *not* a coward," she said. "Lista was very hurt when she realized Julian's misconception of the situation and she said... well, I know he is not a coward. I told her so. I think he was falling in love with Lista, Mama. I know she was falling in love with him. She is a good woman with a good heart and she only saw the good in Julian. But he's hurt her terribly with his behavior. She feels that if he really cared for her, then he would have asked her to clarify what he saw with Louis."

Kellington reached out, stroking her daughter's dark head. "But he ran instead."

"He did. I had to come home quickly to try to fix the damage done. We left your carriage at Felkington so we could move faster."

Kellington sighed faintly, thinking on her second-eldest child and his fragile heart. "The carriage is of no concern. Julian is a man grown now and has been for years," she said. "It is time he stopped behaving like that bullied squire. Addie, have a servant summon Julian to my solar. I will speak with him."

Addington nodded, scurrying off to find a servant, who was never very far away from the heart of Pelinom, the very solar that had been witness to so many battles and deeds and transitions. She returned quickly only to find her mother seated behind the big table where her father, and grandfather, used to conduct their business. Kellington had a vellum in her hand, reading it.

"I sent for him, Mama," she said. "Shall I remain?"

Kellington nodded, still looking at the vellum. "You shall," she said. "Where is Ashton?"

"I do not know."

"Send for him, also," Kellington said. "He met the de Rhos knight?"

"He did."

"Then I want him here, too."

Addington sent for Ashton, settling back into the solar in tense silence as her mother seemed to be occupied with whatever was on the table. The door to the solar was cracked open and they could hear the servants moving around, going about their business, but they also heard her sister's voice. No voice carried like Effington's. Addington pushed the door open, catching her sister's attention.

"Effie," she hissed, waving to her. "Come here."

Effington had her twins with her, one in each hand, and the boys weren't happy about it. When one of them tugged, trying to escape, she grabbed the boy by the ear and he howled.

"Do you know what these two have been up to?" she asked, aghast. "Stealing from some of the soldiers! Ross is the scout while Reid and Rigg rob them blind."

Addington bit her lip to keep from laughing at her naughty nephews, who were defiant to the end. "Where is Ross?" she said, trying not to grin.

Effington cocked a dark eyebrow. "Rod is taking a switch to him out in the yard," she said. "He ran from his father and that guarantees a fatherly beating."

"You'll not beat my grandchildren, Effie."

Kellington had spoken from behind her table, her voice rising from the solar like the Voice of Doom. Effington and

Addington looked at each other, grinning.

"Just a little one, Mama," Effington called into the chamber. "He shall not suffer overly, I promise."

"I will ask Ross and if he tells me otherwise, then you had better tell Rod to hide from me until my anger has abated."

Effington and Addington broke down into soft giggles just as Rod de Titouan, Effington's husband, entered the keep with a small boy in tow. Rod was tall, excruciatingly handsome, with wavy, black hair and bright blue eyes. He also had an easy smile, something that appeared the moment he saw his wife.

"Ross has convinced me that a beating will do no good," he said, referring to his six-year-old son. "You'd think after six boys, the youngest one would not be smarter than I am, but he evidently is. I have agreed not to punish him this time."

That gave hope to Reid and Rigg, who looked at their father with great anticipation. But their mother wasn't of the same opinion.

"They have three older brothers who have taught them to be thieves and scoundrels," she told her husband. "Rafe, Reese, and Roan have taught their younger brothers terrible things and you do nothing about it, so it is left to me to do the discipline."

By this time, Reid and Rigg had gravitated over to their father, hiding behind him as their angry mother scolded him. But Rod did what he so often did; he simply smiled and took Effington into his arms, embracing her sweetly as she resisted him. She didn't want to be held, not even by her handsome husband, who laughed as she tried to push him away.

As this was going on, Julian emerged from the stairwell, having been summoned to his mother's solar, and the younger de Titouan boys rushed him purely out of habit. Julian saw them coming and tried to protect his knees, but Ross got in behind him again and he ended up pitching forward as Reid and Rigg pulled him down. At nine years of age, they were big for their age and strong as well. Julian ended up grabbing the twins by the hair as he stood up, staggering because Ross was punching the back of his knees.

"Effie," he said severely. "Control these wild animals you have produced or I shall cage them."

Effington was still trying to pull away from her husband. "Then cage them," she said. "It would serve them right since their father will do nothing about it."

Julian didn't have time to lock the boys up, so he dragged them over to their parents, forcing Rod to let go of Effington. He shoved the boys at them, slipping past and into the solar as Addington ran after him. She was the last one in the chamber, shutting the door and bolting it, listening to the de Titouan boys yell and pound on the door because they wanted in.

Julian shook his head.

"Effie is going to have trouble with them when they get older if she does not discipline them now," he said, rubbing at the back of his right thigh where Ross had pounded him. "Those three are monsters."

"They are the grandsons of Ajax de Velt," Kellington said. "Did you expect them to be docile creatures?"

She had a point. Julian fought off a grin as he finished rubbing at his sore leg. "Probably not," he said. "But I think I am crippled."

"You'll survive."

That was as much sympathy as he was going to get and he rolled his eyes, changing the subject. "I was told you wished to speak with me."

Kellington nodded, sitting back in her chair and fixing her

son in the eyes. "I do," she said. "This is a continuation of our conversation from the wall walk."

Julian couldn't help but notice that Addington was still in the chamber. He cast her a long look, suspecting immediately what it was all about. She never could keep her lips shut. With an unhappy grunt, he turned to his mother.

"I have said all I wish to say about it," he said. "I mean no disrespect, Mama, but I do not wish to discuss this further."

He started to move to the door but a few words from Kellington stopped him. "But I do," she said firmly. "Sit down, Julian. Please."

He paused and, sighing heavily, moved for the nearest chair. Addington tried to stay away from him even though she knew he would never harm her in any fashion, but an angry Julian was a frightening thing. She didn't want him pulling hair or pinching, as he used to do when they were young.

He still wasn't beyond such things at times.

"What is it?" he said as he sank back in the chair, putting fingers to his forehead as if to rub away the headache that was sure to come. "Say what you will and get it over with."

Kellington watched her son as he massaged his forehead, his unhappiness at the subject matter radiating from him like a fog. "I have heard your side of the story regarding what happened at Felkington," she said. "I have heard what Addie has to say, also, and I must say that the two versions differ tremendously."

Julian sighed sharply. "What does it matter?" he said, looking to both his mother and his sister. "What does any of this matter? It is my life and I do not need or want any interference."

He caught Addington's eyes and she frowned. "Julian, I do not understand how you cannot admit when you are wrong," she said. "You thought you saw Lista and Louis in an embrace and I told you that he was carrying her because she hurt her ankle. That is the only reason he had her in his arms – so he could help her. What was he supposed to do? Leave her on the ground?"

Julian's jaw ticked dangerously. "I've heard the lies before, Addie," he growled. "I will not believe them again."

"Even if they are the truth?" Addington fired back. "You are blind, Julian, and what's worse is that your foolishness is of your own making. You created this misery for yourself because you created a situation in your mind that does not exist."

"You don't know what you're talking about."

"Neither do *you*!" Addington said. "That's the problem – neither do you but you're too stubborn to admit it!"

Julian looked at her, his eyes flashing. "Don't tell me what to think."

"Lista was falling in love with you, you idiot!"

They were starting to shout and Kellington put her hand up to silence them both. Frustrated, Addington turned away while Julian sat there and clenched his teeth.

"Julian," Kellington said quietly. "A wise and reasonable man would have asked for an explanation of what he saw. Addie seems to think that Lista and Louis de Rhos are honorable people. Would they not tell you the truth if you asked?"

Julian wouldn't look at her. "Why should they?" he said. "There is sport in making me the butt of jokes."

"But how would they know that?" Kellington said. "More importantly, what do they have to gain by doing it? You seem to think they are out to punish you or humiliate you for some reason, but my question would be why? What would be their motivation?"

Julian hissed and stood up, abruptly. "You just do not understand."

"Sit down, Julian."

It was not a request. Julian sat back down but he perched on the edge of the chair, refusing to look at his mother.

"As I was saying," Kellington continued. "They have no reason to make a fool of you. Addie says that Lady Lista is falling in love with you, so why would she want to humiliate you? When you were told she'd hurt her ankle, did you even look after her to see if she was well? She could have hurt herself quite badly and de Rhos was the only one available to help her. Does that mean they were deliberately trying to humiliate you?"

Julian's jaw ticked faintly. "Mayhap not."

Kellington leaned forward, folding her hands on the tabletop. "Tell me exactly what you saw that led you to believe they were carrying on behind your back."

Julian was starting to calm but he was still grinding his teeth. He didn't want to answer his mother, but he knew that wouldn't end well. She'd break him down and force him to answer in the end. Therefore, it was easier to simply get it over with.

"I came through the garden gate," he muttered. "There is an archway in the garden that leads to the vineyard. Through that archway, I could see them with their arms around each other."

"Were they standing?"

"De Rhos was."

"Where was Lady Lista?"

Julian shrugged. "At his feet," he said. "Mayhap she was sitting."

"Or mayhap he was picking her up from the ground where she fell."

Julian didn't say anything. He didn't have to because the logic was sound. He knew it so there was no sense fighting it. Kellington watched her son's profile for a moment.

"Julian, I know you've been bullied in your life," she said quietly. "I know there are people who have betrayed you and I know that is why you protect yourself. But you are going to protect yourself into a celibate and lonely life. I know it is difficult to trust people, but you must learn to do that. You must learn that not everyone is out to hurt you. I do not believe Lady Lista or Sir Louis were out to hurt you, but by your behavior towards them, you have hurt them a great deal. You have become the very thing you hate – rigid, cruel, and judgmental. Do you understand that?"

Julian shook his head, briefly, closing his eyes as if there were a sharp pain somewhere in his torso. His entire face rippled with pain.

"I know what I saw," he finally said.

"Do you?" Kellington fired back softly. "Or did you just assume?"

He did look at her, then. "I saw the woman I wanted to court in the arms of another man," he said. "I'd lowered my guard and was knocked back for having that trust. Now you are telling me I must learn to trust people?"

Kellington could see he wasn't going to relinquish what he considered the last vestiges of his control over his version of events. "You are trying so hard to protect yourself that you are going to strangle yourself with your good intentions," she said. "Long ago, your father had to learn to trust me. He'd grown up not trusting anyone, so it was very difficult for him. But he did not regret it. As it turned out, it was the best thing he ever did. All I am asking you to do is give Lady Lista that same opportunity."

"I may regret it."

"You may *not* regret it, too. Is she not worth the risk?"

Julian's focus drifted to Lista. He'd tried so hard not to think of her that when thoughts of her came flooding back, so did the angst and confusion and hope. So many things swirling in his chest. He could see Lista's smile and hear her laughter, the silly way she had of flirting with him that made him feel giddy. Like he was the only man in the world.

Was regaining all of that worth the risk?

It was.

But he was terrified.

"I thought she was worth everything," he finally said. "I was willing to risk everything. In a sense, I did. I let her get under my skin and I've never let anyone do that before."

Addington, listening to what seemed like a break in Julian's harsh stance, stepped forward.

"Julian, you know I would never lie to you," she said beseechingly. "Have I not always been your greatest protector?"

Julian looked at his younger sister. They were very close and he knew her heart, and she had always been fiercely protective of him. She was annoying and pesky at times, but she loved him.

He knew that.

"You have," he said.

"Then believe me when I say that if I thought for one moment that Lista and Louis were lying, I would be the first one to condemn them," she said. "I would tell you to run away and stay away. I would do what Papa did and put them on pikes so the birds could pluck out their eyeballs. Therefore, please believe me when I say that I believed them when they said nothing untoward happened. Lista hurt her ankle and Louis was simply helping her. I would not tell you this if it were not true."

Julian's gaze lingered on her and he could feel his guard lowering. As much as he wanted to continue his stubborn stance, even he knew that it was only because he was hurt. Shocked by what he had seen, he'd assumed the worst. That was the bullied, frightened young boy in him. The one who didn't want to be hurt again and again.

But maybe that young boy had been wrong this time.

The realization made him feel sick.

"You know that I trust you, Addie," he finally said, unable to look at her. "I know you would not deceive me."

"Nay, I would not."

He looked at her then. His broad shoulders lifted helplessly. "What should I do now?"

Addington breathed a sigh of relief, looking to her mother for guidance, but Kellington was fixed on Julian.

"Go back to Felkington," Kellington said without hesitation. "Go back and apologize for behaving rashly. Even if she does not accept your apology, at least you made it. That is what a mature, reasonable man would do. It is what your father would have done."

Now that Julian had realized he may have been wrong, all he could feel was remorse. Remorse and the slightest bit of panic. Addington had been absolutely right – he had been feeling something for Lista, probably more than he realized, which was why he had reacted so badly.

"Leave when the sun rises," Addington said. "I spoke to Louis after you left... he was very offended, Julian. He said that you did not deserve Lista and I fear that his resentment will cause him to pursue her even though he told you that he would not, so you cannot wait. You must return as soon as possible."

Julian looked at her. "What else did he say?"

Addington was reluctant to tell him. "I said that you were a good man," she said. "I told him that you had been hurt before and you were keen to protect yourself, but he said a good man would not have done what you did. A good man would not have been so quick to judge."

Julian's gaze lingered on her for a moment before he finally shook his head. "And he would be correct," he said quietly. "A wise man would not have reacted so abruptly, but I am not yet a wise man. I can be rash and stupid. Mama, I think you were right."

Kellington stood up from her chair. "About what?"

Julian watched her come around the end of the table. "You said that when Papa told me that I must find my greatness, mayhap he really meant that I must find my happiness," he said. "I do not know why that never occurred to me. I always thought he meant becoming the greatest warrior in the north, a great leader, someone well-esteemed like Cole. But mayhap that's not where I shall find my greatness. My path is different from my brother's."

"Indeed, it is," Kellington said. "If you realize that, then you are indeed growing as a man. That is all your father wanted for you, Julian. To not be afraid of *life*. To embrace it and to find your happiness. Even if it is not with Lista, you must give yourself that chance and not be afraid of it."

Julian hung his head even as he nodded. "I realize that," he said. Then he forced a smile, but it was a nervous smile. "It is difficult to allow myself to be vulnerable. I will admit that to you, but to no one else. You have always seemed to understand me better than Papa ever did."

Kellington put her hand on his cheek. "He understood you more than you know," she said. "You are his son with a tender heart, deep feeling and compassionate. Cole and Cassian cannot claim that, but you can. Whatever your greatness is, Julian, I have confidence that you will find it. Mayhap it is at Felkington. You will never know unless you try."

Julian nodded. Kellington kissed him on the cheek and left the solar, leaving Addington still there, still watching her brother, who seemed to be summoning his courage to return to Felkington and face what he had done.

She took a few steps towards him.

"Do you want me to go with you?" she asked. "Back to Felkington?"

Julian turned to her. "Nay," he said, though he was smiling. "Ever my champion, Addie, but I must do this on my own."

Addington smiled at him. "May I give you some advice?"

"Why not?"

Addington sobered. "Appeal to Lista," she said softly. "I do believe she is falling in love with you, so appeal to her growing feelings for you. Show her what I know – show her what a good man you are. I know she will make you happy, Julian. You must give her that chance."

He sobered, too. "I will," he said. "And thank you… for everything, Addie. I do not know where I would be without you."

Addington grinned as she turned away. "Lonely and bitter," she said. "No one else will pester you like I do until you have a wife, although Mama will try. But she does not pester as well as I do."

"That is very true. You are annoying."

"And you are dense."

"I love you, Addie."

Addington paused at the chamber door, giggling. "And I love you," she said. "But you are an idiot sometimes."

Julian just stood there and chuckled because she was quite correct. He really *was* an idiot sometimes. But he intended to change that if he could.

If Lista would allow it.

He was going to find out.

CHAPTER SEVENTEEN

Felkington Castle

"IT SEEMS TO me that you two have manipulated this entire situation," Lista said. "You saw Julian and Louis as potential suitors for me and then you somehow manipulated the circumstances so that one or both would ask to court me."

She was standing in the doorway of that filthy, smelly tower chamber, glaring at her mother and aunt, who were gazing back at her in various stages of bewilderment and defiance. At least, Meadow appeared bewildered while Flora seemed defiant.

The woman didn't bend easily when it came to her niece.

"If you had done your duty as the daughter of the House of de la Mere, we would not have had to manipulate anything," Flora said. "Do not blame us for your lack of duty, Lista. Be fortunate that we found two viable candidates. Now, you have the son of an earl who wishes to court you and any normal girl would be thrilled at the prospect."

After speaking to Louis, Lista knew her aunt and mother had arranged that entire encounter in the vineyard but hearing her aunt confess to it made her blood boil.

"I should have suspected," she said coldly. "It did not occur to me when Louis came to the vineyard and said that he'd been told I wanted to bid him a private farewell, but it should have. I should have known you were behind the entire event that sent Julian fleeing from Felkington."

Flora snorted and turned back to her jumble of pillows on the floor. "Then he is unworthy," she said. "Only the strongest shall survive and that is Louis, the earl's son. He has permission to court you so I suggest you get on with it. Your mother and I are eager to return to the grandeur that we are used to, so do your duty. Marry the earl's son."

Lista thought that was an odd comment and she peered at her aunt as the woman plopped down on her collection of dirty pillows.

"Grandeur that you're used to?" she repeated in confusion. "What does that mean?"

"What do you think it means?" Flora said as she lay back and put her arm over her eyes. "Our mother was the daughter of an earl. You are aware that your mother and I spent our early years at court, something you did not do so you do not know what you are missing. It is time we reclaim our social status and the Sunderland son will accomplish that. Your husband's father will be a well-placed man and that will get us into the finest houses in England."

Lista couldn't believe what she was hearing. "So this was a ploy for you to regain social standing?" she said, appalled. "Is that what you are telling me?"

"A de Velt is good enough, but he is only the son of a great battle lord," Flora said. "The family is prominent, but there is no grand title. No earldom. De Rhos is perfect if you will only do as you are told. He does not seem like an unpleasant man and he is handsome. It should please you that he is interested in you."

Lista stared at her aunt in disbelief but it also occurred to her that Flora was the only one talking. So far, her mother had remained silent so she turned to Meadow, who was sitting on a small chair, dazed because of all the hemp smoke she'd inhaled. Lista moved so that she was in her mother's line of sight.

"Do you hear what she is saying?" she asked. "Is this why you gave permission to Louis to court me? Because you wanted social standing?"

Meadow looked at her daughter as if she didn't understand the question. Then she abruptly nodded her head. "De Rhos seems pleasant enough," she said. "Don't you like him?"

Lista was quickly becoming exasperated. "He's very nice, but I do not want to marry him," she said. "I want to marry Julian but your little plan chased him out of Felkington. He saw me and Louis together and he thought… Mama, did you come up with this scheme? Or was it Flora?"

Meadow blinked as if startled by the question. She looked nervously at Flora, who by now was sitting up again and glaring at her ungrateful niece.

"We thought…" Meadow said, stammering. "There were two eligible knights and you must marry, Lista. I wanted to speak to you about it but I gave my permission for Louis to court you. He asked first. He seems like a nice enough man and he is the son of an earl."

Lista listened to her mother stutter over her words, knowing immediately that her mother more than likely had been bullied into giving her permission. If, in fact, she even gave it at all. Flora was known to tell the servants and even Lista that she had a directive from Meadow when, in fact, her mother knew nothing about it. The whole situation was convoluted but Lista knew one thing – Flora was behind it. That little comment about reclaiming their social status clued her in. Flora had seen an opportunity with Louis. Now, her ambition was showing.

Lista's rage began to build.

"I will not be forced into marriage by anyone," Lista finally said, mostly to Flora. "It is Julian I want, not Louis. At least, I did want Julian but now… now, whatever scheme you've tried to bring about has ruined everything and I'm not entirely sure I shall ever forgive you for that. Julian was kind and considerate and there was something about him that I found endearing and attractive. Now you've made it so he's gone home and he'll never come back, but that does not mean I want the earl's son. I'm not sure I want anyone at all."

"You are going to be a spinster if you do not marry soon," Flora said. "Stop being stubborn and understand your duty, Girl. Your mother wishes for you to marry."

Lista whirled on her aunt. "I want to be very clear to you so you understand what will happen when I marry," she said through clenched teeth. "Be it a pauper's son, a warlord's son, or the son of a king, I will make sure you are nowhere near me. If you show yourself, I will have the guards throw you in the vault and toss the key in the nearest river. What I do will not elevate you in any way. I have told you this before, Flora – I owe you nothing. You mean nothing to me. And you shall get nothing from me no matter how much you try to manipulate the situation. Is this in any way unclear?"

Flora's mouth worked as if she wanted to say something but she ended up falling back on the pillows, grumbling about her ungrateful niece. Lista's gaze lingered on the woman for a moment, waiting for her to get up and start arguing, but she remained on the floor.

Lista finally turned to her mother.

"Stop allowing Flora to make your decisions for you," she said. "Send her back to The Filey, Mama. Send her home. She has done nothing but drag you down into her pit of despair since Simon's death and although I am sorry for what happened to my brother, you and I can get along without him. And without Flora. So please send her home before she ruins your life and my life along with yours. She's already caused Amaury's death. What more will she do before you realize how terrible she is? *Please*, Mama."

Meadow smiled tremulously at her daughter, reaching out to grasp her hand. Lista took it, squeezing it tightly, but even as she did so she knew that her mother would never send Flora home. Flora was too strong for her, too demanding, and Meadow submitted to her every time. That left Lista defending her mother and all of Felkington against her mother's ambitious sister, which was only growing worse as the days passed. Until Julian de Velt appeared a few days ago, Flora was relatively benign, but now... now, she had a taste of what her life could be like should her niece marry well. And Amaury, once an ally against Flora, was gone.

Now, Lista had a reckless woman on her hands and if she wasn't careful, Flora was going to make a bargain that Lista wouldn't be able to get out of. Perhaps she already had.

It was time for a heartfelt discussion with Louis.

Leaving her mother and Flora wallowing in the last of their hemp smoke, she quit the chamber and went in search of the earl's son.

LOUIS KNEW THAT Lista wasn't happy about the situation.

Standing on the roof of Felkington's enormous structure, he was looking up at the stars and thinking of the Felkington heiress stashed in a quiet corner of Northumberland. It wasn't as if he had a problem finding women – quite the contrary. He had a few he was fond of, and one lass in Lincoln in particular, but there was something about Lista that had his attention.

Truthfully, he wasn't sure what it was. He was coming to wonder if it was the competition with Julian that had spurred his interest. Certainly, a woman sought after by another knight was a woman worth having. He might have believed that it was only because of the competition but for the fact that he felt something when he looked in Lista's eyes. What beautiful eyes they were. He wasn't quite sure why she seemed to make him the slightest bit giddy, but she did. Coupled with the fact that she was intelligent and witty, she was a rare jewel, indeed.

But he was fairly certain she wasn't keen on him.

It was because of Julian and he was well aware. She'd told him she was fond of Julian, so that was established. De Velt was a god among men and certainly from one of the most important families in the north, so Julian de Velt had much to offer to a potential wife and Louis had a great deal of respect for him in that regard.

Truth be told, he was rather disappointed with the way things had worked out with Julian. He thought he'd made a friend in the man and was disappointed to realize that had been ruined. He'd come to like the big man with the quiet wit. When

Julian's sister had tried to defend his actions, Louis had told her that a good man wouldn't have behaved the way Julian had behaved, by assuming a situation before he knew the facts, but that wasn't entirely true. It wasn't like Louis' behavior was perfect.

He certainly couldn't cast the first stone.

Still, he had permission to court Lista and he didn't take that lightly, but he knew he had a task ahead of him making her forget about Julian and having her focus on him. He knew he could do it given time, and hopefully her willingness, and he felt strongly that this was something he wanted very much. Whether or not Julian deserved her was immaterial.

It boiled down to the fact that Louis wanted her.

"I was told you were up here." Lista suddenly appeared from the stairwell, her soft voice breaking into his thoughts. When Louis turned to look at her, she smiled politely. "Although I admire your sense of duty, I'm not entirely sure the night watch is your responsibility. Looking for more Scots?"

He grinned. "One can never tell," he said. "There were a few grapes left on the vines. They might return for those. You never know."

Lista's smile turned genuine. "Quite true," she said. "They might return for the last apple or the last grape. We have a cherry tree at the edge of the garden, so surely, they would want to strip that, too."

He was leaning on the wall, looking at her over his shoulder. "Are the cherries ripe?"

"Almost."

"I like cherry pudding. I just thought you should know."

Lista chuckled. "They will give you a bellyache if you eat them now," she said. "Cherry pudding will have to wait."

"I can wait."

It was a statement with many different meanings. Lista sensed that right away because her smile faded. With a sigh, she leaned against the wall a few feet away from him.

"Louis, I think we must talk," she said. "I have just come from my aunt and mother."

He nodded. "I see," he said. "And how are Lady Felkington and Lady d'Orbec?"

Lista shrugged. "How are they ever?" she said. "Inhaling hemp leaf smoke. Or sometimes, it's eating the fungus that grows in the forest. Other times, it's licking the green moss on the walls in the hope it will give them visions or make them giddy. I could go on and on, but suffice it to say they will never change. Any husband I have will need to accept that burden and it is too much to bear."

Louis grunted softly as he returned his attention to the silver-cast landscape. "Don't you think he should be the one to make that decision?"

Lista shook her head. "Nay," she said. "I do not think he should. I think *I* should. Louis, you may as well know that the only reason my mother and aunt wish for me to marry you is so that they can re-establish their social standing. That is all they want you for, I am sorry to say, and that is unfair to you. You are a man of integrity and kindness and you deserve far better than the ravaged baggage I would bring with me."

He looked at her again. "Do you try to scare me?"

"I try to warn you."

"I do not need to be warned," he said. "I am a grown man. I understand this situation. Your aunt is a desperate woman, desperate enough to give me permission to court you when I suspect your mother did not."

"How did you know?"

He shrugged. "Call it a suspicion," he said. "Was she like this with de Velt?"

Lista shook her head. "Not at all," she said. "Mayhap she simply didn't have time. We had not known Julian long before you appeared. All she had to hear was that you were the son of the Earl of Sunderland and you became her prime objective."

Louis scratched his neck pensively. "I am not troubled by the Lady d'Orbecs of this world," he said. "It does not change my interest in you. I am still very interested in courting you but, of course, given the fact that your mother did not give her permission, I will seek yours instead. I realize you had your heart set on Julian, my lady, but all I ask is that you give me a fair chance, too. I promise I will not disappoint you."

It was an earnest plea. Lista found herself looking at him, his handsome face beneath the moonlight, but try as she might, she simply couldn't feel any inclination to agree with him. Had there never been a Julian, she could easily see herself being agreeable towards him. But Julian was a ghost between them, a ghost that would never leave. Although she hadn't known him for very long, the man had marked her enough so that she knew she wouldn't be able to easily forget him. If at all.

Sighing heavily, she averted her gaze and leaned back against the wall.

"I simply do not know," she said honestly. "All of this has happened so quickly. I do not know what I am feeling or what I am thinking other than I am extremely disappointed and sad that Julian left. I am quite fond of him."

"Do you love him?"

It was a blunt question. Lista lifted her head, turning to look at him. "Don't you think that's between Julian and me?" she said softly.

But Louis shook his head. "Nay," he said. "I have a stake in this, too. I think it is a quite reasonable question given the circumstances."

He said it rather firmly. Lista could see that he meant it and she struggled to come up with an answer.

"I do not know the answer to that question," she finally said. "All I know is that Julian is in my thoughts every moment of every hour, every hour of every day. He was hurtful when he left and I'll not deny it, but I've had time to think on it. I cannot say that if I hadn't come upon him with some woman in his arms, no matter how innocent, that I might not have reacted in the same fashion. I do not think you can say that, either – where the heart is concerned, we're all fragile. The heart is the most valuable part of us and if it is wounded, we weaken. If it is broken, we die. Right now, my heart is wounded. Julian's departure did that. I told you once that my heart no longer belonged to me and that is still true. I cannot give it to you if someone else has it, Louis."

Louis listened to her rather impassioned speech and although she didn't give him a direct answer to his question, the implication was clear. A weak smile finally creased his lips.

"I understand," he said. "But if Julian is gone, he will not have your heart forever. Gradually, you will reclaim it again and when you do, I want to be there. I think you are a remarkable woman, Lady Lista de la Mere, and I will not give up on something so remarkable that easily."

Lista sighed faintly. "It is at your own risk," she said. "I am not making you any promises. I could feel the way I do forever."

"Or not," he said.

She conceded the point. "Possibly," she said. "No one

knows what the future will hold. But I will ask you not to push me, please. That cannot go well. Whatever happens will happen in its own time."

Louis nodded but the truth was that he was trying not to feel a sense of discouragement. Whatever Lista and Julian had between them was strong; he could see that. But he had to believe he was just as good as Julian de Velt. Perhaps even better. That was something he intended to prove to Lista if she would allow it.

But all he could do was promise not to push.

"As you wish," he said. "For now, mayhap we can simply be friends. Mayhap that is all we can be at the moment."

"I would like that."

His gaze lingered on her in the darkness before he turned, gesturing off towards the south. "There is a place called Iowick Castle to the south," he said. "Have you heard of it?"

Lista shook her head. "I do not think so," she said. "Why?"

He leaned against the wall. "Because they breed ponies that are no bigger than a large dog," he said. "My sister has one for a pet and it sleeps with her. From one friend to another, I was thinking you might like a pony no larger than a big dog as a pet. They are very sweet little animals and finely bred ladies covet them."

Lista was greatly intrigued. "Little ponies?" she said. "I've not even heard of something like that."

He grinned. "I will take you there tomorrow," he said. "Pick out the pony you like and it will be my gift to you. From one friend to another, of course."

"But why such a gift? It is not my day of birth."

"It does not matter. Gifts are for any day of the year."

Lista thought about that but, somehow, she simply didn't

feel like indulging in something that was supposed to bring her joy. At the moment, she couldn't manage to feel any joy. Julian was gone, her aunt and mother were concocting schemes behind her back, and she simply didn't feel like being happy or joyful, not even with something as sweet as a tiny pony. Besides… something told her that Louis was perhaps trying to endear her to him with a gift.

Buying her affection, perhaps.

That wasn't something she was willing to do.

"It is a very kind offer," she said. "But not tomorrow. I have much to do here and with the raid yesterday, I would not feel comfortable leaving Felkington for any length of time. I'm sure you understand."

Disappointment rippled across Louis' face. "As you wish," he said. "If the Scots return, I will be here for you to command."

"How long do you plan on staying?"

"You were agreeable for me to remain a few days."

"I know, but I also remember that you said you had business for your father in Kelso."

"Would you like to go with me?"

Lista smiled at him, shaking her head with regret. "Nay," she said. "But you are kind to ask."

He wriggled his eyebrows. "It was worth a try," he said, grinning. "You cannot fault a man for trying."

"I have a feeling it will not be the last time you try."

"You would be correct, demoiselle."

Lista chuckled. "Do not try too hard or you will annoy me," she said. "We will not stay friends for long."

He snorted and turned away from the wall. "I am finished trying for tonight, so you may rest easy," he said. "But I was thinking that I should go to Kelso on the morrow. I will return by evening. Then, I can remain a few days before I must return home."

It seemed to Lista that he wanted her to give him some encouragement, some hope that when he returned, she would be glad for it. No matter how much she explained to him that her affections were with Julian, Louis wasn't inclined to surrender. He was looking for a ray of hope, a hint of encouragement, where she could give him none and no matter how much he told her that he would be content with friendship for the present, Lista knew he couldn't keep to that vow. Frankly, she didn't need the pressure.

Nor did she want it.

Perhaps suggesting they remain friends had been too ambitious.

"Louis," she finally said. "Would you do something for me if I asked it of you?"

"Of course I would."

She faced him. "When you finish your father's business in Kelso, I want you to go back home right away," she said, lifting her hand to silence him when he opened his mouth to protest. "I know I told you that you could stay for a few days, but I have changed my mind. I am afraid I must ask you not to come back. For a while, anyway. I know you believe that you can win me over and you speak of being friends, but I do not think you can keep to that vow and I do not want to get to the point where I avoid you because I do not want to feel as if you are pressuring me to accept your suit. I need some time to reflect on my thoughts and feelings and I cannot do that if you are here. Please do not think me cruel. I think it would be even crueler to let you stay, knowing I cannot give you the answers you seek."

Louis sighed faintly. "May we discuss this again in the

morning?" he asked. "Mayhap you should sleep on it and see how you feel on the morrow."

"Nay," Lista shook her head. "It would be better if you go. Please. Go home to Herrington and I will send you word if, and when, I am ready to speak on the subject."

"How long should I wait?"

"That is a fair question," she said. "The answer is that I do not know. It could be a month, a year... I do not know. But if you meet another young woman in the meantime, please do not refuse her because of me. I would wish for you to accept her and be very happy for it."

He gazed at her in the moonlight. "That sounds as if I will never hear from you again."

Lista shrugged. "As I have told you, I do not know," she said honestly. "You are kind and bright and thoughtful, a rare man and one of great value, but my feelings are with another and I do not know if those feelings will ever go away."

Louis looked at her a moment longer before averting his gaze. He'd tried so hard to be understanding, but the truth was that he was a man used to having his way. He was convinced he could sway Lista if she'd only allow it, but it was becoming increasingly clear she didn't want to.

That was a difficult pill for him to swallow.

"I am as good a man as Julian de Velt, my lady," he said quietly. "I would make a good husband."

"I know you would," Lista said. "An excellent husband. But it may not be for me."

He simply nodded his head, but Lista could see that he was clearly unhappy. Even in the torchlight, she could see his jaw twitching faintly. Since there wasn't much more she could say, and she certainly didn't want to delve into the subject of his suit again, she turned back towards the stairs.

"I hope I will see you on the morrow," she said. "But if you are gone when I awake, then know that I wish you safe travels and the very best life has to offer. You deserve everything good, Louis. I mean that sincerely."

He didn't say anything, nor did he respond much other than a tight smile. Lista limped back towards the stairwell but his deep voice stopped her.

"Wait," he said.

Lista paused, trying to stay off her right ankle, as he made his way over to her. He put himself in front of her and gestured to his back.

"Jump on," he said. "Let me take you down the stairs so you do not trip and kill yourself."

He meant to give her a ride on his back and, considering that she had to go down three flights of stairs, it was a rather welcome offer. Without another word, she put her arms around his neck and climbed onto his back as he gripped her with an arm. The other arm was used to steady himself as he made his way down the steep spiral stairs, down to the third floor where Lista's chamber was.

Louis carried her all the way to her chamber door, setting her down carefully when they reached it. With a soft word of thanks, Lista went inside and shut the door, quietly bolting it and listening for Louis to leave.

He stood outside her doorway for a solid hour before she finally heard him depart.

More than likely, for good.

CHAPTER EIGHTEEN

F OR A NIGHT that had been heavy with mist towards the early morning hours, as the sun began to lighten the eastern sky, the mist seemed to dissipate with astonishing speed.

Julian was nearing Felkington as the sun began to rise and the gray morning began to take on color. It was cold and damp from the mist and his nose was pinched red from the chill and his breath hung in the air in puffs of fog. He wasn't wearing his great helm because it was like a block of ice when it got cold. Instead, he had a padded hauberk on his head and shoulders because it was warmer. It sat on top of his de Velt tunic and had kept him cozy on the ride south. As the sun peeked over the horizon, signaling the dawn of a new day, the imposing walls of Felkington Castle came into view.

Truthfully, Julian didn't even know what he was going to say to Lista when he saw her. All he could think of was a groveling apology. The word "sorry" would be the first word out of his mouth and whatever came after that… well, her reaction would dictate much of it. He braced himself for words of anger and even hatred and he was fully prepared for her to tell him to leave and never return. If that happened, he had already decided that he would return to Pelinom and send Addington and his mother back to Felkington in his stead. He wasn't beyond asking his mother and sister for help in this instance because he was so unused to dealing with women, and especially a woman he was fond of, that he was the first to admit he needed help.

Fond.

Aye, he was fond of her but it was more than that. Addington said that Lista had been falling in love with him and Julian knew that he felt very much the same way. He knew because he'd never felt this way in his life and the thought of a future without Lista made him feel hollow inside.

A dark future he didn't want to face.

She was strong and beautiful and resilient. She had demons of her own, something he understood about her. An aunt and mother who behaved like animals and Lista was in the middle of it, trying to keep body and soul together, ensuring the survival of Felkington. She was ashamed by her situation and that was something Julian understood very well.

Shame.

Perhaps her shame wasn't the same as his, but they were kindred spirits in that shame was part of their lives. Shame and the fear of humiliation had driven him away from Felkington when he had rushed to judge a situation that he should have investigated before making up his mind. That kind of thing was a habit with him – a bad habit – that may have cost him dearly, but he was hoping Lista was more mature than he was and, in that sense, more forgiving.

He could only hope.

Around him, birds were coming alive, actively searching for their morning meal, as Felkington loomed closer. He took a moment to admire the structure in the early morning light, this massive fortress in the lap of a bucolic area of Northumberland that would be his someday, God willing. As he drew closer, he was already thinking about how he would improve it, making it more secure without losing the charm it had. Those lovely gardens and the unique vineyard were something he would gleefully show his family. Something he could be proud of.

A wife he could be proud of.

Was it really possible he was going to finally know some joy in life?

Julian could see sentries on the roof of the castle as he drew closer and he was certain they had seen him by now. He was on a narrow road from the northeast, with heavy foliage to his right, a downward sloping meadow to his left, and the sky-reaching bastion of Felkington directly in front of him. From this road, he could see the entry and even at a distance, he could tell that the double-portcullises were down.

But that didn't hold for long.

As Julian came near enough to be in shouting distance, he could see the portcullises lifting, one after the other, and a horse and rider passing through the entry. It didn't take him long to recognize Louis as the man came through, heading in his direction because he was coming from the northern road. Last he'd heard, Louis had business in Kelso, so he had to use the same road to make his way north. It wasn't as if Julian could, or would, hide from the man or head in another direction simply to avoid him. Nay, he wouldn't do that even if he could. For a man who had grown up avoiding confrontation, he was going to stand his ground on this one.

He owed Louis an apology, too.

The horses came closer.

Julian pulled his to a halt.

"Louis," he said. "I've come to…"

Louis didn't give him a chance to finish his sentence. Suddenly, a big, gloved fist came flying out at Julian's face and without his helm, he was vulnerable. Louis hit him squarely in the nose, sending his head snapping backwards. Unable to keep his balance, Julian went over onto the road and landed in a heap.

Seeing stars dance before his eyes as blood poured from his nose, Julian was up in a flash, or at least as quickly as he could. By the time he landed on his feet, Louis had dismounted and was coming for him with another balled fist. He was moving faster than Julian was, mostly because Julian was rather dazed, and clobbered Julian in the jaw this time. Julian staggered backwards but he didn't go down.

Shaking the bells from his ears, he went on the offensive.

Louis might have been more agile purely because he hadn't just been hit in the face, but Julian was far more powerful. Louis got in another blow before Julian let loose on him, pounding him twice in the head so that Louis ended up on his back. Bleeding all over him, Julian reached down and yanked him to his feet only for Louis to ram a knee into Julian's gut.

After that, the fight continued in earnest.

It was a nasty brawl, with both of them throwing, and landing, heavy blows. Louis wasn't as strong, and not quite as skilled simply because he hadn't the battle experience that Julian had, so it was only a matter of time before Julian gained the upper hand.

That's when the fight became truly nasty.

The soldiers from Felkington came out of the castle to watch. A group of them made their way down the road, watching Julian pummel Louis. He tossed him onto the wooden roof of a small stone shed, only for the roof to collapse. In a spectacular crash, Louis ended up in a heap of wood and rubble, but that didn't deter Julian. He dragged the half-conscious Louis out by his feet, dragging him out onto the road again and then grabbing him by the neck and pulling him to his knees. The fight had caused quite a stir, enough so that the entire castle was aware of it. More men, and even servants, were pouring from the entry to watch.

A knight fight was truly a brutal sight to behold.

Julian ripped off Louis' helm, grabbed him by the hair, and was about to land a blow to his face that would surely knock him unconscious when they heard shouting from the direction of the castle. Bloodied and battered, Julian ground to a halt, fist cocked, only to see Lista rushing out of the entry, skirts hiked up to her knees as she ran towards them. It was more like limping very quickly, but she was doing her best to move swiftly.

"Julian, stop!" she cried. "Stop fighting!"

Exhausted, with blood still seeping from his nose and a cut over his right eye, Julian immediately let go of Louis and stepped away from the man as he collapsed to the ground. By this time, Lista was upon them, looking at the pair in astonishment and horror.

"What are you doing?" she nearly shrieked at him. "Why did you do this?"

Julian wiped the blood from his eye because it was stinging. "I did not start this, I assure you," he said, winded. "Louis threw the first blow. I am allowed to defend myself."

Lista looked at him in shock before returning her focus to Louis, who was struggling to sit up. "He struck you first?" she said. "But why? Louis, why did you strike Julian?"

Louis wasn't really capable of answering at the moment. Julian put his hand to his jaw, thinking he had some loose teeth, before sighing sharply.

"In response to the insults I dealt him, I am sure," he said. "In fact, I was returning to Felkington to apologize for my behavior. I acted poorly and had come to seek forgiveness, but I can see that de Rhos is not in a forgiving mood. Not that I blame him, but I had hoped he was a man of mercy. I had hoped you are a woman of mercy, too, but if you have a notion to put your fist in my nose like de Rhos did, then know that I will not let you. I am certain your words of anger will do more damage than any blow ever could."

Lista's gaze was drawn to Julian, who was fairly battered. His right eye was starting to swell and there was blood all over his chin and neck, down onto his tunic. A panicked servant had found her in her chamber as she'd finished dressing, only to tell her about the vicious fight that was going on just outside the entry. The servant hadn't told her who was involved, so seeing Julian and Louis trading brutal blows had been a shock.

But a strange thing happened after that.

Seeing Julian for the first time since his departure had her bloody well thrilled to see the man. Yesterday, she wasn't sure she'd ever see him again, so his surprise appearance wasn't unwelcome in the least.

At least, to her.

But Louis' reaction in seeing Julian was entirely another matter.

"Nay," she said after a moment. "I have no desire to put a fist in your nose, nor do I have any intention of spouting off angry words. I know why you left, Julian. Addington told me. I suppose that I should be furious that you thought I was capable of such deceit and, to be truthful, I was quite irate when I first learned of it. But I am not irate any longer. I've had time to think about it and I'm sorry that others have hurt you so badly that you thought the worst when you saw Louis helping me stand. It was a polite action and nothing more, I swear it."

Julian let out a grunt of disbelief. "You are apologizing to *me*?" he said, incredulous. "Lista, you have nothing to apologize for. God's Bones, woman, why would you even do such a thing? I am the one in the wrong here which is why I suspect de Rhos went after me. I was so very wrong and I behaved horribly. I would beg for your forgiveness but I do not blame you if you do not wish to give it. I am not entirely sure I deserve it."

Lista smiled timidly. "I forgave you long ago," she said. "You needn't worry about me."

Julian could hardly believe it. He thought he was going to spend the day on his knees, at the very least, begging for her understanding and the fact that she forgave him so easily had his head spinning.

He shook his head in wonder.

"Is there really such forgiveness in this world?" he murmured. "Is there really a woman of such grace, of such understanding, that she would absolve me of my horrible deeds so easily? Truly, Lista, I do not deserve it but God bless you for being so merciful."

Tears were starting to pool in Lista's eyes as she looked at him. Battered, emotionally scarred Julian could hardly believe there was forgiveness for him. It only underscored the trials and tribulations the man must have had to go through in his life, of the unjust people he surely must have known.

Poor, sweet Julian.

But he'd found his forgiveness now, as easily as if the transgression had never happened. It was at that moment that the healing between them began, something that patched any cracks in their budding relationship. If there was mercy, there was hope, and they both had an abundance of hope. Just as Lista took a step towards Julian, and he towards her, Louis suddenly lurched to his feet.

"That is not why I struck you," he said, slurring through his swollen mouth. "I struck you because you do not deserve this good woman, yet you have returned and she will fall into your arms regardless of what you have done. I struck you because she seems to think you are more worthy than I am. I struck you because you judged my act of compassion without even knowing the facts. I thought we were becoming friends, de Velt, but you severed that infant friendship without any reason whatsoever. I struck you because you deserved it."

Julian was out of arm's length, but Louis was so badly beaten that he probably couldn't have taken much more of anything. Julian was quite certain he could topple the man with little effort.

But nothing he said was untrue.

"I know," he said simply. "I judged you badly, Louis, and I am deeply sorry for it. Mayhap you are not in a forgiving mood now, but mayhap you will be someday. I hope you will reflect upon the short time we spent together and the pleasant conversations we had and realize I had simply made an error in judgment, one that you did not deserve. It was my own insecurity that caused me to behave that way and although it is a weak excuse, it is the truth. You are a decent man and there aren't many of those in this world. I recognize that."

Louis wiped at his mouth, clumsily. "Up until this moment,

I did not think you were a man of good character after what happened," he said. "But it seems to me that only a man of good character would recognize his failings."

"I hope so."

"Did you return to apologize and claim Lista?"

Julian looked at Lista. Her gaze was moving nervously between him and Louis. "Only if she'll have me," Julian said, the warmth in his eyes reflecting the emotion he was feeling for her. "But after this, I would not blame her if she would not."

Louis snorted, an ironic sound. "I suspect that is something you need not worry over," he said. "I asked permission to court her, you know. After you left, I went to her mother and asked. I was given permission, though by whom is debatable. Nonetheless, by rights, she is mine to court."

The warmth faded from Julian's eyes as he looked at him. "Then it is little wonder that my return was an unwelcome sight."

"Unwelcome, indeed. But in hindsight, not entirely unexpected."

That bit of news put a new light on the situation and the warmth and hope in Julian's eyes went out completely. He felt sick in the pit of his stomach to realize that Louis had jumped his claim on Lista. His delay in asking permission to court her had cost him. Now, that right belonged to Louis.

He remembered his conversation with Addington when she told him that she feared Louis might pursue Lista simply out of anger and it seemed that his little sister had been correct. Until this moment, he'd held out hope that it hadn't happened, but now he knew the truth.

He'd lost.

Everything.

"Then I will not interfere," he said, though he nearly choked on every word. "As a man of honor, I will surrender any claim or intentions I had towards the lady. You were correct when you said that I did not deserve her. I am a most unworthy man of such a magnificent woman. You *are* worthy, de Rhos, and not just because you are the son of an earl. You are a man of integrity and I respect that. Pray... be good to her. And do not think too poorly of me in the years to come."

With that, he turned away, looking for his horse, feeling a lump in his throat as he did so. Although it was well and good to return to Felkington to seek forgiveness, it was clear that was all he *could* seek. He'd made a mistake and Lista was now spoken for.

But not to him.

His horse was several feet away, grazing on a patch of fat, wet grass, so Julian headed in that direction. Tears began to fill his eyes because behind him, he could hear weeping and he knew it was Lista. She was weeping for him, for what they could have had. For what would never be. Blindly, Julian grabbed for his horse's reins, desperate to get clear of Felkington before he broke down completely. He had to get out of there before he lost himself.

"Julian, wait."

Louis was calling after him and he staggered to a halt, making sure there were no tears on his face before turning around to see that Lista was wiping the tears from her cheeks. Louis looked at her, his swollen face registering concern.

Compassion.

When Louis spoke, it was to Lista.

"Part of courtship is understanding if you and the lady you wish to court are fond of one another," he said. "I know that you were fond of Julian before you ever met me. I know that you wished for him to court you. You told me yourself. Had you not forgiven him when he came seeking your grace, this would not have been an issue. But clearly, you have forgiven him. As much as I want you to be fond of me and not him, I cannot in good conscience push this courtship any further. You would be miserable and I could not be the cause of it. I would much rather see you happy, even if it is at my own expense."

Lista wiped the tears from her chin. "Do you mean that?"

"As difficult as it is for me to say it, I do."

Lista stared at him a moment as if waiting for him to change his mind, but he simply looked at her. There was regret in his expression, but he wouldn't go back on his word. When she realized this, a smile spread across her lips.

"Louis," she said, reaching out to put a soft hand on his battered face. "That is the greatest gift you could give me. You have given me back my happiness and, for that, I shall always be grateful."

Louis forced a smile, feeling her warm hand against his face and knowing it would be the one and only time he would feel her flesh against his. But he wasn't sorry. He knew he'd done the right thing.

"Prove it to me by being truly and deliriously joyful all the days of your life," he said, turning to look at Julian, who was standing there in shock. "And take care of that big dolt. He needs it."

Julian was indeed in shock. His gaze was fixed on Louis in disbelief. "Never has anyone done something so completely selfless for me," he finally said. "I do not deserve it, but I will strive to be worthy of that gift. My heart may belong to Lista, but my sword and loyalty belong to you. Whatever you need,

Louis, truly… all you need do is send word to me. I will come."

Louis smiled weakly. "One de Velt brother already had a woman taken from him by a de Rhos," he said. "I could not repeat history. Take her and welcome her, Julian. When I marry, I want it to be a woman who looks at me the way Lista looks at you. I know that now. I was trying to force something that would have made us all miserable."

"It is a wise man who realizes his follies."

"If you realized yours, I can realize mine."

Julian smiled at the man. He couldn't help it. Louis smiled in return, as much as his swollen mouth would allow, and moved away from Lista, heading off to find his horse who had bolted away during the fight. As Louis wandered down the road, calling for his steed, Julian turned to Lista.

One moment he was looking at her and in the next, she was in his arms.

He didn't know how it happened, only that it had. The first real touch, the first real embrace, and the first real kiss all came together in a clash of flesh and blood and emotion. Julian could feel Lista alternately weeping and giggling as he kissed her furiously, realizing that he was weeping and giggling, too.

It was joy.

It was bliss.

It was all things delirium.

In the arms of Lista de la Mere, Julian found his everything.

CHAPTER NINETEEN

Pelinom Castle
Four weeks later

"AND THAT'S HOW we met," Julian was saying. "She yelled at me and told me I was a terrible commander because my men were undisciplined. One moment she was shouting at me and in the next, I was in love with her. In speaking to Mama, she says nearly the same thing happened with you."

He was speaking to an enormous crypt in the small chapel of Pelinom, the one Julian's grandfather, Keats, had built against the outer wall of his fortress. It was tucked back by the kitchens, half-moon shape in design, and it had two crypts in it – Keats Coleby and Ajax de Velt.

Jax had never wanted to be buried far from his family.

Which was a good thing considering a loud and expensive wedding was going on at Pelinom. Jax was part of it because the family kept coming in to celebrate with him. At the moment, it was Julian, who had put two full cups of wine on the crypt because he was marrying the woman he loved and he wanted to celebrate the event with his father. Cole and his family had arrived for the celebration, as had sisters Allaston and Effington, all the way from Wales. Julian had more nieces and nephews running about than he could count, more boys to take him down by the knees and try to steal his coin purse.

But there were other guests, as well.

Christopher de Lohr was among them. The man had come north with his brother, the Earl of Canterbury, and a host of knights and friends, all of them gathering to celebrate Julian's marriage to Lista, who was a truly sweet and humorous woman. The word from the de Lohr women was that they most definitely approved of Lista and held her in great esteem, much like her husband, who was rarely away from her side.

But for this task, he wanted to be alone.

It was a moment between father and son.

"I brought a drink for you, Papa," Julian said, picking up one of the two cups on Jax's crypt. "I wanted to celebrate my marriage with you, just the two of us, because I know you would be giving me fatherly advice right about now. This would be your moment to tell me how to be a good husband because you were one for all of those years. But instead, Cole felt the need to take your place and tell me how to treat a wife. I think he lied because he told me that women like to have their hair pulled and appreciate love bites on their buttocks. I think he was drunk when he told me that because I'm fairly certain he's trying to get me into trouble with my wife."

Julian chuckled as he brought the cup to his lips and drank deeply, a very fine Belgian wine provided by Lady Felkington on the event of her daughter's wedding. Somehow, Flora hadn't gotten to the wine before it was shipped to Pelinom and even now, Lady d'Orbec was back at Felkington, in her chamber and under guard from Julian's own men. He didn't trust the woman not to make his wedding a fiasco, so she hadn't been invited. She'd been restricted to her chamber until Julian could decide what to do with her.

Lista had been grateful.

While Flora's fate was still up in the air, Meadow had come to Pelinom and Kellington had spent nearly every minute with her. She still wanted to drink and forage in the trees for fungus that would give her a wildly intoxicated feeling, but Kellington had managed to keep her away from those things and she had actually enjoyed herself at her daughter's wedding. Meadow removed from Flora seemed to be a saner and more stable lady, now with the renewed friendship with Kellington Coleby de Velt, who was a much better influence on her. It was another thing that Lista was deeply grateful for.

And Julian was, too.

"You'd like Lista, Papa," Julian said softly, running his hand over the great stone crypt. "In fact, I know you would grow to love her because I think she's that greatness you once spoke about. If you will recall, as you lay in Mama's arms, you told me I needed to find my greatness. I've wondered for six years what you meant by that and I always thought it was something to do with strength or honor. It never occurred to me that my greatness was a person. I found my greatness and her name is Lista. I just thought you'd like to know."

He was smiling by the time he finished, giving the cold granite one last pat before setting down his empty cup and picking up the one he'd left for his father. It was a poignant moment with his father, one he would remember for the rest of his life. Having a big brother like Cole explain the ways of married men and women to him had actually been quite sweet, a bonding moment between brothers, but there had been something missing without their father present. They both felt it. But it had been a beautiful moment, nonetheless.

"I thought I'd find you in here."

Julian heard the voice over near the chapel entry, turning to see Cole standing there with two more cups in his hand. He came in, handing one to Julian even though he already had a cup.

"Papa and I were just having a conversation," Julian said. "Somewhat one-sided, but I swear I hear his voice now and then."

"Oh?" Cole said, taking a drink from his cup. "What did he tell you?"

"That women do not like love bites on their arses."

Cole nearly spit his wine out, managing to salvage most of it as a droplet ran down onto his chin. He wiped it off as he swallowed the drink in his mouth, grinning at his younger brother.

"If you truly believed me, then you are in more trouble than I realized," he said. "But coming to know Lista as I have, I suspect she would not tolerate bites to her arse."

Julian snorted. "Probably not," he said. "But I intend to find out... gently."

Cole chuckled. "Cori likes her a great deal, you know," he said. "So do Allaston and Effie and Addie. Next to Cori's younger sister, Gaia, Addie considers Lista her best friend in the entire world. I would not be surprised if she moved into Felkington with you two."

Julian shook his head. "I love Addie, but she is staying here, with Mother," he said firmly. "I am not sharing my wife right now. I do not need my sister tagging along with everything we do. God, do you remember how Cassian used to do that to us when he was young? Everywhere we went, there he was. We would go hunting and he'd cry to Mother so she would make us take him along. What an annoyance he was. Addie has the potential to be just like that."

Cole grinned at the memories of a little brother who was born when Cole and Julian were twelve and ten years of age, respectively. As they grew, Cassian wanted to do everything with them, which greatly annoyed the boys who were becoming men.

"He used to be like that until we got older and that dynamic changed," Cole said. "I do not remember when it became me and Papa against you and Cassian, but that's when we found out just how cunning and ruthless Cassian was. I never told you this, but you were fortunate to have him as an ally."

Julian was still smiling at the recollection of his little brother who was tough and fierce, even at a young age. "I know," he said. "I miss those times very much."

The smile faded from Cole's face. "I know," he said. "Actually, that is why I've come. I know you wanted to be alone with Papa for a while, but I just had a conversation with de Lohr that I think you should know about. It's about Cass."

Julian's good humor fled. "God, what now?" he said. "We already know about his bastard son, whom I fully intend to see at some point."

"I know. Me, too. We shall go together."

"Then what else is there about Cass?"

"He's alive."

That wasn't what Julian had expected to hear. In fact, he was expecting to hear anything but that, so the news was like a blow to his belly. He actually had to grip the side of the crypt to steady himself, setting the cups down so he wouldn't drop them.

"Say that again," he said as if not trusting his own ears. "What did you just say?"

Cole put a hand on his shoulder. "Cassian is alive," he said. "De Lohr's men have seen him on the tournament circuit and they have confirmed that he is alive and well, competing as a tournament knight who calls himself The Dark Conqueror."

A hand flew to Julian's mouth. "He's truly *alive*?" he hissed. "And they're certain?"

"They are."

Julian stared at him, shocked to the bone, but along with that shock came a question. It spewed from his lips before he could stop himself.

"But why?" he demanded. "Why is he on the tournament circuit and has not sent us word? Why has he let us think that he has been dead all these years?"

Cole was shaking his head even as his brother asked those terrible questions that he had asked himself. "I do not know," he said. "Christopher does not know, but he is going to find out. He plans on attending a tournament to see for himself. He said he would send us word as soon as he had spoken to Cass. I would like to think our brother has a very good reason for doing what he's done but, at the moment, I cannot think of one. All I can think of is Mother's face when she thought Cass had been killed on his way to visit Papa's grave after he was killed and I want to throttle Cassian. I really do."

Julian did, too, and he wasn't satisfied with that answer. "He'd better have a damned good reason for all of this," he said. "Mayhap he was knocked on the head by outlaws and forgot who he was, or mayhap…"

"Mayhap what?"

Julian cast him a long look. "Mayhap he is one of William Marshal's spies," he said. "Mayhap The Marshal commanded him to feign his own death."

Cole shook his head. "Nonsense."

"Why?" Julian wanted to know. "You served William Marshal and his ring of spies. Mayhap the man got to Cass and forced him into service."

Cole held up a hand to silence him. Although it was true that Cole had indeed served William Marshal in his spy ring for several years, Julian and Cassian had never been part of that. Still… he wouldn't put it past William Marshal to sink his claws into the youngest de Velt son.

Perhaps Julian had something, at that.

"De Lohr will tell us when he sees Cass," Cole said. "He asked that we remain out of the situation until he can settle it."

Julian frowned. "Why should we stay out of it? Cassian is *our* brother."

"But he has a child with Brielle. It's complicated, Julian. De Lohr will handle it far more diplomatically than we could."

He had a point. "I suppose," he said begrudgingly. "But… Cass is really alive? I simply cannot believe it."

Cole couldn't disagree with that. He was feeling a great deal of shock himself. "I know," he said. "Meanwhile, I suggest we not tell Mother yet. I do not want to shock the woman, nor do I want to get her hopes up until we know something more."

Julian knew that his brother was correct. "Agreed," he said. "But, Cole?"

"Aye?"

"It would be nice to have our little brother home again."

Cole patted him on the side of the head. "It would, indeed," he said. Then, he took a deep breath and swept his hand in the direction of the chapel door. "Mayhap we should go drink a secret toast to the return of Cassian as we celebrate your marriage. Papa is taking up all of your time and I would like some of it."

Julian was still digesting the news of Cassian but, in the same breath, he felt some joy. Joy and relief that his little brother hadn't been killed those years ago. But the joy was tempered with confusion, something he was desperately trying to shake. This was his wedding celebration and he wouldn't be distracted from his beautiful bride by the revelation of his brother's reappearance, as important as it was.

Tonight belonged to him and Lista.

"Then let us return to the hall," Julian said as Cole led him from the chapel. "I think my wife is with Cori and Addie."

Cole grunted. "Where else would she be?"

"I think I'm going to have to fight them off when I try to take her up to my chamber for the night."

They looked at each other and started laughing as they quit the chapel and headed for the keep. As they crossed the shadowed bailey, a lone figure emerged from the alcove near the altar of the chapel. There were two entrances, one for the family and one for the priest, and the priest's door had been opened. In fact, the figure had been standing there for quite some time, long enough to have heard Julian's conversation with Jax and the subsequent news from Cole.

Kellington's tear-stained face came into the light.

It was sunset, with the last rays of light penetrating through the expensive stained-glass window that was one of three on the east side of the chapel. The light caressed her features as she made her way to her husband's crypt, a gentle hand upon the stone as her lips kissed the effigy on the head.

She sniffled.

"I hadn't meant to hear all of that," she said, her voice trembling from weeping. "I had only meant to have a private word with Julian until Cole came in, but did you hear what he said? Cass has been found. My little boy has been found. I thought he was with you, but as it turns out, he is still with me. All of our sons are with me and I could not be more grateful. And you... *you*, my pet, are always with me. You are with us all. I heard what Julian told you and he was right... his greatness *is* Lista. She is what he has been searching for all of these years. I wish you could see them together, Jax. Then you would know it is true."

Kissing the effigy one last time, Kellington followed her sons' path from the chapel, heading back towards the keep that was lit up with the glow of a thousand candles. There was light and music, food and drink, and the chatter of people celebrating a truly happy occasion. It was all things glorious and although Kellington was joyful in her son's marriage, she couldn't help but feel that something was missing.

Some*one* was missing.

Jax.

She had been with the man more than half her life. Losing him as she had in battle those years ago had been a shock, one she still wasn't over. His abrupt departure left a hole that no one else could fill, as if a large piece of her heart had broken off, a piece she would never get back. *That's why they call it a broken heart*, she mused. Broken or not, however, it was still full enough and strong enough to love her children, their spouses, and her grandchildren.

Even the naughty ones.

How Jax would have loved them.

With a smile, Kellington stepped into the great hall, confronted almost immediately by Ashton. The tall, blond de Royans knight nearly bowled her over, startled when he realized he had been rather abrupt.

"Lady de Velt," he said, clearly fortified by alcohol. "I was hoping I might have a moment of your time. I have a very important question to ask you and I do not take it lightly. I have thought long and hard about it and it is time that I speak with you."

Kellington already knew what it was before he even asked. She'd been expecting that question for the past two years, only Ashton had been too skittish and cowardly to bring it up. Seeing Julian married, however, must have fortified his courage and Kellington fought off a smile at the young knight who seemed to be sweating quite a bit.

"Of course, Ashton," she said. "What would you like to ask me?"

His eyes widened. "Now, my lady?"

"You asked for a moment of my time. Now you have it."

Ashton looked around nervously, making sure no one was listening, before refocusing on her. "My lady," he said. "I would like to ask permission to court Addington. I am a de Royans, my father's heir, and I will inherit Bowes Castle upon his death. I have much to offer a wife so I hope you will consider this when rendering your decision."

Kellington opened her mouth to reply when Anteaus was suddenly in front of her, trying to push Ashton out of the way.

"Lady de Velt," Anteaus said, shoving Ashton back by the chest. "I would like a moment of your time, if you will. I must ask you a question of the utmost importance."

Kellington almost laughed. She could see Ashton's enraged

face and Anteaus' determined one. Before a fight could erupt, and the pair had been building up to it all day as Addington flirted with both of them, Kellington stepped back and took charge.

"Anteaus," she said firmly. "Find Cole and escort him to my solar. Ashton, you will go to my solar immediately and wait for me. Do this now."

The knights split off, automatically carrying out her command without hesitation. When Lady de Velt gave an order, it was not meant to be disobeyed. Kellington watched them head off for a moment before seeking out Julian, who was in conversation with a de Lohr knight. She pulled her son away from the conversation and pointed in the direction of her solar.

"Ashton has finally summoned the courage to ask for Addie's hand," she said. "Unfortunately, so has Anteaus. I need your help, Julian. Get into the solar and keep Anteaus calm. God's Bones, I wish your father was here. He could settle them down."

Julian's eyes glimmered. "You think so, do you?" he said. "Mother, the real commander of Pelinom is, and always has been, you. But I do agree that we are in for trouble if this gets out of hand. I have no desire to spend part of my wedding celebration breaking up a fight between my sister's suitors."

An idea occurred to Kellington. "I do not think you will have to," she said. "Send Cori and Lista into my solar. No man would dare fight in front of them and they'll be able to calm them down better than anyone else can. Hurry, now. Do as I say."

Julian did. That greatness he'd finally found, his beautiful wife in her pale blue wedding gown, ended up helping broker a betrothal between Ashton and Addington, and not a drop of blood was spilled. Julian watched his wife, a natural organizer and negotiator, take on two love-struck knights and win.

It was the most amazing thing he'd ever seen.

As Anteaus drowned his sorrows in more wine, having lost out on the last eligible de Velt daughter, Julian finally took his wife to his chamber, high atop the fortress of Pelinom, and retreated from the world. It was the first day of the rest of his life, a life that had finally come full circle in more ways than he could have ever imagined. That bullied boy with eyes of different colors had finally found his greatness in the arms of a woman he loved more with every breath he took. A woman of poise, of grace, and of genuine kindness.

A woman who loved him with all her heart and soul.

Julian de Velt, and all of his inner demons, had finally found the peace he'd been looking for.

On this night, all was finally right in his world.

EPILOGUE

Six years later
Felkington Castle

"TAKE ME NOW, Julian," she breathed.

Julian's hand was on the door latch of their warm, comfortable chamber. It was dawn and he'd been trying to leave for the past half-hour, but Lista wouldn't let him. At seven months pregnant, she was like an animal in heat at this stage. For some reason, it had happened with every one of their children. Being that this was her fourth pregnancy, he ought to know. Not that he minded, because he didn't. Not in the least. But they'd already made love twice last night and once this morning as soon as they woke up. He was dressed now and trying to get out of the door, but Lista was on her side, nude, as the soft firelight illuminated her beautiful figure. Her gently swollen midsection drew his lust.

Rolling his eyes and surrendering to the inevitable, he began to strip off his clothing as he made his way back to the bed, but Lista didn't even let him get halfway undressed before she was on top of him.

"Wait," he said, trying to remove his boots as she straddled him and latched on to his mouth. "Sweetheart, give me a few moments to get my boots off."

Lista was already unfastening his breeches. "I do not care about your boots," she said. "Only your breeches. Remove them!"

She was kissing him passionately and he was succumbing like a weakling, but he started laughing because she was being so forceful. When her hands moved into his breeches, invading warm and intimate places, he was instantly aroused and the laughter stopped. Boots on, breeches down around his hips, he put his enormous arms around her and lay her on her back, covering her with his massive body.

"Take me, my angel," Lista said breathlessly, parting her legs for him as he wedged himself in between them. "Now, darling. Do not make me wait."

His mouth moved down her body, to her delicious breasts. "Not yet."

"Why not?"

Her demand was cut off when his lips descended on a swollen nipple. His hands massaged her, pulling at her breasts and pinching her nipples until she was writhing with passion. His massive hands still splayed on her breasts, his mouth blazed a trail down the center of her torso, losing himself in her scent and texture. Every curve was explored with his tongue, every inch of flesh touched or caressed.

He had to experience *all* of her.

Julian's mouth moved to her tender groin area, tasting and kissing. His hands left her breasts and he moved between her thighs, bringing up both of her legs and spreading them wide.

Lista's head came up. "What are you doing?"

He lowered his head to her throbbing core, a wolfish grin on his face. His gentle fingers delicately traced the dark curls, tenderly spreading the thick folds.

"You like this," he murmured.

Lista had her fingers in his hair. "I do not want your tongue there," she said. "I want your…"

She was cut off when his hot mouth descended on her sensitive core. A moan spilled forth from her lips and she arched her back with the force of her passion, staring up at the ceiling. Frozen in that position, legs spread and over her husband's shoulders, she felt every lap of his tongue, every suckle, as if nothing else in her world existed.

Julian's hands held her buttocks, trapping her against him as he continued his onslaught. Her sharp pants of passion excited him terribly, driving him mad for want of her. When she was hot and ready, he released her buttocks and stood up, thrusting his throbbing member into her slippery flesh.

Lista was already climaxing as he came into her, only enhanced by his enormous organ. His thrusts were firm and complete, prolonging her pleasure. The harder he pushed, the stronger her contractions until she began the inevitable downslide.

But Julian didn't let up. His arms were braced on either side of her, his body aloft from hers as he thrust into her again and again. When his release finally came, it was with the most powerful of blasts. He spilled deep, still moving, feeling her juices and his combine and making her unbelievably wet. Still, he continued to move, wanting to feel her around him, still wanting to be within her until out of sheer exhaustion, he came to a halt.

He lay atop her, gathering her into his arms, feeling her big belly between them. Not wanting to smash the child, he shifted so his weight was off her belly, but he was still wedged in between her legs, still joined to her. As he gently kissed her neck and shoulder, Lista took one of his hands and put it on her belly.

His head came up.

"He is kicking strongly," he said, grinning as he felt the baby move. "Soon, I will no longer be able to touch you until the child is born."

Lista made a face. "And then you will not be able to touch me for weeks afterward," she said. "I love giving birth to your children, Julian, but I do not like it when you are not permitted to touch me. That is the worst part about it."

He chuckled, feeling the baby roll around beneath his hand. "It is no joy for me, either, but as it was explained to me by four midwives and a physic, if we continue relations up until you give birth, it could harm both you and the child," he said patiently, considering he explained this same thing with every child they'd had. "And I am not to touch you afterwards because you must heal. Having a child wreaks havoc on a woman's body, especially in the area where a man gains his pleasure. You *know* this, sweetheart."

Lista did indeed know all of that, but she still didn't like it. Pregnancy had made her quite moody, too, and Julian lived in fear of her tears and rages. Four pregnancies in six years meant she had been with child a good deal of the time simply because they couldn't keep their hands off one another and were quite fertile together. They had three boys already and Julian was convinced the child she carried was the fourth. He was so in love with his family that there were times he would watch his boys sleep, tears in his eyes as he thought on how fortunate he really was.

More of that greatness his father had spoken of.

"I know all of this," Lista said, interrupting his thoughts. "I know that I must be allowed time to heal and, truthfully, I do not feel much like having you touch me right after the child is born. But still... I miss that time together. Our moments alone are few and far between sometimes."

He smiled and kissed her, his hand on her belly when something crashed into the chamber door. Had it not been bolted, it most certainly would have swung open. In fact, Julian bolted it with a purpose because his sons couldn't seem to remember to knock at their parents' door. To them, a closed door was simply a vague suggestion that those on the other side might need or want privacy.

The de Velt stampede had begun.

"Mam!" Someone was pounding on the door. "Mam, open the door!"

Lista sighed faintly, looking to Julian, who started laughing. He disengaged from his wife and rolled off the bed, pulling his clothing together again as Lista struggled to sit up. Julian saw her efforts and he paused in redressing, pulling her into a sitting position.

"Stop pounding on the door," he called to the hooligans in on the other side of the panel. "We shall open it in a moment."

Lista was on her feet, pulling a heavy shift over her head. Julian quickly finished dressing and helped her don a heavy robe and slippers. When she was completely dressed and hastily braiding her hair, Julian went to the door and released the bolt. The door flew open and three young boys spilled into the chamber.

Boys with their father's two-colored eyes.

"Mam!" the biggest one went to Lista, pulling on her sleeve. "Mama! Mam!"

Lista stopped mid-braid and put her hand over her eldest's mouth. "Quinton, please," she said. "I can hear you perfectly well without shouting. What is it?"

Quinton de Velt, or Quin as he was called, was the image of his late grandfather. He had Jax's eyes, his dark hair, and his dark eyebrows. There was nothing about the boy that didn't scream of Jax de Velt.

He also had his grandfather's legendary impatience.

"He's here!" Quinton said. "Louis is here! He's brought the small ponies! Mam, he promised me for my day of birth and he came! He really came!"

Lista looked at Julian in surprise. Now, she knew what the chaos was about. Louis, who had become a good and true friend to both Julian and Lista over the years, had promised Quinton a dog-sized pony for his day of birth and now he'd evidently shown up with the goods. Julian met his wife's surprised expression, with two boys crawling on him and demanding their own tiny ponies. In fact, Julian had the youngest boy, Simon, in his arms as his middle son, Tybalt "Ty" de Velt, tugged on him.

"Where is Louis?" Julian asked his eldest.

Quinton was pointing to the door, out in the general direction of the courtyard. "In the stables," he said excitedly. "Come and see, Papa!"

Quinton bolted from the chamber, followed by Tybalt. Simon pushed himself out of Julian's arms, ramming a little hand into his throat and causing his father to cough. All three boys charged out, excited, as Julian and Lista brought up the rear.

"I hope he's brought three little ponies or there is going to be a battle," Lista muttered. "Why would Louis do this? Did you not tell him no ponies for Quin?"

Julian fought off a grin as he took Lista's arm and carefully helped her down the stairs. "My dearest darling, I know you still look at them as babies, but Quin and Ty are old enough to ride," he said. "Simon is still a little young, but they are de Velts. They are born to ride and bear arms. Besides, these ponies aren't for riding. They're pets."

The statement displeased Lista immensely. They reached the third level, the one with the great hall, and they could hear the boys in the hall as they clamored around Meadow, who had evidently demanded they break their fast before going outside to see the ponies. Simon seemed particularly upset and his wailing could be heard echoing off the walls.

Lista shook her head in resignation.

"Go to the stables and tell Louis that if he has not brought three ponies with him, then he had better flee for his life," she said. "I am going to make sure my mother does not take a stick to the boys. She's been known to do that when they argue with her."

Julian's grin broke through. "Your mother was born to tend a gaggle of young lads," he said. "She's happier than I've ever seen her."

Lista had to concede the point. "She is," she said. "All she needed was some children to love to give her a reason to stay away from the wine and live again. I can hardly remember that drunkard she used to be when Flora was around."

"Have you heard from her lately?"

Lista shook her head. "Nay," she said. "She's gone back to The Filey and she evidently has a new companion to drink her days away with, so she has no more need of us."

"Not even our social connections?"

It was a sarcastic question and Lista grinned. "Not even our social connections," she said. "Now, go. Tell Louis that I am greatly displeased. And also ask him what he has done about the de Chevington lass. We met her during the summer when we visited Sunderland at his invitation. Remember?"

Julian nodded. "I remember," he said. "She seemed very keen on him."

Lista nodded. "The man needs to get married. He's not getting any younger." A scream rose up, catching her attention. "I must go save my children from my mother. Or would you rather do it and let me see to Louis?"

Julian shook his head firmly, pulling her close for a tender kiss. "I'll take the knight," he said. "You take the wild animals. And then later tonight, I will take *you*."

Lista giggled, kissing him again, gazing into those eyes she loved so well. Six years of bliss with a man she loved with every fiber of her being, a man who was the most perfect father and husband imaginable. A man she thought she'd lost once, but a man who had learned from his mistake. Their love had healed that weakness inside of him, the lack of confidence that had taken a chunk out of his soul. Everything about their love had been healing and glorious, timeless with wonder.

Theirs was the stuff that dreams were made of.

It was the greatness Julian had finally found.

And Jax would have been proud.

෬ THE END ෭

Children of Julian and Lista
Quinton
Tybalt "Ty"
Simon
Romulus "Rom"
Daphne
Nessa
Brenan
Denys
Jasper
Amaury
George

KATHRYN LE VEQUE NOVELS

Medieval Romance:

De Wolfe Pack Series:
Warwolfe
The Wolfe
Nighthawk
ShadowWolfe
DarkWolfe
A Joyous de Wolfe Christmas
BlackWolfe
Serpent
A Wolfe Among Dragons
Scorpion
StormWolfe
Dark Destroyer
The Lion of the North
Walls of Babylon
The Best Is Yet To Be

De Wolfe Pack Generations:
WolfeHeart
WolfeStrike
WolfeSword
WolfeBlade
WolfeLord

The Executioner Knights:
By the Unholy Hand
The Mountain Dark
Starless
The Promise (also Noble Knights of de Nerra)
A Time of End

Winter of Solace
Lord of the Shadows
Lord of the Sky
Splendid Hour

The de Russe Legacy:
The Falls of Erith
Lord of War: Black Angel
The Iron Knight
Beast
The Dark One: Dark Knight
The White Lord of Wellesbourne
Dark Moon
Dark Steel
A de Russe Christmas Miracle
Dark Warrior

The de Lohr Dynasty:
While Angels Slept
Rise of the Defender
Steelheart
Shadowmoor
Silversword
Spectre of the Sword
Unending Love
Archangel
A Blessed de Lohr Christmas

The Brothers de Lohr:
The Earl in Winter

Lords of East Anglia:
While Angels Slept
Godspeed

Lord of Light
Realm of Angels

Saxon Lords of Hage:
The Crusader
Kingdom Come

High Warriors of Rohan:
High Warrior

The House of Ashbourne:
Upon a Midnight Dream

The House of D'Aurilliac:
Valiant Chaos

The House of De Dere:
Of Love and Legend

St. John and de Gare Clans:
The Warrior Poet

The House of de Bretagne:
The Questing

The House of Summerlin:
The Legend

The Kingdom of Hendocia:
Kingdom by the Sea

Regency Historical Romance:
Sin Like Flynn: A Regency
Historical Romance Duet

Gothic Regency Romance:
Emma

Contemporary Romance:

**Kathlyn Trent/Marcus Burton
Series:**
Valley of the Shadow
The Eden Factor
Canyon of the Sphinx

**The American Heroes Anthology
Series:**
The Lucius Robe
Fires of Autumn
Evenshade
Sea of Dreams
Purgatory

**Other non-connected
Contemporary Romance:**
Lady of Heaven
Darkling, I Listen
In the Dreaming Hour
River's End
The Fountain

Sons of Poseidon:
The Immortal Sea

**Pirates of Britannia Series (with
Eliza Knight):**
Savage of the Sea by Eliza Knight
Leader of Titans by Kathryn Le
Veque
The Sea Devil by Eliza Knight
Sea Wolfe by Kathryn Le Veque

Note: All Kathryn's novels are designed to be read as stand-alones, although many have cross-over characters or cross-over family groups. Novels that are grouped together have related characters or family groups. You will notice that some series have the same books; that is because they are cross-overs. A hero in one book may be the secondary character in another.

There is NO reading order except by chronology, but even in that case, you can still read the books as stand-alones. No novel is connected to another by a cliff hanger, and every book has an HEA.

Series are clearly marked. All series contain the same characters or family groups except the American Heroes Series, which is an anthology with unrelated characters.

For more information, find it in **A Reader's Guide to the Medieval World of Le Veque**.

ABOUT KATHRYN LE VEQUE

Bringing the Medieval to Romance

KATHRYN LE VEQUE is a critically acclaimed, multiple USA TODAY Bestselling author, an Indie Reader bestseller, a charter Amazon All-Star author, and a #1 bestselling, award-winning, multi-published author in Medieval Historical Romance with over 100 published novels.

Kathryn is a multiple award nominee and winner, including the winner of Uncaged Book Reviews Magazine 2017 and 2018 "Raven Award" for Favorite Medieval Romance. Kathryn is also a multiple RONE nominee (InD'Tale Magazine), holding a record for the number of nominations. In 2018, her novel WARWOLFE was the winner in the Romance category of the Book Excellence Award and in 2019, her novel A WOLFE AMONG DRAGONS won the prestigious RONE award for best pre-16th century romance.

Kathryn is considered one of the top Indie authors in the world with over 2M copies in circulation, and her novels have been translated into several languages. Kathryn recently signed with Sourcebooks Casablanca for a Medieval Fight Club series, first published in 2020.

In addition to her own published works, Kathryn is also the President/CEO of Dragonblade Publishing, a boutique publishing house specializing in Historical Romance. Drag-onblade's success has seen it rise in the ranks to become Amazon's #1 e-book publisher of Historical Romance (K-Lytics report July 2020).

Kathryn loves to hear from her readers. Please find Kathryn on Facebook at Kathryn Le Veque, Author, or join her on Twitter @kathrynleveque. Sign up for Kathryn's blog at www.kathrynleveque.com for the latest news and sales.